RISE OF THE STRONGEST SOVEREIGN

BOOK 5

RISE OF THE STRONGEST SOVEREIGN

BOOK 5

KAZ HUNTER

Podium

Published in 2025 by Podium Publishing
www.podiumentertainment.com

RISE OF THE STRONGEST SOVEREIGN

BOOK 5

CHAPTER ONE

[Level: 50]

[Name: Jason Lee]

[Skills:]

[Monster Trainer: Tame a wild monster of an equal or lower power.]

[. . .]

[Weapons:]

[Beowulf's Dagger]

[Incendiary Dagger]

[Ascalon]

[Dagger of Friendship]

[Dagger of Doom]

[Dagger of Kings]

[Initializing Livestream . . .]

[Connected.]

Energy swirls around me as I'm shot through the long

interdimensional straw that connects Mr. Wang's penthouse-club-thing to the dungeon that we *believe* Krak is going to be attacking soon. I've only traveled through interdimensional space in this manner once before, and I have to admit that this is no more pleasant than the last time I did it. Getting sucked through portals is always awful, but with these . . . Well, you're inside this little tube that stretches across interdimensional space, surrounded by an immense black void dotted with little bursts of light. That light, of course, comes from the fires of the dungeons, so they're not exactly pleasant places to visit. The short explanation is that I'm not going to be getting a whole lot of comfort for the foreseeable future.

Ahead of me, the tube stretches out and connects to a particularly brilliant light. I know that's my destination and do my best to prepare myself. Closer and closer I draw . . . and then, with a flash of light, I go shooting through.

Flash!

Lightning explodes across my body as I tumble out the other side of the portal. I hit the ground hard and roll for several moments, then get up and glance around. With luck, no one noticed. I am, after all, trying to bait Krak.

"*Grrrrrrrrrrrrrrrrrrr . . .*"

A low growling noise echoes all around me, and I slowly climb to my feet. It would seem that luck has abandoned me today. I'm standing in the middle of a broad, dusty crater, with a hot sun beating down upon me as if trying to melt my bones like wax. There are small cavities in the side of the formation, which have been lined with sharp rocks, rather like nests. And, of course, inside those nests are lions.

At least two dozen of them, maybe more.

"Hello." I glance back at the portal, only to find it closing. "I don't suppose you all might want to help me get rid of an oppressive and rather aggressively ambitious dungeon boss? If you survive, I'll pay you well."

[ChaosRider: Don't offer them what you can't provide, Jason!]

[ShadowDancer: And moreover, cut the banter! We want to see blood, not listen to you make jokes.]

[IceQueen: Yeah! FIGHT!!!!]

"Oh, is that so?" As I keep talking, I slowly draw out Beowulf's Dagger with my right hand. The words are keeping the lions slightly distracted, which is useful for ensuring that I'm able to get a good strike on them. "If you're so excited about seeing blood, you ought to hop in here and see how you'd fare against these things."

[DarkCynic: I could totally do it if my powers would just awaken! I know I have them. I do!!!!!!!!]

[LunarEclipse: Yeah, Jason. We're stuck. We didn't get lucky like you. Just go kill stuff so we can live through you vicariously.]

[ViperQueen: Please please please!!!]

"Well . . ." I sigh as if deliberating things. "If you insist."

One of the lions takes that opportunity to spring forward, and I leap at the thing, ducking under its blow to slash the monster along the underbelly. The lion howls as Beowulf's Dagger carves a long gash in its stomach, then I race forward as the lions all leap forward and begin to attack.

And that's when I notice that they're not lions. Their tails are snakes instead of . . . well . . . *tails.*

These are chimeras.

The closest chimera snarls and rears up on its hind legs, slashing wildly at me. I pause, only for another one to hit me from the side. It knocks me to the ground, slams a paw into my chest, and opens its mouth wide. Quickly, I slash upward with the dagger and cut clean through its paw before rolling to the side.

FOOOOOM!

A great blast of fire explodes across the rock where my head was just lying. I stagger back to my feet as the monsters all converge upon me and quickly throw myself into the battle.

The next several moments are a desperate struggle for survival. The chimeras are swarming all around me, biting and clawing and blasting me with flame. I'm forced to spend all my time ducking and dodging. I can't land a single strike against any of them. They're pressing too hard, coming too fast. Quickly, I throw myself down, then roll desperately underneath them. The monsters don't seem to expect it, and I pop up near the edge of their formation. I prepare myself as they spin in my direction, then back up toward the edge of the crater.

"Come on, everyone. Come to me!"

I gesture at them, and the monsters snarl and charge headlong at me. This time, though, they're spread out in a line, and I prepare myself for impact. The first one lunges, and I duck underneath the blow and slash it across the neck. The second one claws at me, and I leap to the side and cut off its paw. A third one bounds straight down at me, and I leap up into the air and snatch hold of its mane as I pass clean over its head. As

I come down, I stab deep into its neck, and blood bursts from the wound and splatters down onto the ground.

[Condition: Poisoned. You will take 2 HP of damage every second for the next 00:05:00.]

[IceQueen: Actually, if snakes bite you, it's *venom*, not poison.]

[ShadowDancer: Yeah, but for the sake of brevity in a video game, it's easier to just say poison for everything.]

[ChaosRider: THIS ISN'T A VIDEO GAME!!!]

I don't feel the stinging in my shoulder until after I notice the notification. Quickly, I slash backward with my dagger and cut the snake clean through, then leap from my perch atop the monster. As I come down, I stab another chimera through the shoulder, then charge forward.

"Burnie! Someone! I could use some help!"

With a flicker, my pocket dimension opens, and Burnie flies out, flames trailing from his feathers. He immediately launches a white-blue fireball that hits a chimera in front of me.

Foo—BOOM!

The blast of fire completely incinerates the chimera's head, and I leap over the body and cut the snake's head off the tail before the dying monster can bite me. Suddenly, I sense another of the monsters coming up from the side, and I spin as it snarls and jumps.

There's no time to dodge, so I fall flat on my back. It passes mere inches over top of me. The claws seem to glint with light, and I gulp. The moment it's gone, I leap back to my feet and snarl and stab upward as another of the monsters snarls and lunges at me.

I stab the dagger up through the underside of its chin and pin its jaw to the top of its mouth. At that moment, it unleashes a great blast of flame. Beowulf's Dagger turns white from the heat, and while the closed mouth does contain a lot of it, an immense amount of flame still does manage to pour out and scorches me in the face. I groan and stagger backward as I rip the dagger back out, which *does* kill the thing, thankfully. A footstep patters behind me, and I spin, but not fast enough. My dagger hits the side of the chimera's head just as it hits me, and I'm sent flying.

I imagine that I do look rather like a ragdolled NPC as it flings me high over the floor of the crater. I come down hard on the other side, landing mostly on my head, which doesn't allow me to get up quickly. Before I can right myself, a massive paw hits me on the side of the head. I'm sent rolling across the ground, then slowly stand up as the monster snarls and approaches.

FOOOOOOOOOOM!

Burnie shoots past me as he hits the chimera with a fantastically powerful fireball. The monster falls, and I turn back to face the crowd. Nearly all the chimeras are sporting injuries now, but there are more alive than dead, which isn't how I'd like it. I check my status condition.

[Condition: Poisoned. You will take 10 HP of damage every second for the next 00:03:28.]

Apparently, I've been bitten a few more times. My health bar drops as I watch it, and I quickly open my inventory and pull out a couple Pumped! bottles. The other chimeras in the area snarl and begin to circle, watching me closely. They don't want to get hurt, that's for sure. I just need to keep my head down, and—

Wham!

Something hits me from behind, and I'm thrown forward further down into the crater and slam to the ground. I don't know what it was, and I frankly don't care at this exact moment. My health is down in the red, and that's a problem.

[Skill: Bearing of a Knight.]

[Peril Detected.]

[Increasing Strength by 200%.]

[Increasing Dexterity by 300%.]

[Increasing Health Regeneration by 1,000%.]

[Increasing Damage Resistance by 500%.]

[. . .]

My health suddenly stabilizes, though it doesn't really begin to rise, and a new strength fills me. I slowly climb back to my feet, dagger gleaming in the sunlight. The chimeras snarl and bend down, then attack en masse.

[DarkCynic: Ahh, yeah!!! This is what I'm talking about!!!]

[ViperQueen: GO JASON!!!!!!!!]

[RazorEdge: Kill those monsters!!!]

My body moves so fast that I can barely see it myself. Overhead, Burnie swoops back and forth as he continues to rake the chimeras with as much fire as he can produce. I hack and slash, hack and slash. Nothing can touch me; no claw is fast enough to hit my skin. One by one, the bites wear off, and my health begins to rise as the poison no longer affects me. Soon, I'm getting close to full health again, and there's only a single chimera left. Bearing of a Knight wears off, and I take a deep breath as the lone chimera snarls and prepares itself for battle.

"Bring it on," I mutter. "Burnie, hold off."

Burnie flies down to land on the edge of the crater, and I charge forward to meet the chimera. It opens its mouth and lets out a piercing blast of flame and fire, and I drop to the ground as it flashes over my head. My skin burns from the close proximity to the flame, but I push on, nonetheless. I come out of the slide and leap back to my feet just next to the thing and slash upward just behind its ear. A great chunk of its mane falls to the ground, and it spins as it tries to hit me. I duck under the blow, then stab it just behind the other ear. The monster sways, and I snarl and lunge forward as I thrust the dagger right at the middle of its face.

CRUNCH!

The dagger smashes through the skull and pierces down into the brain. Bits and pieces of gore trickle down the front of its face, and the monster groans and falls to the side.

[You have leveled up!]

[Congratulations! You are now Level 51!]

"I'm still a long way from level one hundred," I mutter as I wipe off the dagger. "Now, Burnie, what hit me while I was facing off against those things?"

It hasn't come back, so I assume that it was more of an environmental effect to keep me within a certain area, but it's hard to know for sure. I glance around, then walk up to the edge of the crater and look around.

The crater itself is situated in the bottom of a small valley, which, based on the position of the sun, seems to run in a more or less north–south direction. There are a scattering of cacti and Joshua trees throughout the dusty bottom of the valley, while red stone walls rise up on either side. To the south, the valley seems to open up into an endless desert. To the north, though, I can see a mesa rising up from the dust, and I squint my eyes. At the top of the mesa there's something, though I can't quite tell what it is.

"Huh." I shrug and sheath my dagger. I'm sure I'll need it again, but I could use a moment to rest my hand. There will be time to snatch it out before I run into any trouble, I'm sure. "I don't see any monsters, but the rest of this valley is a *prime* place for an ambush. Any input, anyone?"

[FireStorm: I bet they're going to come out of the rocks!]

[GoldenShield: Yeah, you're going to be facing some sort of sand monster. Maybe a dust golem or something!]

[IceQueen: I think it'll be a flying creature! It's going to be an epic fight, whatever it is!]

I frown as I think over the possibilities. Now, the most important thing—far more so than just what monsters I have to fight in the dungeon—is what exactly I should do. I entered the dungeon to face off against Krak in the hopes that he would target this dungeon. My plan had been to enter quietly, but that didn't happen. Was that just because the portal accidentally opened up into the wrong area, or was that by design? Does the dungeon boss know I'm coming? Does *Krak* know I'm coming? I don't know, and that fact is more annoying than anything else.

Suddenly, from high on the mesa, I see a small flash of light. It's followed by a whole series of lights, some longer, some shorter, in a rapid series of pulses.

"It's Morse code," I murmur in recognition. "Can anyone on the chat translate?"

[DarkCynic: I could translate it if I had ever been taught it, but the school system doesn't teach cool stuff like that anymore.]

[ViperQueen: I know how to send S-O-S!]

[ChaosRider: My dad is in the military. Hang on, let me go grab his book.]

There's a long pause, and the light continues to flash.

[ChaosRider: Yeah, let's see . . . So, that's saying, "Jason, I know you're here. Come and get me. We need to talk. Please pardon my minions."]

"Great," I mutter. "So much for the ambush. Alright, let's get this over with." I draw in a deep breath, then take a step forward out of the crater and onto the floor of the valley.

WHAM!

Something hits me from beneath, and my health drops down into the orange as I'm sent flying high into the sky.

"Pardon my minions," I snort. "Yeah, I'll bet he wants a pardon. When I get to him . . . he's going to regret that."

CHAPTER TWO

Okay, so the previous line was something that ran through my head, but I probably shouldn't say that I *said* it. I'm currently flying head over heels through the air above the valley, desperately trying to get my bearings. Down below, something starts to slither about, and Beowulf's Dagger begins to glow on my belt.

[Serpentine creature detected.]

[Additional Damage will be dealt.]

[All stats increased.]

Strength flows through me, and a smile spreads across my face. A moment later, though, I hit the ground and my health falls all the way into the red.

[Skill: Bearing of a Knight.]

[Peril Detected.]

On one hand, it's *really* nice to have all these buffs and things. On the other hand, the fact that they're activating means that I'm in trouble. I slowly climb to my feet in the shadow of a Joshua tree as a creature pulls itself up from the dust.

Okay, so you know those flat fish you see in aquariums sometimes? The ones that are the color of sand and lie flat on the ocean floor to hide themselves? Yeah, so this is a dragon that is doing the same thing on the floor of the valley. It snarls and roars, then shakes itself, causing an immense torrent of dust to come tumbling down. This dragon is immense, probably a hundred feet long from tip to tail with a wingspan that's just about as impressive. It has long spiky horns protruding from its head that go both forward and back, and . . . Well, it's just big, alright? Slowly, it stretches, then comes down on all fours and stares at me with beady yellow eyes. It seems to be waiting on me, and I sit back to wait for it.

And then I realize that it's probably waiting for me to heal enough that my buffs wear off. Dragons are terribly intelligent creatures, you know. I grit my teeth and charge forward, flashing across the ground just as fast as I can.

[Skill: Bearing of a Knight.]

[Peril no longer detected.]

With that, my buffs wear off. I'm still mighty strong, don't get me wrong, but it's less than before, and I stumble as my legs suddenly struggle to keep up with my body. The dragon senses this and lashes out with its tail as if it was batting away a fly. The tail hits me in the chest and flings me backward into the stone wall of the valley, and I groan and sink to the ground.

"And here I thought you would be a more worthwhile

opponent," the dragon sneers as I groan and push myself off the wall. "You defeated twenty chimeras without dying. I would have thought you could have at least injured me before succumbing."

I draw in a deep breath and wipe a bit of blood away from my mouth. "You'll see just how resilient I can be."

[ShadowDancer: That's your epic comeback line? Come on, that was lame.]

[ChaosRider: Yeah! Jason, I know you can do better than that!]

[FireStorm: Please??? Give us a good quip!]

"I thought you guys didn't *want* me to be quippy," I snort. I don't actually mind the razzing. The moral support of the livestream has kept me going more than once, and as a viewer of other forms of entertainment, I've certainly lent my opinion to the entertainer a good number of times. The chat quickly launches into a defense of their assorted actions, and I grin and slowly start forward.

It should be noted that my health is *really* low right now. That dragon's tail-whip is powerful, that's for sure. That said, unless I were to sit back and heal all the way to full health, a second hit would kill me. I just have to go in while it's expecting me to hang back, and that's all there is to it. Quickly, I race across the ground, leaping over the dust and rocks and cacti, and the dragon eyeballs me with interest.

"You attack again, do you?" the dragon snarls softly. "Back for more pain? Or are you really that eager for death?"

"I'm not eager for death, no," I answer. "No more eager for death than you are for treasure."

The sentence is chosen carefully. Everyone knows that dragons hoard treasure and only ever leave their hoard for the sake of raiding kingdoms for food or for more treasure. In this case, though, the dragon was just lying around on the valley floor without a hint of treasure to its name. I can only assume that there's a reason for that.

"How do you know how eager I am for treasure?" the dragon snarls. It lifts its tail and strikes down, and I dodge out of the way. As it strikes, a powerful shock wave explodes outward and shakes the valley floor, but I ignore it and keep coming. I'm getting close to the dragon, but still not close enough to actually kill it.

"Well . . . you don't have any, so . . ." I shrug.

"That means nothing!" the dragon snarls. Then it spins. It's like a snake, so it spins *fast*, and the tail lashes out at me once more. I fall to my back, and the tail passes just above me. The wind from the tail's passing actually sends me rolling across the valley floor, and I come up in the shadow of a large cactus. "You are an impudent little cretin, and I will crush you like a bug."

"You'll certainly try."

I race forward, moving just as fast as my legs will carry me. I'm behind the thing now, and it doesn't see me for a few crucial seconds. Those are just enough, and it snarls as I approach to within just a few feet. Once more it tries to spin, but I leap up and stab my dagger deep into its rear right leg.

The monster howls and flaps its wings. A concussive blast of wind slams me into the ground, and I groan as the thing flies up into the sky. It begins to circle the valley, then slowly drops down and begins to make a downward run. I know exactly what that means, and I brace myself.

[GoldenShield: Quick, Jason! You need fire resistance!]

[IceQueen: Does he have anything that can grant fire resistance?]

[ShadowDancer: YEAH!!!!!]

With a flash, my pocket dimension opens, and Bjorn steps out. He already looks a lot better than just a few hours earlier, and he tilts his head back and lets out a powerful howl that shakes the valley. Rocks come tumbling down, and the air cools so rapidly that I start to shiver. With that, the dragon opens its mouth and lets out a piercing blast of flame, and suddenly, I don't feel so cold anymore.

Flame and fire rage against the icy howl, and as the dragon passes overhead, I slap a few flames off my clothes. I'm alive, though, and that's the important part. As the dragon circles, I nod to Bjorn, who's swaying from the exertion.

"Do you think you could ask Balder out here?"

Bjorn nods and retreats into the pocket dimension, then his son, Balder, steps out. I nod up at the dragon, and Balder understands instantly. He snarls, then emits a sharp bark as the dragon comes around for another pass.

A shock wave erupts outward through the air, flashing up through the sky, and hits the dragon head-on. Its wings buckle, and it suddenly spins rapidly through the sky as it begins to fall. With a tremendous *crash*, it hits the ground and sends up a terrible spray of dust and gravel and stone. Balder snarls, and the cloud of debris hits a force field that has suddenly formed around me. As the dust dies away, the dragon snarls and slowly starts to stand up, but Balder emits another bark. The dragon's head is slammed back into the ground, and I take that as my cue.

I race forward as fast as I can go. As the dragon lifts its head again, I jump upward and land between the eyes. My dagger flashes, and I slash the thing across its forehead, then slice off one of its horns. My weaker daggers couldn't have even begun to do such a thing, but Beowulf's Dagger is *powerful*. With that, I leap over the back of its head and slide down its neck, then do something that I hope will be clever.

I yank out the Incendiary Dagger.

I haven't had a chance to test the thing yet, so this is going to be a good way of knowing whether or not it actually works. I stab Beowulf's Dagger into the neck of the monster, causing a great eruption of blood and gore as I continue the path down to its back, and then stab the Incendiary Dagger in right next to it.

Almost instantly, a great torrent of flame explodes through the dragon, and I feel the beast tremble beneath me. Smoke hisses up between the scales, from the tail, the wings, the nostrils, and the eyes. It howls and begins to thrash about, and I swing down and catch hold of the base of one of the wings. Quickly, I hack it off, then fall to the ground along with the wing to land next to the dragon's feet. It stagers about, seemingly blinded, at least in part, and tries to flap its wings to escape. The motion only makes it stagger and fall flat, and I seize my chance.

Without abandon, I charge at the monster, ready for anything. It looks up and sees me coming and flicks its tail once more. This time, as a sonic boom erupts from the tip of its tail, I can see that its aim is true and that there's not a chance in this world that I'm going to be able to avoid it. There's only one chance I have, and I have to take it.

I'm going to try and block the tail.

Quickly, I hold up both of the daggers, come to a stop, and brace my feet. There's a single breath of anticipation, and the tail slams into me with the force of a mountain.

WHAM!

I'm sent flying—of that there's simply no doubt—and slam into the valley wall once again. As I peel myself off the wall, though, I see something else stuck in the red stone only a few feet away.

The end of a dragon tail.

A flash of victory passes over me, and I look up to see the dragon howling in pain once more. Blood drips down from the tail to the ground, and the monster snarls and turns to look at me. I check my health, noting that I have a fraction left, maybe around ten points. The dragon certainly has a whole lot more, and that's a problem. Slowly, carefully, I charge forward, knowing that it's now or never. Bearing of a Knight kicks in and begins to heal me slowly, but it's not going to be enough, and we both know it. I'm either going to do something clever and get out alive, or it's going to do something and squash me like a bug, just like it promised.

"Anyone?" I gasp out. "If you're in my pocket dimension, and you feel like you can assist, I'd sure appreciate it."

There's a sharp crackle as my portal opens and Blub floats out. I snatch him out of the air as he inflates, then spin and throw him up at the dragon with all my might. There's an explosion against the dragon's face a moment later, and the beast howls. Astrid comes out as well, already splitting the air with a powerful howl. The ground splits open, and lava comes exploding upward and splashes over the feet of the great monster. The dragon snarls and draws back, and she follows it for a second. Burnie swoops overhead and hits it with a blast of flame, but the attack doesn't do much through the scales of the beast.

While the dragon is distracted with the lava, I bolt forward, seizing my opportunity. Suddenly, Lightfax races up next to me, and I swing up onto her back. The noble steed shoots forward as if she's been launched from a cannon, and we go sweeping around the side of the lava pool. The dragon doesn't notice as we race up underneath its belly, and I stand up.

"*Ahhhhhhhhhh!*" I slam both daggers into the belly of the beast and carve a long path down its body, allowing a torrent of blood to come pouring out. As we reach the end, I jump off my noble steed and swing onto the dragon's back. It thrashes around angrily, but I hold on tight and stab it several more times. Blood flows more and more freely. Finally . . . slowly . . . the dragon tips over and falls to the ground with a powerful *thud*. I sigh and climb down off the thing, then look it over just to make sure it's dead.

[You have leveled up!]

[Congratulations! You are now Level 52!]

"Yup. It's dead." I sigh and turn away, then slowly walk down the valley floor toward the mesa. My pets all go back inside my pocket dimension to heal, and I cross my arms in thought.

[DarkCynic: Hey, Jason! You should go take trophies from the dragon or something!]

[FireStorm: Yeah! Like its claws or something!]

[GoldenShield: Or the dragon eyes! Dragon eyes are cool!]

I laugh and shake my head. "First of all, where would I put them? I don't exactly have a house at the moment. Besides, eyes will just rot." I shake my head. "Plus, that was a pretty weak dragon. I'm sure I'll fight more dragons that are far cooler. I can take trophies from them."

[RazorEdge: That's our Jason! Epic as always!]

[ChaosRider: Or just lazy.]

I shake my head as the chat continues to debate the merits of my actions. They can say what they will, but truth be told, I just don't want anything to do with the beasts. I've seen what they can do, and it's not pretty. It's dead, and that's the important bit.

Ahead of me is a mesa and a long climb to reach the top. I don't know what I'm going to have to face on the way up the side of it, but I'm certain that it's going to be quite a lot. I just have to keep my head down and charge forward and I know I'll make it in one piece.

And I'm not going to let *anything* distract me or stand in my way.

CHAPTER THREE

The walk across the floor of the desert is a long one, but I'll admit that it's quite beautiful. Southwest America, which seems to be what this is styled after, is one of my favorite places in the whole world. If I ever do wind up defeating this whole apocalypse, I have every intention of heading that way to spend some well-earned time relaxing. In the meantime, I fight my way through a handful of smaller monsters that pop up to challenge me. Little things like giant scorpions and a few large cobras. Once, such creatures would have set me back enormously. A few of them are so large that they would be mini-bosses in smaller dungeons, but at this point, I hardly even notice them. After a good thirty minutes of walking, and after passing up a handful of side locations that I'm sure hold mini-bosses, I come to a long walkway that shoots sharply up the side of the mesa toward the top.

"And here we are," I murmur as I stare up at the thing. "Anyone see anything that might be of concern?"

[IceQueen: It looks to me like you're going to have to pass right by a pretty big cave! I bet there are loads of things hidden in there.]

[DarkCynic: Yeah, and there are some nests up near the top. They'll have giant bird monsters that you'll have to fight, for sure.]

[FireStorm: And I bet there are snakes! Loads of snakes.]

"Hmm." I think for a moment. "And what about shortcuts? Anyone see any shortcuts?"

Before anyone can answer, the area suddenly grows darker. I look up at the sun just in time to see it eclipsed by a large dark cloud rippling across the area. A cloud that seems to be pouring outward from a single central point.

As the cloud spreads outward, a light forms at the center, and a beam of crackling energy shoots down and hits the top of the mesa. The ground shudders under the impact, and stones come rattling down. I grit my teeth.

[GoldenShield: THAT'S KRAK!!!]

I have to agree with the assessment. More lightning shoots down from the portal, striking the ground behind me. As each strike fades away, I find myself looking at warriors. Most of them are lizardmen, though there are a handful of spider-folk, skeletons, werewolves, and other sorts of monsters. They immediately strike out across the floor of the desert, and I draw in a deep breath.

Krak has commenced his invasion. Trap or not, he's here, and that means I need to get to the point of the action just as quickly as I can.

With that, I charge upward as fast as possible, all sense of restraint gone. The red stone flashes past under my feet, and I climb higher and higher at a speed that I'm sure must be a record. Ahead of me, some stones clatter together to form a small stone golem, but I punch it in the face right as I reach it. The figure explodes under my fist, and the monster collapses before it can even fully finish forming. I continue climbing, knocking aside a few smaller monsters as I do so.

Suddenly, I come upon the entrance of the cave, which is dark and quite foreboding. A gust of wind blows out of it, which tells me that it probably leads somewhere. Maybe the top of the mesa? I'd sure love a shortcut, so I take a step inside. Something rumbles from within, and I get an odd sense that I'm about to have company.

"So, you've made it this far," a slithery sort of voice echoes. "You must be a very powerful warrior indeed."

"I know how to make an account of myself," I answer cautiously. "Come out where I can see you."

There's a pause, and slowly, a serpent emerges from the darkness. The monster is huge, probably twice the size of the basilisk that I fought in Harold's dungeon. It has piercing red eyes, and a massive forked tongue flicks from its mouth. It draws itself upright, then slowly leans forward.

"I will tear you into bits, cut you apart, and—"

A sharp squeal echoes through the air as a black arrow flashes out of the depths of the cave and hits it in the back of the head. It falls forward, slams into the ground, and begins writhing about. I step out of the way, and in its grisly death dance, it flops out of the cave and goes tumbling down the mountainside. Now *that* has me concerned. I make sure that

Beowulf's Dagger is held tightly in my hand as I turn and face the darkness.

A fire flickers to life an instant later, and a figure slowly emerges. He stands a good seven feet tall and is humanoid, though not terribly so. He looks to be a knight, though he wears black armor instead of steel. Flames pour forth from his helmet, flickering upward from the visor and from beneath the rim. A strange rune is scratched onto his breastplate, likely some demonic symbol of protection, and he holds a sword that's long and red.

[RazorEdge: WOW!!!! I've never seen one of those in person before!!!]

[ViperQueen: I did! LadyKiller ran into one in a seaside dungeon just yesterday. It killed her in like three seconds. RIP.]

[ChaosRider: Yeah, I remember when the news of it hit the internet. Jason, be careful!]

I spare only a quick glance at the chat. I don't know exactly what they're talking about, but I can sense the evil nature that's radiating off this thing like a mist. My stomach churns just looking at him. This thing was built to kill, and to draw whatever he's killed down with him to hell.

[FireStorm: IT'S A DEMON KNIGHT!!!]

"Alright." I slowly take my stance. "So, you're here on behalf of Krak. Any message from him?"

The demon knight doesn't answer for a moment as he slowly walks forward, unconcerned. Then he raises his sword and gives the weapon a twirl before settling into his own stance.

"Only one," the knight snarls softly. "If you survive, he

would like a word with you over the body of the current dungeon boss."

"Tell him that I'll gladly accept."

"You'll have to tell him yourself."

The demon knight lets out a piercing scream, one that chills me to the bone, and charges forward. His sword flashes with a dark light—I know that sounds paradoxical, but that's the best way I can explain it—and he swings at me.

I dodge backward, then raise both of my daggers. As he attacks a second time, I raise them again and catch the sword between them. The blow knocks me backward several feet, and pain flares up my arms as if I've been hit by a truck. The monster doesn't stop there, but seizes the offensive and attacks with a blistering flurry of strikes, driving me steadily backward toward the edge of the cave.

[ShadowDancer: Jason, don't give him ground!!!]

[ViperQueen: Oh, you let him be.]

[DarkCynic: No, you listen to ShadowDancer, Jason! Don't let the demon win!!!]

I grit my teeth and try to ignore the chat. Frankly, if the demon wasn't forcing me backward, I probably would have tried to draw him out anyway. Night vision isn't one of my skills, so if I get into the cave, I have little doubt that he'll be able to see better and have a distinct advantage. Out in the sunlight, I doubt he'll have any major debuffs, but I'll at least be able to see what I'm doing.

As I exit the cave, I turn to allow him to force me up the path. The high ground is always an advantage, though the longer reach of his sword prevents me from being able to make any use of it. For the moment, though, I'm mostly just trying to feel him out. I can sense his power, and I can tell that he's holding back. I'd rather know more about him before I really—

Crack.

Something moves behind me, and I spin as another rock golem rises up and takes form. I spin on a dime and punch it as hard as I can, making stone crack and explode. The demon knight seizes the opportunity and rushes forward to stab at me in a lightning-fast blur.

I, however, am just a *hint* faster.

I spin out of the way as he passes by me and stab at his helmet with Beowulf's Dagger. The blade glances off the metal without doing much damage, though the impact causes a loud, hollow *bong* that echoes up the side of the mesa. The demon passes by me, the flames from his body making me shudder, and he turns and faces me, this time from above.

I'm not given a chance to reclaim the offensive as he strikes again, and this time, with the high ground, I'm forced to back-pedal much faster. His blows are impossibly strong, and he can attack so fast that even with my daggers it's hard to block or anticipate them. That said, I'm starting to see patterns, and I think I find a gap in his attack. As I come up close to a sharp turn in the path, I feign a step backward, then lunge forward as hard and fast as I can go.

My intuition was right, and as he slashes downward, I come up to him right behind the blade. I slam my shoulder into him, making the demon stagger, and plunge both daggers into chinks in his armor, one under the armpit, one under the chin. The resulting fire damage from the Incendiary Dagger doesn't really hurt him, but Beowulf's Dagger certainly packs a punch. The demon howls and staggers backward, and I rip out my daggers and attack with fury.

Suddenly, I have the offensive, and I don't let up for even the briefest moment. My attacks come hard and fast, and I force him steadily back down the path toward the cave. He flails about, trying to block my double-wielded stance, and I strike at his wrist with Beowulf's Dagger. My aim is true, and I cut clean through the hand holding the sword.

Dark energy explodes outward as black blood drips down, and the demon howls in pain. His hand clatters to the ground and the sword falls from his limp grasp over the side of the cliff. The demon snarls, then clenches his remaining hand. A dark energy pulses from the stump of his wrist, and slowly, new black flesh grows out to form a new hand. The monster hisses, then raises the naked hand and mutters a few words in a dark language.

[ChaosRider: Uh-oh.]

[IceQueen: Yeah, that's not going to go well for you, Jason.]

[LunarEclipse: Hope you survive!]

Ka-BOOOOOOOOOOOOOOM!

A bolt of dark flame shoots from his palm and flashes right by my head. I only narrowly dodge, and it hits the cliff face, causing a resounding explosion. I charge forward at the demon, swinging both my daggers, and he snarls and raises his hands. Black fire swirls through the air around him and then hits me, which burns me quite badly, flames licking at my face and my arms and my feet. I ignore the pain, leap onward, and slash both daggers across the monster's neck.

Once more, my aim is true, and both blades bite deep into the black flesh. The resulting explosion flings me backward, and I bounce down the path before sliding clean off the edge of the cliff right where the path turns. I fall a foot or so before catching hold of a protruding stone and gasp as my Incendiary Dagger tumbles from my grasp and plummets down to the ground far below. The stone cuts into the palm of my left hand, and I grit my teeth and slowly start to pull myself up.

Clunk.

A black boot echoes on the stone, and the demon knight steps into view at the top of the cliff. He stares down at me for a long moment, flames now trailing from his neck where he was injured. A new black fire forms in his palm, and he raises his hand.

"You will now die. You've been a worthy opponent." His voice sounds almost pleased. "My master will give you a good place in his kingdom."

"I don't serve your master," I answer. "I serve only the light!"

With that, I heave myself upward and sling to the side just as he launches a fireball right down the face of the cliff. Stone melts into lava under the blast, but I swing up just fine. I land at the feet of the monster, sweep them out from under him, and rise up.

Blam!

A blast of energy knocks me backward into the wall, and stone cracks under the impact. My bare left hand catches hold of a large fragment, and without thinking, I sling it down at the monster as hard as I can. The stone slams into his helmet, denting it inward, and the demon groans. He lets out a concussive blast of energy that slams me back into the wall, then climbs back to his feet.

"I'm going to enjoy—"

"*Ahh!*"

Yelling as loud as I can to amplify the effect, I push myself off the wall and kick the demon in the chest with all my might. He's knocked backward, where he slips and slowly falls off the cliff. I groan and step forward to gaze over the edge of the stone. I watch the demon tumble down . . . down . . .

Thud.

A shock wave ripples outward from the point of impact on the ground, flattening Joshua trees and blasting cacti into slivers.

[Demon Knight defeated!]

[XP Awarded: 10,000,000]

[. . .]

[Notice: S-Ranked creature defeated!]

[First Kill of a Demon Knight from planet Earth!]

[Extra XP Awarded: 5,000,000]

[. . .]

[You have leveled up!]

[Congratulations! You are now Level 53!]

[. . .]

[Extra reward granted for First Kill of a Demon Knight!]

[Rank: S]

With a flash, a small token appears in my hands. It looks almost like a coin with a depiction of wings on either side. I frown, then look at the effects.

[Michael's Wings (passive): Grants an extraordinary increase in power when fighting against demonic creatures. Also, grants an increase in XP gain from such creatures.]

"Now that could be useful." I smile as the chat explodes. I'm starting to accumulate a laundry list of passive skills and buffs against different creature types; though, in all fairness, several of them are linked to specific weapons and could be lost if I were to drop said weapon—which seems to be a perpetual issue that I face. Slowly, I turn toward the top of the mesa. "Onward and upward I go. Let's find Krak and *crack* his head open."

CHAPTER FOUR

Okay, so it's a cheesy line, but I think it's funny. With that, I quickly start upward, though I do still go slow enough to ensure that I don't walk into any ambushes.

It takes me around thirty more minutes to get to the top of the mesa. I fight my way through a handful of giant insects, along with an assortment of golems and living plants and other such things. They're all fairly easy to slay, and I soon come up to the top of the trail—I decided to avoid the cave, due to the tricky nature of the darkness. As I arrive at the top, the ground shakes, and I slow to a crawl.

"Get out of my territory!" a loud voice roars. I glance through the small entry to the boss arena, which seems to occupy the vast majority of the mesa's peak. A red dragon, the same color as the stone all around, snarls and stamps back and forth. Fire erupts from its mouth here and there, but it doesn't attack directly. Meanwhile, a fifty-foot-tall Krak stands directly beneath the swirling portal in the sky, a fierce look upon his face.

"I will depart when it becomes *my* territory," Krak snarls right back at the dragon. "You will yield to me and pledge allegiance, or you will perish."

"Abandon this dream," the dragon snaps back. "We both know that the queen could kill you in a heartbeat if she so chose. She's allowing this rampage of yours because it suits her, not because she's helpless to prevent it."

"And that's what she wants you to believe!" Krak almost screams. "She presents herself as all powerful, but in reality, she can be killed just like you and me. Join forces with me, and we can topple her."

"In doing so, I would only exchange one tyrant for another," the dragon hisses in return.

"If that *is* the case, which tyrant is challenging you right now?" Krak threatens.

"All I can do is remain loyal and hope that my queen will remain loyal to me."

Krak rumbles, low in his throat, "So be it."

With that, he draws his sword and mutters a few arcane words. Fire swirls around the weapon, churning and swirling and preparing to erupt, and the dragon flashes forward on darkened wings. I wince, as I have a pretty good idea how things are about to go.

As it happens . . . Well . . . I'm actually wrong.

The dragon lets out a piercing blast of flame that hits Krak in the chest and knocks him backward. He stumbles, and a bolt of lightning suddenly shoots down from the sky. The bolt is brighter than any I've ever seen before, and it hits Krak in the shoulder. A great burn sears down his arm, and he howls and stumbles before falling to his knees with a great cry of pain.

The dragon reacts instantly with a spin and whips Krak with its tail. I see sharpened barbs draw a great deal of blood on Krak's face, and the lizardman hisses. A great blast of dark magic erupts from his maw and blasts the dragon across the mesa. He raises his hands and demon knights emerge from swirling portals across the whole of the landscape as he staggers back to his feet.

"If your queen was so powerful, she would have killed me then and there, not simply injured me!"

Another blast of lightning hits Krak in the chest, and he's knocked backward once again. He growls, then turns and stares me dead in the eye. Blue energy swirls around him, and he's sucked up into the portal. Other energy swirls as well, and most of his demon knights are sucked up along with him. A few are left, maybe five, and they converge upon the red dragon.

The beast slowly pulls itself up and lets out a great blast of flame that rolls across the mesa. One of the demon knights withers and vanishes under the blast, but the others form dark shields out of their black energy and keep coming. The dragon crouches low and snarls softly, and I step out into view.

"Jason Lee." The dragon's voice is thunderous and powerful. "Join me in defeating these foes, and I would have a word with you."

[ShadowDancer: Ahh, yeah! Jason, check that out! An alliance with a DRAGON!!!]

[GoldenShield: Hmm. That seems to me like a bad idea.]

[RazorEdge: Bad idea? That would be EPIC!!!]

I grit my teeth. I don't like the idea of talking with a dragon either, but I also know that trying to fight the dragon *and* the demon knights isn't going to go well. "I'll agree that these things need taking care of before we take any further action."

"I understand."

With that, the dragon launches itself into the air and lets loose another blast of flame. I open my pocket dimension and call out Astrid, then race forward. Astrid lets out a howl, which sends cracks rolling across the surface of the mesa. Lava boils upward and sucks down two of the demon knights. A third one spins around to look at me, and the sword and shield in his hands suddenly transform into a bow.

Twang!

A piercing black arrow flashes past my head, and I drop to the ground as he fires another. The arrows come hard and fast, and I find myself dodging frantically. As I come up from the last one, I throw Beowulf's Dagger at the demon and hit him squarely in the visor. The blade sinks in up to the hilt, and the demon lets out a scream.

[Skill: Michael's Wings.]

[Activated.]

A great blast of light explodes from the dagger, and the demon's head simply vanishes in a great torrent of radiation. As the light fades, the monster sways and collapses, and I rush past and snatch up Beowulf's Dagger once more. Suddenly,

Burnie flashes overhead with my Incendiary Dagger in his claws. He drops it down to me, and I grip the two weapons as I charge toward the last knight standing.

The demon glances back and forth between me and the dragon, then snarls and thumps his chest. The rune there glows a brilliant and bloody shade of red, and his whole body erupts into flames as he grows several feet taller. I gulp.

"Well, that's not good."

The demon knight snarls, then begins to throw fireballs at me. They're fast and powerful fireballs, and as I dodge and bound about, they blast large craters into the ground. The dragon swoops down, and the knight spins and throws several more fireballs up at it. They strike the serpent up and down the length of its body, and it comes crashing to the ground with a spray of rubble. The knight glowers, then spins toward me.

The next several minutes are among the most terrifying of my life. The knight unleashes a blistering combination of attacks that drive me backward, until, finally, he runs out of time.

With a flicker, the enhanced demon knight collapses and crumbles into ash. I come to a stop and stare down at the remains of the corpse. I walk up and kick it, but I only cause a little puff of ash to drift across the mesa top.

[DarkCynic: It was a suicide skill! It activated when the demon realized that he couldn't win!]

[ViperQueen: Hmm. A desperate attempt to ensure that his opponent was taken down too.]

I shudder a bit at that thought. I can't imagine doing

something that I know will result in my death, but I suppose that's the length that some people will go to. Slowly, I turn toward the dragon, which is struggling to rise. It turns and looks at me as I approach, and I draw both of my daggers and place them upon its throat as I reach its head.

The beast is massive—the head alone is the size of my body—but it's injured. The blast from the demonic fire seems to have hindered the thing's ability to regenerate, judging from some odd flashes of light that aren't healing the open wounds. The dragon lets out a hiss, and I nod down at it.

"I trusted a dragon boss once. I regretted it. You'll forgive me if I don't inherently trust you."

"We share a common enemy," the dragon hisses.

"And that's not enough. Common enemies only bond opponents for a certain time, and I'm not here just to get rid of Krak. I'm here to kill anything and everything that lives in these portals," I answer, staring down into the dragon's eye. "If we forge a pact, you'll learn things about me, and when we inevitably become enemies again, you'll be in a much better position to kill me. I'd rather not risk it."

"Do what you will. Just know that if you abandon me, you abandon an ally in a time of your greatest need."

I stare down at the thing for a long moment. I desperately want to trust the dragon, to take its advice. "What do you mean?"

"I will not give away my information for free," the dragon snarls. "I desire to, and I desire to do so quite strongly, but I have no guarantee that you won't just kill me and be done with it. We are not so unlike, you and I."

I don't lower my weapons, but I give it a nod. "Would you turn from your ways? Leave the dungeons behind? Take on a life of fighting on the side of Earth?"

"You would have me become a human," the dragon sneers.

I shrug. "If that's what it takes. Let me put it this way: You say that I'm in an hour of great need. I already know that. If I kill you, I'm going to head on my way and keep killing monsters, and when I come to the next problem, I'll face it and kill *that*. I'm not all that worried, you know? You need me more than I need you."

The dragon growls softly. "That is . . . that is true."

The beast doesn't move for a long moment, then slowly pushes itself upright. It rises to its full height, something that seems to me to be quite painful, then mutters something in a language that I don't understand. A thunderous crash of light and energy swirls across the beast, and it shrinks down to form a human body. As I gape, a man slowly walks forward where the dragon once stood. His eyes are cold and dark, and shaggy black hair hangs around his head. He's wearing a tattered trench coat, and just . . . I don't know. If you were to custom create someone who just looks creepy, this would be the guy.

"I now renounce my skills. I renounce my abilities. I transfer all my XP and assets to the care of Jason Lee."

More lightning and thunder crash across the landscape, and a bolt of lightning suddenly connects the two of us. In that moment, the man softens. His hair becomes brown instead of black, and his eyes become a soft bluish color. His trench coat is transformed into a more dapper coat that might be worn to a casual dinner party, and a fedora settles onto his head.

And in that moment, I gain a *lot* of XP.

[You have leveled up!]

[You have leveled up!]

[You have leveled up!]

[You have leveled up!]

[. . .]

I blink in surprise, and the man sighs and rolls his shoulders around in his sockets. When he catches me staring at him, he shrugs.

"Come on. You were going to make me do that sooner or later. *Now* do you trust me? I'm a helpless little meatbag of a human. I couldn't even turn back into a dragon if I wanted to. The queen wouldn't allow it, but even if she did, system rules are pretty strict. If you lose your status as an Awakened, you're not allowed back into the game."

"Why'd you do it so willingly?" I ask, though I'm pretty sure I know the answer.

"You were about to kill me, or the queen was going to, or Krak or someone," the man answers. He looks momentarily angry but suppresses it. "This gives me the longest chance of survival, even if it *is* only a paltry few decades instead of millennia."

"I'll take it. It's really not so bad, and the constant threat of death actually makes life a bit more exciting." I flash a smile at him.

"So you say." The man sighs and shifts on his feet. "Well, that constant threat of death is telling me that we need to get out of here, and we need to do it quickly. There will be more monsters coming, I'm sure of it. My own minions won't recognize me and will brand me as a traitor. If they don't come, whatever forces Krak left in here will certainly come to finish the job."

[Moneybags: Don't worry, Jason! We're getting a portal linked up to your position at this very moment!]

"We'll be out of here shortly," I answer. "In the meantime, tell me as much as you can."

"If you'll forgive me, I'll save most of it until we're safe. It gives you a bit of incentive to get me back in one piece." The man lifts an eyebrow. "That said . . . this dungeon is among the more powerful of those linked to Earth at present. I have—well, I *had* scouts that I was able to send into other dungeons. As Krak began his little crusade of darkness, I sent out people to determine just what was happening and how concerned we needed to be."

"And what did you discover?" I ask.

"He's building an invasion force, but I imagine you already know that." The man crosses his arms. "He has plans of toppling the queen and taking her place."

"Right." I nod slowly.

"The problem is that she's a level-one-hundred creature, which she's absolutely not going to allow anyone else to reach." The man bites his lip, as if trying to think of what to say. "Because of that, Krak is building a weapon. A powerful weapon. One that he intends to use to kill the queen without a direct fight. She's too powerful to engage one on one. The problem is that this weapon is *so* powerful, I suspect that it will kill a whole lot more than just the queen. In my estimation . . ." He pauses, for dramatic effect, I suspect. "It will destroy the Earth, countless thousands of dungeons, and more. In a word, it will bring complete and utter chaos to the nine realms, wiping out billions of lives, and that"—he shrugs—"is something that I cannot allow."

CHAPTER FIVE

I mull that over for some time while we wait on the portal to open to allow us back. It takes a good thirty minutes before Mr. Wang is able to get it powered up, but the man refuses to say any more except that he'll gladly go by the name of Paul. I don't really know why he chose that name, but I'm not going to argue if he's giving us good information.

In any case, the portal soon opens, and Paul and I step through. If you've been following my journey for some time now, you know that I absolutely *hate* portal travel. When you hit the boundary of the portal, it feels like your whole body gets liquefied, at which point you just get slurped up through an interdimensional straw. When you get spat out the other side, you never quite know if the flesh making up your arms might have come from your gut, or if the matter now composing your brain might have come from your feet. It's terribly disorienting, and I hate it beyond belief.

When we stagger back out of the portal, I find that Mr.

Wang's club-cum-warrior-support-room is quite the hive of activity. Workers have fully installed an enormous array of weapons, training dummies, tables, food stands, and various other things that could be used by warriors in their assorted quests. Mr. Wang stands there, a broad smile on his face, and holds out a hand.

"Welcome back, Jason! Welcome, Paul! I do hope that you find Earth agreeable!" He whisks us over to a nearby table, where a bottle of wine is instantly poured for the three of us. Food is placed before me and Paul—I'm always hungry after completing a dungeon—and I tuck in just about as quickly as I can.

"You're . . . you're giving me food?" Paul frowns down at the hamburger in front of him.

"You're a human now. Until you give us reason not to trust you, we'll give you our full cooperation and hospitality," Mr. Wang answers.

I lean over and whisper in the former dragon's ear, "Also, he totally wants to pump you for information. Giving you food and drink is a good way to get your lips to loosen."

Paul flashes a small smile, then takes a bite of the food. "Well, it's not quite the same as raw mutton, but I suppose it'll do." He glances over at me, then whispers, "Actually, this is incredible. Way better than raw mutton."

Mr. Wang folds his hands and seems to be waiting, and I nod at him.

"Paul, I don't mean to push you, but I imagine that we *do* need to have at least a bit of haste. Krak left that dungeon in an awful big hurry, which I assume means that he's up to something."

"Yes," Paul answers. He takes a sip of the wine, and his eyes almost pop out of his head. When he manages to get ahold of himself, he takes another bite of food, then begins again. "You'll have many questions. I have a few answers, though not as many as I assume you'll want. In short, the weapon that Krak is constructing is a gun of sorts, one that shoots energy." He brightens slightly. "Actually, I've seen a movie from Earth that has something similar. There's this space station, and it blows up planets."

"Ahh, yes. *Space Battles*." I nod. "A classic, for sure. At least until RatHouse got their hands on the IP."

"Yes, a tragedy indeed." Paul frowns.

[RazorEdge: Wait . . . Are we saying that monsters can stream movies from Earth???]

[ViperQueen: They have to do *something* while they're waiting for human warriors to stumble into their dungeons.]

[DarkCynic: That's probably how they found Earth in the first place. All those radio waves blasting out into space, we were practically just begging for a more advanced race to come along and eat us.]

[ViperQueen: Uh . . . Don't mean to be a pain here, but what's a radio wave? We don't blast things out into space, we just stream them through the internet.]

It takes me a moment before I'm able to drag my attention away from the chat. When I do, I find Mr. Wang and Krak deep in a discussion about the nature of the weapon.

"He's building it inside an Astral Dungeon," Paul explains. "He chose the dungeon because of the ease with which it can be moved around, as well as the fact that Astral Dungeons haven't been unlocked yet. I imagine that Jason is getting close to unlocking them, but it'll still be at least a little bit."

"What level does he need to reach for that to happen?" Mr. Wang asks.

"Sixty-five," Paul answers.

"And what level are you at now?" Mr. Wang asks as he turns to me.

"I don't know." I shrug, then open up my interface. "I'm . . ." My eyes nearly bug out of my head. "Sixty-four! I was only *fifty-four* a few minutes ago!"

"Enjoy it," Paul mutters. "It took me centuries to amass all that XP."

"Then I just need to gain one more level." I glance over at Paul. "What will that do, practically?"

"On a functional level, Astral Dungeons, and therefore the weapon, are currently on a different level of the dimensional playing field. When you unlock them, they'll move down to this level. They'll still be hard to access—Astral Dungeons are tremendously difficult to track down—but they'll be brought within range. Like I said, they can move around a lot."

"My technology still struggles to pin down dungeons unless they stay in place for at least three or four hours," Mr. Wang mutters.

"Yeah, if you're going to take him down, you're going to need to cut that time down by a *huge* margin." Paul nods. "The way I see it, your best bet right now is to try and take down Krak's main dungeon, the one he uses as a flagship. He'll jump ship long before you have a chance to kill him, but doing that will almost certainly send him running back to his

Astral Dungeon. You'll level up in the time you're in his flagship dungeon, which will knock the dungeon down within range of Mr. Wang's portals. As soon as you come out of the flagship, you can jump into his Astral Dungeon and engage the weapon properly."

There's a flash of light, and my pocket dimension opens. Elrith steps out, a smile upon his face.

"Forgive me for intruding, but I may just be able to help."

"You?" Paul glances over at the elf. "What exactly could you do?"

"Elves are highly intelligent beings. I have a great deal of mathematical prowess, and I know a good amount about the dungeons and their movements through interdimensional space," Elrith answers. "It's possible that I could assist with the tracking software, perhaps cut down on some unnecessary operations."

"We'd sure appreciate any help we can get, wherever it comes from." Mr. Wang nods in approval. "Thank you, Elrith."

"Of course." Elrith bows his head and starts to walk away. One of Mr. Wang's technicians catches him and pulls him over to a bank of computers, where I see him start to talk quickly as he types on a keyboard there, his fingers flying far faster than I've ever seen a human able to do. I have to admit that it's impressive, but the conversation pulls me back away from the spectacle.

"The next question I have, then, is how we can find Krak's flagship dungeon, as you put it." Mr. Wang frowns in thought. "Do you know where it might be found? We saw it on our radar when he attacked that wasteland dungeon, but then he managed to make his escape. We don't have a clue where he's at now."

Paul lowers his head and closes his eyes. "Hmm. That's a tough one, but . . . maybe I can help." He stands up. "Could you show me to your computers?"

Mr. Wang gives a nod, and we quickly stand up. We're taken to the computers hooked up to the portal generator itself, which still show all the dungeons present in the New York area. A particularly large one seems to be circling around the southern side of the map, though it doesn't seem to be attaching anywhere.

"Is that it?" I ask, pointing at the thing.

"No." Mr. Wang shakes his head. "We've seen that one appearing over the last several days, but as of this moment, we don't know what it is or who it belongs to."

"I believe I might be able to answer that question," Paul murmurs as he starts to type. The images of the dungeons start to change slightly, almost as if he's looking at them from a different angle all of a sudden. "I believe, though I'm not confident, that that dungeon belongs to a monster by the name of—" He utters a name that I couldn't even begin to pronounce in English. Frankly, I don't even know how all of those sounds came out of Paul's mouth, and it makes me wonder if he really is all the way human. "He's a void behemoth, tremendously powerful. One of the queen's top ten guardians. I'm sure that your activities have alerted him to your threat and has brought him to examine the situation closely."

"A void behemoth," I mutter. "That doesn't sound like a terribly pleasant creature."

"Let me put it this way: in his dungeon, I would be one of the low-level grunts that warriors rip through without thinking about it." Paul snorts. "He's fantastically powerful. Level ninety-something, I think. If he came through, he would be essentially unstoppable."

"We'll just have to see about that." I crack my knuckles. "If I'm going to get all the way up to the queen, I'm going to have to go through him first."

"Ahh, yes." Mr. Wang holds up a hand. "As long as we're on that subject, and since you're a person who might actually know, who *is* the queen? When Jason met with Beowulf, it was insinuated that we would be able to determine who the queen was, though all my experts haven't yet been able to pin it down. If you'd be able to point us in the right direction, I'd sure appreciate it."

Paul suddenly freezes, and he slowly turns and looks first at me, then at Mr. Wang. "You don't know who the queen is?"

"At this point, all I know is that she sometimes shoots lightning bolts at monsters that she takes a strong dislike to," I answer with a smile.

"Oh, that's not her. That's her top general, her brother." Paul shakes his head. "She isn't going to lift a finger unless she *absolutely* has to. Now, when she *does* lift that finger, you're going to regret it."

"So, who is it?" I press. "Come on! I'm sorry, but we really do need to know."

"I suppose that you do." Paul bites his lip. "If I tell you, you have to promise not to hold it against me."

"We promise." I sigh in annoyance. "Please, just…Who is it?"

Paul bites his lip once more, then turns back to the computer screen. "Hella."

There's a short pause, and my chat explodes.

[DarkCynic: Hella? Like the goddess of death?]

[ViperQueen: Hey, I saw a movie about her! She was actually pretty cool.]

[ChaosRider: I would wager a guess that the real-life version is a bit more evil than the movie version.]

[GoldenShield: This is going to be great!!!]

"Hella," I finally answer. "Like the Norse goddess of death? Ruled the underworld and all that?"

Paul nods his head. "She's the one. Terribly unpleasant lady. I've only met her once, and that was enough for me."

"And you're a dragon," I mutter.

"*Was* a dragon. Let's not get things mixed up," Paul points out.

"Then"—Mr. Wang crosses his arms tightly—"her brother would be Thor."

"Yup," Paul agrees. "To get to her, you're going to have to knock through Thor, Loki, and probably Sif and Odin, and a few others too."

"Wonderful." I start tapping my toe. "This is going to be rough."

[IceQueen: You can do it, Jason!!!]

[ShadowDancer: Yeah! I mean, if you can take down a god, you can take down anything!!!]

[FireStorm: You'll be the most epic warrior ever on the face of the Earth!!!]

I can't disagree with the sentiment of the chat, but it also means that I'm going to have to fight a god. This is *not* going to be easy, no matter which way you cut it. I close my eyes and try to think. There are a lot of factors to mull over, that's for sure.

Finally, I open my eyes and nod at Paul.

"What exactly do I need to do to be able to fight her?"

"That's the spirit." Paul smiles. "Honestly, stick to the plan. She's allowing Krak to go on his rampage, which means that he's useful to her. Maybe she thinks that his weapon will get rid of you, maybe she just thinks that she can commandeer it for herself. Whatever the case, by the time you knock Krak down a few pegs, you're going to be in a much better position."

"Sounds like a plan, then." I draw in a deep breath. "Find me that flagship dungeon."

Elrith comes walking over, a smile on his face. "I've recalibrated the sensors slightly. There's still a lot more work to be done before the technology really becomes viable, but it'll work for the time being."

"Good. Yup, here. I'm getting the new data as we speak." Paul's fingers fly rapidly across the keyboard. "Almost there . . . Here we go."

The images on the screen change just slightly, and I see a small corner of a dungeon that seems to be off to the north of the city. I frown in thought, and Paul nods.

"That's it. He's keeping it close, *just* out of range of what he thinks your capabilities happen to be."

"Link up a portal quickly before he moves." Mr. Wang gives a nod. As I step back across the room, the portal generator begins to wind up. Mr. Wang comes with me, and he lowers his voice as he asks, "Would you like me to call in John or Ali? Someone to come along with you?"

I shake my head. "Ali was underpowered compared to me when I first started fighting alongside her, and I've gotten a *lot* more powerful since then. I can't speak as much for John, but I imagine that my strength stat is almost as high as his now."

"And all your other stats will be a whole lot higher." Mr. Wang frowns.

"Exactly. I don't say that as anything against the two of them, but the monsters are scaling higher and higher, and"—I shrug—"I can't have anyone else getting hurt just because I'd like some company."

"I can understand that. In that case, I bid you well." Mr. Wang nods at the portal, which roars to life. Elrith really *is* getting it to work a whole lot faster than before. "Fight well, Jason. Return a hero and a victor."

"Just be ready to pull me out of there once I clear it," I answer. "I have to imagine that clearing this place out isn't going to be easy, nor is it going to make people pleased with me."

"Probably not." Mr. Wang laughs. "Well, off you go!"

I give him a nod, then race toward the portal. Energy swirls in front of me, and with that, I leap through, on to whatever comes next.

CHAPTER SIX

This trip through the portal tube is the longest I've yet taken. I'm sucked across the dimensions, swirling and whipping this way and that, past dungeon after dungeon after dungeon. I do my best to look around as I go, but due to the nature of things, I don't exactly have the best muscle control. I *do* catch a glimpse of the really big dungeon, the one that Paul said was ruled by a void behemoth, but it grows more and more distant as I fly in the other direction.

Then, ahead of me, I see my target growing near. It's huge, the size of a rift, and pulses with an enormous amount of energy. I have little doubt that I'll be fighting for my life the moment that I enter, and I brace myself for whatever happens. Closer and closer it comes . . . And then, with a flash, I explode through the outer wall of the dungeon and come tumbling out of the portal.

Flash!

Lightning explodes across my body, and I draw out Beowulf's Dagger as a torrent of noise and chaos starts to rumble around me. It takes me a moment to get my bearings, but thankfully, it also takes the monsters a few moments to get *their* bearings.

I've landed in what seems to be a computer room. Frankly, it looks like something from NASA, with row after row after row of desks lined up through a large room. The only real differences are that the room is actually a small cave, the computers are connected to odd, demonic-looking sensor units, and the big screen at the front of the room—every control room *ever* has a large screen at the front of the room to display progress reports and so on—shows an image of the Earth, with reports of dungeon incursions and other such things from around the world.

Oh yeah, and all the workers are demon knights.

Flames roar up from inside their helmets as they all leap to their feet and draw their swords. There are a dozen of them, if not more, and dark magic starts to swirl throughout the room.

Which only means that I have a bit of a challenge on my hands.

The closest demon snarls and raises a hand. Dark fire blossoms in his palm, and I strike out as hard as I can. My dagger cuts through his wrist, and the hand falls to the floor, where it explodes. Black fire knocks me backward a few feet, but it utterly demolishes the computers and sends the demon knight a few paces back as well. I seize the opportunity and lunge forward to stab the monster under the chin. I rip my dagger back out as hard and fast as I can, then lunge at the next one.

The second demon is more prepared and has a sword in hand long before I get to him. He attacks with fury, but this time, ten levels higher, I find that I'm more or less able to stand against him. My dagger flashes in time to his sword, with neither of us able to gain a clear advantage.

Of course, there are a great many other demons in the room who take that very opportunity as an advantage, so I don't exactly get to milk my victory, but . . . still.

Arrows flash through the air as half a dozen demon knights form bows and start to shoot at me, and I dodge out of the way. The arrows flash past my head and stick deep into the rock, only to dissolve into smoke. I snarl, then lunge forward at the knight with the sword, striking with fury. I don't have time to be dealing with him, and he knows it. He blocks frantically, and I throw myself at him with all my might. His sword is knocked backward, and I duck inside his reach. With that, I stab him in the gut, then grab his helmet with my free hand. It burns my palm terribly, but I ignore the pain and slash the dagger across his neck. His head comes clean off, and I spin and throw it as hard as I can.

My aim is true, even in my haste, and I fling the helmet straight into the head of another knight nearby. The demon is knocked backward, and I leap over a row of desks. On a whim, I grab one of the computers there. Metal crumples under my grasp, and I sling *that* through the air just as hard as I can. Wires are torn out of the table and ripped from the wall, and the computer smashes into the face of another nearby knight. I don't know that it does all that much damage to him, but it blinds him for a few moments while I leap on him. My blade flashes once more, and I stab him three times through chinks in his armor, and he falls to the ground with a loud thud.

I hear a hiss from behind me and turn around as two more of the knights come charging forward. They have daggers as well now, each wielding two. I brace myself for impact, though I'm actually saved as an arrow flashes at me. I raise my dagger, rather on instinct, and the arrow is deflected off the blade and through the visor of the closest demon. He groans as he falls, and I spring upon the next one.

For a brief moment, the two of us lock together. He's fast, and I'm not really any faster. Dagger rings out against dagger, blade against blade, as both of us seek the advantage. The knights with the arrows stop shooting, which is handy. I know it's just because they don't want to hit their own, but I'll take whatever break I can get. I press my attack, forcing the monster steadily backward, but after a moment I'm forced to retreat as he manages to gain the advantage and forces me backward under a blistering offense. I have a feeling that it's going to come down to a battle of endurance, and this guy is proving to be *quite* durable.

Which just means that I have to come up with a way to knock him down to size a bit. What could wear out a demon knight?

I don't come up with any brilliant answers, though something does ring out in the back of my mind. All the way back when I was first fighting against Harold, back in the early days of the apocalypse, I killed an undead ape using a whole bunch of healing medicine. Undead things are generally killed by things that heal. I can only assume that demons count as undead, so I open up my inventory as the demon presses another series of attacks.

[ShadowDancer: Be careful, Jason! I'd sure hate to see you go down like this!]

[ViperQueen: For what it's worth, you now have by far the highest number of demon knight kills in the whole world!]

[ChaosRider: That's because no one else has a single victory.]

[RazorEdge: Hey, don't knock his achievements.]

I flash a small smile at the chat, and then, as I'm still blocking the demon's attacks, I scroll down to my healing items. With a flash, a bottle of Pumped! appears in my free hand, and the demon pauses, seemingly confused.

"That's right." I nod. "Come at me, if you dare."

The demon dares, and with a shrill shriek, he leaps forward. I swing the bottle as hard as I can, and the glass shatters against his visor with a resounding *crack*. Soda explodes across the monster, leaking through the eye slits and dripping down around his neck, and the demon lets out a piercing scream that I'm sure damages my hearing something awful. I'll be clear, I don't know whether or not the Pumped! is actually strong enough to kill the thing, but it makes him freeze for just a moment, and that's more than enough for me. I lunge forward and stab him through the neck, and the monster slowly falls.

"Alright." I turn to face the remaining demons, all of whom have bows and arrows. There are almost a dozen of them, and they glance at each other as I take my stance. "Who's next?"

A flurry of arrows flies hard and fast as I throw myself into battle. I duck down underneath one of the tables, slam it upward from beneath, and use it as an impromptu shield as I charge forward. The next several minutes are a crazed fight for survival as I hack my way through the swarms of demon knights charging at me. Arrows graze past me, swords slash at my arms, but onward I fight.

[DarkCynic: He got another one! Go Jason!!!]

[IceQueen: That's 26 . . . Now 27 . . .]

[ChaosRider: He's a demon-killing machine!]

I grit my teeth as another of the monsters slashes at me with an enormous broadsword. I duck under the blow and lunge at his midriff, where I stab him a dozen times in the blink of an eye. He tumbles backward, and I receive a notification.

[You have leveled up!]

[Congratulations! You are now Level 65!]

[Please accept from the following rewards:]

[. . .]

I don't have time to worry about a reward as I spin around the room looking things over. There's one more knight left, and he's standing in the entryway of the room, barring passage. He snarls at me, and the flames around his helmet burn a bit brighter. I have a feeling that I know what he's about to do, and it rather terrifies me.

[IceQueen: Brace yourself!!!]

[DarkCynic: Huh. This might actually be the end of our dear Jason.]

The monster bursts into flames an instant later, then grows a couple feet taller and lets out a roar that shakes the walls of the place. He's activated the suicide skill, which means that he now has absolutely nothing to lose and is so powerful that it'll be almost impossible to stop him anyway. With a mighty scream, he charges forward. No weapon, no magic, just raw brute force.

The thing throws a punch at me, and I duck under the blow, dive out of the way, and roll under a table. The monster simply smashes through the table with an overhand blow and grabs at me, and I'm *just* able to skate away. Suddenly, a burning hand latches down on my arm. Pure and utter pain lances through my body, and the world whirls around me as he suddenly spins and throws me up into the large screen at the front of the room.

Now, it should be pointed out that the screen is actually a plate of marble upon which the image of the Earth is being projected. I suppose it was cheaper that way. Anyway, the stone cracks under the impact as I slam into it. I groan as I tumble down, and the monster throws himself forward.

[Skill: Bearing of a Knight.]

[Peril Detected.]

Strength flows through my body, and I rise as the knight snarls and throws a massive punch at me. I come up to meet it and throw a punch of my own. Fist meets fist, and a resounding *boom* shakes the entire room.

What few computers haven't already been destroyed are instantly obliterated, and shards of glass explode through the area. Smoke rises from the fried electronics, and the monster snarls and throws another punch. I dodge that one, then throw an uppercut that hits him in the chin. His helmet is blasted clean off, and for a moment, I find myself staring at the beast, face to face.

His skull is entirely wrapped with flames, and what little flesh he possesses is black and charred. His eyes are tiny points of darkness sunk deep within the bone, and horns protrude from his chin, his forehead, his cheeks—I mean, this guy just *looks* like a demon. He roars, exposing fanged teeth, and I stab him in the face.

[Skill: Michael's Wings.]

[Activated.]

The blade lights up with energy as it slams into his skull, and the demon is blasted backward across the room. He reels as he climbs back to his feet, and I run forward to slash at the monster with all my might. He reaches up and catches my right arm with a flourish, but I drop the dagger, snatch it with my left, and stab him again.

This time, down on the ground, there's nowhere to go. Light explodes through the room once more, and his skull is blasted into nothing but ash. There's a long pause, and I slowly rise as smoke drifts up from the point of impact.

[Berserker Demon Knight defeated!]

[XP Awarded: 20,000,000]

[. . .]

[Notice: S-Ranked creature defeated!]

[First Kill of a Berserker Demon Knight from planet Earth!]

[Extra XP Awarded: 5,000,000]

[Michael's Wings upgraded to Rank II.]

I whistle softly. Now that's a nice bonus that I wasn't expecting. Unfortunately, my level is high enough now that even twenty-five million XP won't instantly level me up, but

I suppose that I really shouldn't complain about a thing like that. Slowly, I look around the room making sure there's nothing else left alive.

As near as I can tell, the room has been entirely destroyed, and I turn toward the door. That's one room down and countless more to go. All I can do is keep my nose to the grindstone and my feet to the floor.

And, hopefully, my blade to the throat of any monsters that stand between me and Krak.

CHAPTER SEVEN

When I emerge from the cave, I find myself in a small, winding tunnel that stretches off in both directions as far as I can see. Torches hang from sconces on the wall, and I do a quick check to see if anyone is going to be coming up on me immediately. I can certainly hear footsteps off in the distance, along with startled shouts and calls to arms, but they're nowhere close, which gives me some hope.

[ChaosRider: Hey, Jason! You ought to see what new reward you get! That'll be cool and fun!]

[ShadowDancer: YEAH!!! DO IT!!!]

There are other messages that have the same general idea, and I shake my head.

"I'll get to that just as quickly as I can, but for the time being, I really need to get to safety." I glance back and forth. It seems to me that the voices are largely coming from the left, but I can't be sure. Cave echoes can make noises seem like they're coming from a whole host of directions, so it's really a toss-up which way I should go. "It wouldn't work so well if I drew out a Dagger of Snot or something right as another demon knight jumped me. Which way should I go?"

A poll goes out to the chat, and a few moments go by as numbers are tabulated. It comes back that I should go left—after all, that's how you find your way out of any maze you get stuck in—so I nod and slip off in that direction. I keep Beowulf's Dagger at the ready but leave the Incendiary Dagger in my inventory. I'd rather not put it to the test when one of these demons is actually immune to fire.

Of course, I also don't *know* that I'll only be facing demons, but it does seem for the time being like Krak has employed a lot of them.

In any case, I steal down the hallway just as quickly and quietly as I can. I pass a few small cave entrances and alcoves, all of which seem to lead to storage rooms. One of them I suspect might hold a mini-boss, but I don't mention that suspicion out loud so my chat doesn't try to make me go fight it. Soon, I come up to a larger entrance, where a handful of stalactites partially block the view. I drop to the ground and creep up to peer out through a small crack between them.

On the other side of the entrance is a massive room, something that might be a hangar bay if it were on a spaceship. Indeed, there are loads of vehicles strewn all throughout the room. Chariots, war elephants, even a handful of tanks and airplanes that seem to have been stolen from militaries all around the world. It's really quite the sight, and my eyes nearly bug out of my head as I take it in.

[ShadowDancer: WHOA!!! That's so cool!!!]

[LunarEclipse: Cool? That's the invasion force being prepared for planet Earth! Those are going to be knocking on our doors soon enough!]

[ChaosRider: Nah, Jason will stop them before they have a chance to invade. Besides, I see a panzer in there. If a demon driving a panzer rolls down my street, I'll be okay with it, all things considered.]

I snort a bit at that comment. The vehicles are impressive, I'll give them that, but that's not what really concerns me. Lining up in front of the entrance are a *great* many demons. They're forming up in ranks and units with larger demons patrolling behind them. Several of the demons practically look like trolls, they're so large, while a particularly horrid-looking archdemon stands at the rear on a small platform. He holds a trident and has a crown made of burning fire. Suddenly, I realize that these demons were probably the residents of an infernal dungeon that Krak convinced to join him. The archdemon would have been the dungeon boss. If I can take him out, I'll probably take out most of the demons through the rest of the dungeon—maybe even all the demons that Krak has been accumulating. Now, there are pros and cons to doing a thing like that. On the bright side, all the demons would be gone. On the less bright side, I'm starting to be able to deal quite a bit of damage to the things, so it would be nice to keep fighting them in order to make better use of that, but . . . beggars, choosers, and all that.

In any case, they're waiting on me, which is probably a smart tactical move on their part. That said, it also gives me a chance to plan, so I slip back down the hall to one of the side hallways. There, I pause, then open up my reward. It doesn't look like I received any rewards for the levels that Paul essentially gave to me, but I imagine that simply receiving said levels was really enough of a reward. Carefully, I scroll through the options. They're the same as normal:

[Weapon]

[Monster]

[Skill]

Normally, I just choose the weapon. After all, I have a massive laundry list of skills that I can never remember to use anyway, and my creatures are a formidable fighting force. But in this case, I suddenly find myself more drawn toward the monster option.

[LunarEclipse: I'm telling you, Jason, go for the weapon! You lose daggers like I lose pencils.]

[ViperQueen: No, do a skill! You might get an S-Ranked skill that lets you turn into a dragon or something for five minutes!]

[GoldenShield: No, no, no!!! You should absolutely choose a weapon. If you don't, you're stupid.]

"I'm going to choose a new pet," I answer. "Let's hope it's something good against demons."

There's a flash, and a portal suddenly swirls in front of me. The chat explodes with comments, some positive and some not. There's a long pause, and then, with a flicker, a paw steps through.

My heart sinks just a bit, if I'm being honest. It's a dog's paw. I already have three dogs—well, wolves—and while I certainly love them, I do have to admit that I was sort of hoping for something different. But as my new pet emerges, all my hesitation fades away in an instant.

He stands about as high as my waist and looks like a Great Dane. His hair is a gleaming golden color, and he seems to radiate bliss and peace.

[Hound of Heaven]

[Rank: S]

"Now *you* look like something that would fare quite well against demons." I bend down and scratch him behind the ears. "What's your name?"

Gabe, Master. And yes, killing demons is a particularly favored pastime of mine.

"Then I think you're going to enjoy my first assignment for you." I flash him a smile, then slowly rise. "Want to meet my other pups?"

I'd love to!

I open up my pocket dimension, and Bjorn, Astrid, and Balder all come out. For a moment, the dogs all sniff each other, then they turn to me.

We're ready, Bjorn says. *I think we're all going to go inside and handle this particular problem.*

"I'd be happy for your help," I reply, then glance at Astrid. "You too? You're a fire type, generally speaking."

I can still be of assistance.

"Alright. Well, I'm glad to have you. Just don't exert yourselves too much. I'll need you in fighting condition when we get to Krak. I know the plan is to drive him off to his weapon, but if we can just catch him and kill him here, I'd sure like to do it."

My pups all nod in agreement, and with that, I turn and head back down the hall. As I come up to the end, I crouch down and slide up behind the wall of stalactites, then give a nod.

"You all know what to do. Gabe, how'd you like to lead this one?"

I'd be honored.

Gabe shakes himself, then slowly steps forward. My other pets prepare themselves, and I stand up. The demons catch sight of me, and I hear their armor rattle as they tense up. I raise my dagger, then nod.

"Now!"

Gabe leaps out into the open and charges forward. Demons instantly let a flurry of arrows loose, but with a flash, Gabe doubles in speed, and every last one of the arrows misses him. He bounds across the floor in great leaps, then goes crashing into the front lines.

A powerful howl splits the air, and the demons are thrown backward as if hit by a shock wave. Gabe snarls and spins as one tries to cut him in half, then unleashes a blast of light that sends the demon knight reeling. He's certainly making a dent in their lines, that's for sure, and I charge forward just as fast as I can.

Bjorn takes the right flank, howling as loud as *he* can. Ice spreads across the floor and stabs up into their ranks. Several of the demons succumb and fall as their fire burns out, and they simply clatter to the floor. A few others unleash blasts of dark magic against the ice, but they're still being forced to defend themselves, and that's good news to me. Meanwhile, Astrid and Balder take the left flank. Astrid growls and cracks explode across the floor, opening up great gaps. No fire comes boiling up through them, though I do see flashes of light. A handful of the demon knights fall through, and I see bursts of lightning. Suddenly, I realize that the hangar has been built just above a reactor core. I don't have a clue what the reactor is powering, but I can tell that it's big, and that fact is going to come in handy.

Either that, or it'll kill both me and my pets. I suppose we'll find out!

Balder is a bit more straightforward than his parents and lets out a howl that unleashes a powerful shock wave. It hits the knights dead on and flings them backward as if they were rag dolls. My XP meter climbs as the four canines tear their way into the ranks of knights, and a smile spreads across my face.

Yeah, this is the way I like it.

With that, I throw myself into the fray of things. At this point, the demons are so confused that they've fallen out of their ranks and are just sort of hacking and slashing as desperately as they can. One of them comes up and tries to take my head off, and I narrowly dodge out of the way before stabbing him under the chin. They really need to check those helmets. Another demon knight comes racing up from the side, and I dodge and spin, then kick his leg. He stumbles right into Gabe's path, who unleashes another lance of light, which sends the demon flying as though he was hit by a freight train. Another knight comes up flailing about with a large mace, and I dodge the first several blows. Balder comes bounding up from the side and lets out a sharp yip, and a focused shock wave hits the knight firmly. He's lifted from his feet and tossed through a large crack, and a moment later, a burst of lightning signals his death. I let out a sigh of relief, then continue to press forward.

My canines race back and forth, tag-teaming the demons as only they can do. Bjorn creates slabs of ice that cause the knights to slip and fall through Astrid's cracks. Gabe uses his blasts of light and other holy attacks to corral them so that Balder can crush them. Meanwhile, I dodge about between them, helping out as I can. Our attacks align perfectly, as if we had choreographed the battle. It's really quite wonderful in just about every sense of the word, though one thing does concern me.

In the background, the rest of the demons are staying up. The archdemon remains on his little platform, watching the events play out as if he were watching an opera. The troll-sized demons, who seem to be looking to him for guidance, also stay put. Maybe he just doesn't want to kill his own troops with some sort of special area-of-effect attack, but somehow, I doubt that's the case. Demons don't usually care about hurting their own people. No, he's got something up his sleeve; I only hope that I can see it in time.

Soon there are only a few of the knights left, and they form a circle as we converge upon them. Astrid growls and the ground beneath them cracks and starts to fall apart. They leap out of the way, only for Gabe to emit a splendorous, wonderful howl. Three of them simply crumble into dust right at that moment, and the others tremble in fear and terror. I smile at them, then charge forward. They all turn to run, and the archdemon lets out a snarl.

"Cowards!"

It must be a terrible thing to be caught between the wrath of a powerful enemy and an archdemon. The mighty enemy raises his trident, which suddenly blazes with an immense light. Fire shoots down from the stone roof as if called from the heavens and hits the remaining demon knights. They're burned up in the blink of an eye, and I brace myself. My pups all come and stand next to me, and I stare up at the archdemon.

"Well." The monster chuckles as he leans forward. "I have to say, you've done well."

"You don't seem all that concerned," I answer back. "You either have something up your sleeve, or you're about to offer me a place at your right hand or something."

The archdemon laughs. "You watch too many movies! Let us suppose that you *were* evil, like me, and I thought that our goals could align. I would have to constantly watch my back for fear that you would stab it. As it is, you aren't evil, and you seek to protect the Earth. I could no sooner trust you than I could trust my own mother."

"You must come from a lovely society," I mutter. Something begins to flicker in the back of my mind, and I nod to my pups. "Get back inside, now."

Somewhat reluctantly, the four canines obey. As the pocket dimension portal closes, I brace myself for whatever comes next.

"Alright, then. Do your worst," I sneer up at him. "Shall we do hand-to-hand combat? One on one? What exactly is going through your head?"

"Only the fact that while you're powerful, you're still a

fool," the archdemon snaps. "You're standing on unstable ground. That will be your downfall . . . literally."

The demon trolls snarl, raise their fists, and bring them crashing down. The floor, which Astrid weakened significantly, suddenly shatters into bits. I find myself looking straight down at what seems to be an artificial sun, with nothing between myself and the pure embrace of torrential energy. Down I fall . . . down . . . into what may as well be the fire of hell itself.

CHAPTER EIGHT

I have only moments before hitting the great star, which seems to rest upon three metal beams that jut up into its core. Down below the star are a great many other things, though I can't properly see them at that moment. Before I can hit the reactor core, though, I see a flicker of portal energy, and something comes shooting out.

"Burnie!" I cry out. "You—"

Burnie doesn't answer but throws himself at me. He's traveling at the speed of a falcon, and all the air is knocked out of my lungs as he hits me with an extraordinary amount of force. I'm knocked to the side, and even though the heat sears me rather badly, I pass *just* by the edge of the core. Burnie, though, isn't so lucky, and I catch the briefest glimpse of my noble blue Phoenix tumbling into the reactor core before I come crashing to the ground.

"No!" I scream as I hit the metal floor. I bounce as the metal is dented underneath me, and I slowly sit up. The floor of the cave here seems to be uneven and is covered with a great many snake-like cables and other things you'd expect to see in a reactor. A metal grate has been placed above all of that as a sort of walkway, while computers and other monitoring stations are strewn about the area. They're all staffed by gross centipede things, and I take hold of Beowulf's Dagger as I slowly climb to my feet.

[ChaosRider: NO!!!!!! Not Burnie!!!!]

[ViperQueen: I bet he'll be back.]

[ShadowDancer: He just fell into a REACTOR CORE! There's no coming back from that.]

[GoldenShield: Yeah, but he *has* already died more than once, you know.]

[RazorEdge: More than once?]

I grit my teeth. I'm in no mood now to think about the possibilities of Burnie coming back or not. The odds are against it by an extraordinary margin, and I slowly stalk forward, anger burning in my heart. The centipede things all grab weapons and start to charge at me, and I draw in a deep breath.

Thankfully, they're not hard to defeat. My blade cuts them into bits within seconds, and as the last one falls, I turn to look for a way out. There's a single broad pathway that leads up and away, and I head in that direction.

Boom.

The walkway shakes, and I slowly turn around to see the archdemon drop down from above and land on the ground with a resounding *thud.* His trident crackles with energy, and he sneers at me. His infernal crown burns a bit brighter, and he slowly stalks forward.

"I'll admit, I'm impressed. I've always sacrificed others for my own ends, not had them sacrifice themselves for me. It's far more effective." The archdemon seems to pause in thought. "Maybe I should learn how to do that."

I let out an enraged scream and charge at the thing. He's in the opposite direction I need to be going, but if I leave him alive, he'll only follow me.

Plus, he killed Burnie.

The archdemon simply laughs, then raises a hand and snaps a finger. One of the demon trolls comes crashing down just behind me and slams a fist into the metal walkway. The grate buckles underneath me, and I'm sent tumbling. As I come up, the troll bounds forward—those things can move *fast* when they want to—snatches me up, and throws me into a wall.

I've barely even hit the wall before he leaps over, grabs hold of me again, and spins. This time he throws me into a computer console. Metal folds around me like plastic wrap, glass shatters, and wires spark. I gasp as I peel myself out of the mess, and the troll leaps upon me once more.

He throws a powerful punch at me, which I dodge. The strike blasts a great crater into the ground, and I slash at the thing's arm. My dagger doesn't seem to do a lick of damage, and he snatches me up an instant later. Suddenly, he hefts me into the air and brings me slamming down again, battering me about like a rag doll.

The troll grunts, and with that, he begins to swing me back and forth over his head, smashing me first to one side of his body, then another. I'm mostly helpless against him as the world spins around me. Finally, the attack runs out, and he tosses me at the feet of the archdemon. I roll several times before coming to a stop, and the archdemon slowly snarls and flips his trident over before placing it against my chest.

[Skill: Bearing of a Knight.]

[Peril Detected.]

[Error: Healing is being inhibited by an Infernal being.]

"Struggling a bit, are we?" the archdemon snarls down at me. "You will perish soon enough, and you will know that good will *always* bow to evil."

"You know what's funny?" I gasp out. "You're . . . you're referring to yourself as evil. Truly evil things always think that they're doing the right thing."

The archdemon chuckles, and he presses the tip of the trident into my skin. It only pierces the top layer, but pain radiates outward, and it *burns*. I'm going to be feeling *that* in the morning, I'm certain of it.

"No." The archdemon shakes his head. "No, that's a misconception. *Truly* evil people are the ones who know that what they're doing is evil, and despite that knowledge, they continue to do it anyway. There are few more powerful than me, few who have done the things that I've done. You will be nothing more than another mark on my trident."

"Then why are you still talking to me?" I snap. I know if I move a muscle, he'll stab me, so I decide to humor him for as long as he's interested in continuing our little conversation.

"I like the scent of fear," the archdemon answers. "And you, sir, are ripe with it."

[DarkCynic: Our Jason? No! He's not scared of anything.]

[GoldenShield: He's holding himself together, but come on. Look at that thing. If *that* was standing over you, you'd be scared too.]

[DarkCynic: No, I wouldn't be! I'm not scared of anything either.]

[FireStorm: Sure . . .]

The archdemon continues to snarl down at me and pushes the trident a bit deeper. Now, I'll admit that at this moment, I don't have the faintest idea how I'm going to get out of this. One of my pets will have to show up, I'm sure, but none of them seem inclined to do so anytime soon, and frankly, I don't know that any of them should. Maybe Gabe could take this guy on, but most of them would just wind up getting themselves killed.

As I ponder how to get out of the situation, the reactor core above the archdemon's head suddenly flickers. A strange ray of hope strikes me, and I grit my teeth. The archdemon notices the change, and he lifts his trident.

"Just what do you think you're going to—"

Pzzzzzzzzzzzzzzzzzzzzzzzzzzzzzzew!

A great blast of pure, white energy shoots down out of the core and hits the archdemon in the chest. The mighty creature is thrown backward and smashes into the wall, and Burnie flashes down out of the core to land on the ground next to me. His feathers are pure white now, from head to claw, and his eyes have a fiery, brilliant gleam. The archdemon snarls and stands up as I leap to my feet, but Burnie spreads his wings and fires another blast of piercing energy at the monster. This time he is actually blasted several inches into the stone, and he lets out a cry.

"Don't just stand there! Rip him apart!"

The second demon troll jumps down into the pit, landing not far away, and with that, the battle is on. The first one lunges at me, but Burnie fires a blast of energy and hits the beast in the face. It knocks the creature backward, though not far, and Burnie spins to the second one.

I focus my efforts on the first troll as Burnie flashes over and begins harassing the second troll. He snarls and lunges, trying to stomp me, but that makes him move just a bit slower than normal. I dodge the attack and stab him several times in the leg, then spin out of the way as he rotates and tries to grab me. I'm only narrowly able to dodge-roll to safety, and I come back up to stare at the tank of a demon.

[LunarEclipse: Come on, Jason! You can do it!]

[ViperQueen: Yeah! Just don't let him hit you, and you'll wear him down eventually!]

[RazorEdge: Go for the face! The FACE!!!!]

I glance over at Burnie, who's flashing in circles around his troll. A near-constant beam of destructive power is hitting the monster in the head, which makes the creature simply stomp about as he tries to cover himself up. Now, I can't fly, nor do I have a great many ranged attacks, but I take note of Burnie's tactic.

I'll just have to knock the demon troll down to my level.

As the troll runs forward once more, I come racing up to meet him. I drop to the ground and slide under the first blow, then pop back to my feet and slash upward at the troll's backside. My blade is strong, and my aim is true, and I inflict a long gash that erupts from his left knee all the way up his spine. The skin seems to be softer there, and the monster howls and stumbles. I take the opportunity to charge forward at him and leap up at his back. I slam Beowulf's Dagger deeply right between two of his ribs and snatch out my second dagger as well.

Fire blazes from the Incendiary Blade as I use the two daggers like picks to climb up the demon troll. Fire is also crackling from the troll itself, which burns me severely as I try to clamber all the way up to the top. My health drops, but not terribly fast—after getting away from the trident, my health healed enough that I'm willing to risk a bit of exposure. As I get close to the top of the creature, I grit my teeth, then lunge upward, reach around the great head of the troll, and slam both daggers down into his eyes, one into each.

The troll lets out a powerful scream, one that echoes throughout the whole of the reactor room, and he begins to stumble about. I grin despite myself . . . And then he swings a hand wildly upward and whacks me firmly.

I'm tossed up into the air and sail toward the reactor core. For an instant, the thing fills my entire vision, and I just *know* that I'm going to slam into it. In fact, I very well might have done so, but within inches of the fiery surface of the sphere, the second troll reaches up, snatches my leg, and slams me back into the ground.

"Uh, I thought you had him," I groan as I climb back to my feet and Burnie swoops past me. He responds by firing a blast of flame into the face of the monster, momentarily blinding him, and I dodge out of the way. Once more, I find that the archdemon is simply standing back, watching. That gives me an idea, and despite the fact that I've lost my daggers (again), I charge at him. The sword on my back emits a warm glow, and I reach up to grab hold of the handle.

A mighty *shing* echoes through the room as I draw the weapon and spring forward. I'm not terribly used to wielding a sword—daggers are really my jam—but in this case, Ascalon just seems to know what it's doing. A holy light explodes from the weapon and shines all about the room, and the archdemon flinches backward.

"Ahh! It's been centuries since I last saw that weapon!"

"I'll make you a deal," I snarl. "After this fight, you'll never have to see it again."

I attack the archdemon with fury, slashing down at his head. He raises the trident and blocks, but I disengage and attack once again almost instantly. The trident is slow, and while the demon certainly knows how to use it, my sword is quite a bit faster. He spins his own weapon desperately through his hands as he blocks attack after attack after attack.

The thing is . . . I'm not actually trying to hit him.

I suspect that he'll call his trolls to help, and that's exactly what happens. With Burnie keeping the second troll busy, the one that I blinded is the one that comes leaping to the rescue. It knows roughly where the archdemon is located and roughly where I'm located, and I hear the *whiff* of air as it throws an impossibly powerful punch.

And I simply step out of the way.

The archdemon takes the full brunt of the blow intended for me and is flattened against the wall with a powerful *boom* that shakes the whole area. I quickly leap backward and slash through the back of the troll's knee with Ascalon, making him stumble and fall forward, and he lands on the archdemon with another powerful *boom*. He flails about and tries to stand up, and the archdemon assists.

By, of course, firing a lance of flame straight through the troll's body.

The troll groans as the archdemon blasts him out of the way. The corpse lands just next to me, and I leap upward, sheath Ascalon, and snatch my two daggers out of the thing's head. With that, I charge at the archdemon with every last ounce of energy that I have.

The archdemon snarls and points his trident at me as he fires blast after blast of energy. I drop to the ground and slide under the first one, then come back to my feet and jump clean over the second. The next several I dodge as best I can, and that brings me *right* up close to the monster. He has only a second before he realizes that my daggers are a whole lot faster than his trident, and I duck back behind his guard and stab him in the chest.

For all his power and tricks, the archdemon has surprisingly little armor, and my blade punches clean to his heart. Michael's Wings activates and delivers a powerful punch that erupts clean through his body. Light explodes out of his eyes, and with that, the archdemon groans and falls backward. Fearful that it could be a trick, I don't lower my guard until I've slashed clean through the archdemon's neck. The crown falls to the ground, cold as death, glittering with a handful of gemstones. I know better than to pick it up and instead slowly turn to the last troll.

[Michael's Wings upgraded to Rank III.]

My body fills with newfound strength, and I charge forward. The troll turns toward me, and I throw myself at him. Now, I'm well aware of the fact that Burnie has been working on the thing's health for about ten minutes at this point, but it still feels good to inflict a single slash across the demon troll's belly and watch as he falls sprawling across the floor with one final *boom.*

I loosened it for you, Master.

"I don't doubt it in the least."

A handful of notifications cross my vision, informing me that I've gone from level sixty-five to sixty-seven. No new rewards appear, though, and I open up my inventory to pull out a Pumped! drink.

With that, I turn toward the exit and start slowly making my way in that direction. I'm making a good account of myself, I do believe.

Now, I just have to go find out what's waiting for me around the next corner.

CHAPTER NINE

I walk fairly slowly out of the reactor room. A small part of me wants to try and destroy the reactor, but I don't know exactly what that would *do*, so I restrain myself. After all, it's entirely possible that destroying it would power down Krak's systems and make it easier for me to fight through the dungeon, but it's *also* quite possible that destroying it would simply blow up the dungeon, which, considering that I'm more or less trapped inside, I can't say is my favorite idea in the world.

The path out of the reactor core is a smooth one, which I appreciate. It seems to be fairly well trafficked, which makes me assume that this was likely one of the first rooms that Krak added to the dungeon. Whatever the core is for, I'm sure it's important, and it only adds to the mystery surrounding this odd place.

[ChaosRider: Alright, Jason, keep your head level! There's

no telling what else you'll run into, and we want to make sure we watch you cut Krak down to size!]

[ViperQueen: Yeah! Go for Krak! Knock him dead!]

My chat fills with more general cheer, and a small smile spreads across my face. Suddenly, I see something on the wall, a small plaque, and after glancing around to make sure that nothing is waiting in the shadows, I quickly walk over. My heart leaps as I realize that it's a map! Though I can't read the strange, rune-like text used to indicate what's what, I can certainly tell that the red dot indicates where I'm at and the green dot indicates the command center. I can also locate the reactor room, the hangar bay, and a handful of other places as well.

Importantly, it looks like the hallway I'm in right now leads up to a major hallway, which then leads through a handful of smaller, warehouse-like rooms. From there, I have to go up an elevator shaft—or stairwell, I can't quite tell—to the top floor, where I'll find the command room. Satisfied that I know the route, I turn to start off again, then pause.

Footsteps echo through the corridor, a lot of them, and I glance around. I spot a small alcove and duck inside, and a moment later, a handful of figures stride past. They look like humans, but they're a bit taller and wear black combat robes. I can't tell for sure, but it looks to me like they have weapons concealed under their robes, and I make sure that I have a good hold on my dagger. A moment later, they're out of sight, though I don't dare move.

"I don't see him anywhere," a voice drifts up. It's sharp and has an off tone about it that unsettles me. "He must have fallen into the core."

"No. There are three dead bodies," another voice hisses. "He survived the fall and cut them down. No one else could have taken on the archdemon with two demon trolls."

"Pfft. Anyone could have taken on the archdemon. He was a weakling who pretended to have power."

"He *did* have some spectacular magic."

The conversation grows louder, and I freeze. The figures come sweeping past again, quite business-like. There are five of them, though only two seem to be speaking.

"His main magic stemmed from the fact that he could control the minds of other demons. Hardly something worth bragging about."

"I'll say that he certainly did plenty of *that!*"

The beings laugh, though it isn't really a laugh that has a lot of mirth to it. I shudder a bit, then slowly slip out of my hiding place and stride after them.

Ahead, the figures go around a corner. I creep up to said corner and glance around, where I find them entering the major hallway that I saw on the map. It seems to have been carved through the stone and is plated with metal. There are sliding doors, gun emplacements, and automatic turrets, and that's just what I can see from my limited vantage point. This is going to take some guts to get through.

I just hope that most of the guts I encounter belong to someone else.

The beings sweep up and into the hall. A cart rumbles past, and my eyes just about bug out of my head. It's carrying cannon shells like enormous bullets, mounted in a rack that could have come from any military base on Earth. These beings have been raiding Earth's military installations, stealing tanks and weapons!

[LunarEclipse: Why do they have to take our stuff? Aren't their own weapons good enough?]

[FireStorm: I mean . . . give us a fighting chance, won't you? You're already pounding the Earth into dust. The least you could do is leave us our own weapons to fight back, right?]

I smile at the chat as they begin debating whether or not the monsters had a right to take weapons from Earth. I, though, have other concerns. They're here, and the question is whether or not they'll be employed against me. I've seen people try to use guns against the monsters, even low-level ones, and it doesn't work out well. If a monster were to shoot a gun at *me*, what would the result be?

Frankly, I'd rather not find out, but I suspect that I'm about to get a firsthand demonstration.

"Alright, enough waiting," I mutter quietly, then grit my teeth and step out into the open. Clinging to the side of the passage, I slip up toward the hall. I still don't want to engage them directly unless I have to, but I do need to get moving. "Let's see what these things have to—"

BAM!

One of the automatic turrets spins in my direction and fires. The shot is incredibly accurate and hits me squarely in the chest. Pain flares through my body, and I groan. As I look down, the bullet simply drops to the ground with a *ping*. Another shot rings out and hits me in the exact same place, and I grimace.

They hurt, but they don't do much damage to my health, which . . . I suppose is a good thing?

In any case, startled shouts ring through the area, and I charge forward. Two of the creatures step into view, and they snarl softly, revealing pointed teeth. They both throw off their outer combat robes to reveal much tighter robes beneath. Both of them have wicked-looking swords hanging at their sides, and they draw their weapons as I charge forward.

The swords . . . They're a little hard to describe. They have a curve like a cutlass, but they're a lot thinner, almost like a rapier. In any case, both creatures come running forward, and I prepare myself. Beowulf's Dagger flashes in my hand, and I throw myself into combat.

The first of them slashes at me, a sharp whistling sound coming off the sword. I stop short, and the blade flashes past my face. The tip just nicks my nose, drawing blood, and I lunge forward and stab the thing in the gut. It doesn't have any armor to speak of, which is nice.

It also doesn't seem to register any pain, which is less nice.

In fact, the only result of me stabbing it is that I'm suddenly up close to the monster. Like lightning, it stabs the curved sword deep into my shoulder. I feel the weapon cut along the back of my shoulder blade almost all the way to my spine, which is *beyond* painful. I rip out Beowulf's Dagger and slash the creature's neck through, then the second monster attacks with fury.

It's lightning fast with that little sword, and I only manage to parry three strikes before it slashes me across the gut. I tumble backward and hit the ground with a *whack*. My health drops so low that you would have no idea that I had healed myself after the fight against the demons, and I groan and slowly push myself back up. The first one—which *didn't* die from having its neck cut open—attacks again, and I angrily raise my dagger and slap the curved sword away.

This time, as it attacks with fury, I focus my anger and use my dagger to parry the attack with as much force as I can muster. The sword clatters off to the side, and I stab the monster between the eyes. Bone crunches under the impact, and the thing lets out a hiss as its dark eyes glaze over. Slowly, it slumps to the ground, and I turn to face the second one. I notice that my health is slowly starting to rise again—it would seem that Bearing of a Knight kicked in while I wasn't paying attention—but it's still a lot lower than I'd like.

"And just what exactly are you?" I ask. The creature doesn't answer, but another shot rings out and hits me in the shoulder. I gulp in pain, and the thing lunges, slashing and stabbing once more.

I quickly throw myself into a desperate series of blocks and parries. I'm starting to see its pattern, so I can block more than before, but I'm still being pushed back toward the wall behind me. The monster knows it too and suddenly springs backward and braces itself. I recognize *that* move, so I spin out the way right as it lunges.

Thankfully, this time my intuition is right on point, and the monster executes a speed-based attack that sends it flashing forward at what must be almost the speed of light. I slash at its neck with Beowulf's Dagger at the same moment, and my blade hits it firmly and squarely.

Now, yes, I'm aware of the fact that the last time I cut one of the things across the neck, it didn't do anything. But on *that* occasion, I only severed its throat. This time I chop clean through, spine and all, and the fast-moving body slams into the wall while the head falls to the ground with a *thunk*. The sword sticks fast in the stone, quivering a bit as the body collapses, and I turn toward the hallway.

With that, the gunshots begin to ring louder and faster, and I run forward just as fast as I can. As I tear into the hallway, I hear a sudden whir and notice almost a dozen red dots appear on my chest. Anyone from Earth knows exactly what that means, and I do a *very* quick reconnaissance of the hall.

In the direction that I need to go, the hall stretches out for about fifty feet. In those fifty feet there are six doors on either side, each with a turret mounted above it and one in between. There are also almost a dozen of the odd monsters, each of which is armed with one of those little swords. It does not look good for me, and I quickly spin back out of the way into the tunnel I just came from.

Bam-bam-bam-bam-bam-bam-bam-bam-bam-bam-bam-bam-bam-bam-bam-bam-bam-bam-bam-bam-bam-bam-bam-bam-bam-bam-bam-bam-bam-bam-bam-bam-bam-bam-bam-bam-bam-bam-bam-bam-bam-bam-bam-bam-bam-bam-bam-bam-bam-bam!

A torrent of bullets rips through the air, pulverizing the stone into dust and ringing off the metal. I grit my teeth as I try to think through my options. The turrets wind down once I'm out of the way, and I hear feet ringing on the metal. Those *things* are coming for me, and when they arrive, I doubt I'm going to be able to hold them all off. They're just too fast. If three or four, let alone a dozen, attack me at once, I won't be able to beat them.

"Alright, think," I mutter. "Guns, bullets, crazy things that are insanely fast. Anyone in the chat have any ideas?"

[ShadowDancer: First off, I think those are Nephilim. I can't guarantee it, but they look similar to some pictures I saw in a guidebook that another warrior found.]

[IceQueen: Yeah, I totally agree! Let's see . . . You could always try using holy water against them!]

[ChaosRider: He doesn't *have* any holy water!]

[RazorEdge: You could try stabbing them!]

[DarkCynic: Just be faster than they are! I could probably do it.]

[GoldenShield: Why not just punch them or something?]

Overall, as much as I love everyone in my chat, the answers are utterly and completely unhelpful. I sigh in frustration as the footsteps come closer . . . And then comes a bolt of inspiration.

[GrendleH8tr: Kid, just use what you've got. You'll do fine.]

I'm not sure what it is about that line, but in that instant, everything clicks. A smile spreads across my face, and as the Nephilim come racing into view, I leap back out into the middle of the hall.

In that moment, the guns blaze to life again, and I brace myself. A few of the bullets do hit me, but with a dozen of those monsters bearing down upon me, well . . . there are a *lot* of meat shields between me and the turrets. I watch with a smile as they're hit by what must be hundreds of bullets fired over the span of just a few seconds. Only a few of the Nephilim actually die, but they're all wounded pretty badly, and I settle into my stance, then spin back out of the way.

As the monsters stagger through the doorway, Beowulf's Dagger flashes in my hand, and I carve my way through them one by one.

Plop.

Plop.

Plop.

Heads, arms, legs, they all come crashing down into a growing pile as the Nephilim fall into my trap. A few moments pass, and the last of them dies upon my blade. I rip the dagger back out and let the monster fall headlong across the ground, then let out a long breath and glance around the corner once more.

Two more of the creatures are waiting at the end of the hall, but they're waiting, not attacking. I've bought myself a few precious seconds, and that isn't all.

I've *also* just made the first kill of a Nephilim, and that's something to be pleased about. All things considered, I'm in a pretty good position. All that's left is to make sure that I can capitalize on it and fight my way through to the end of the dungeon.

CHAPTER TEN

Nephilim Grunt defeated!]

    [XP Awarded: 15,000,000]

[. . .]

[Notice: S-Ranked creature defeated!]

[First Kill of a Nephilim from planet Earth!]

[Extra XP Awarded: 5,000,000]

[Skill Acquired!]

[Rank: S]

[Nimrod's Bane (passive): Grants an extraordinary increase in power when fighting against Fallen creatures. Also, grants an increase in XP gain from such creatures.]

I nod in approval at the skill. It's not as flashy as some of the others, but I've already seen how effective Michael's Wings has been in fighting against the demons. It'll work well enough for me, that's for sure! I glance at my XP bar, but I'm still firmly at level sixty-seven. Still not too shabby, but I'd also like to see it rising a bit faster. In any case, I take a deep breath, then glance around the corner once more.

[ChaosRider: You've got this, Jason!]

[ViperQueen: Yeah! Just go really fast so the bullets can't hit you, and then take out those guys!]

[GoldenShield: You know, I bet if you went into one of those storage rooms, they'd follow you!]

That last suggestion actually sounds like a good one, strange as it sounds. If I fight the last two Nephilim in the hallway, I'm going to be dueling both them *and* the bullets, and I can't say I really like the idea of that. I don't know exactly how to get into the storage rooms, though. I have to imagine that they're locked, right? Suddenly, an idea hits me, and I bend down and start sorting through the pile of bodies. It only takes me a moment before I come across what I'm looking for.

"Here we go!" I find a small keycard, which I hold up for my chat to view. It has a picture of the Nephilim on it, and I twirl it through my fingers before poking my head out the door. The two monsters are still standing there, swords drawn, just waiting. They know better than to be baited in by me. In the hall, they have a distinct advantage.

Thankfully, I now have a way to nullify that advantage. Quickly, I place the keycard in my fingers like I'm going to throw a card for a trick and step out into view. With a sharp flick of my wrist, I fling the card at the keycard reader next to the door opposite where I'm standing. It slams into the reader and sticks into the metal, but the reader still gives a sharp *ding*, and the door slides open.

Now *that* gets the dander of those two monsters up. They flash forward, and I leap into motion, diving across the hallway just as quickly as I can. I perform a perfect dodge-roll through the door and pop back to my feet in a warehouse that's just about as chock-full of weapons and ordinance as you could imagine.

There are machine guns hanging on the walls on pegs alongside crates and crates of rifles, shotguns, pistols, and a whole lot more. Tank shells are lined up against one wall, a whole row of different-sized ones. There are jugs and jugs of what looks like gasoline with an Asian script I can't identify written across them, along with a wide assortment of other things. I blink in surprise at it all, only to feel something sharp stab deep into my back.

One of the thin blades of the Nephilim stabs me in the left side and another one hits me in the leg. I throw myself forward as I scream in shock and come up into a stance as best as I can. The Nephilim, both of them, are furious and have abandoned all traces of holding back. I'm in a room where I'm not supposed to be, a room that's likely extremely dangerous for everyone involved. I flash them a grim smile as I lash out and bat the first one's sword aside as it tries to deliver a killing blow. The second one tries to stab at my chest as well, and I just *barely* manage to knock it out of the way. Ignoring the pain, I slowly rise up to standing once more and stare the two of them down. They both back up just the slightest bit, and Ascalon grows warm on my back. My leg wound heals, at least enough so I know that my leg won't buckle when I need it most, and I draw in a deep breath.

"Alright." I keep my voice level. "This isn't *quite* the tour that I signed up for. The brochure made this place sound far more inviting."

The two Nephilim don't budge, but they don't attack me right away either. That's a good sign, at least. I draw in a deep breath, then flinch to the left. Both Nephilim take the bait, and they lunge in that direction. They realize their mistake almost instantly, but by that point, I'm springing into action.

Unfortunately, it doesn't do a whole lot of good, as the Nephilim are just *so* fast. They're both able to recover with ease and block my attacks quite forcefully. I grit my teeth as we come crashing together. A moment later, we break apart, and I attack with as much fury and force and speed as I can manage.

The three of us blur into a torrent of limbs and energy as we try to break through each other's defenses. Finally, I manage to score a small nick across the arm of one of them, and a small blast of light streaks through the air.

[Skill: Nimrod's Bane.]

[Damage Added.]

The Nephilim screams and falls backward slightly, giving me just a smidge more room. Before the second one can fully process what's happening, I lunge forward, swat its sword aside with almost all my remaining strength, and stab it in the chest. Light explodes off my dagger and erupts cleanly through its back, and it staggers backward and falls in a heap.

[GoldenShield: WHOA!!! That's epic!]

[ViperQueen: Yeah!!! Again, again!!]

[FireStorm: You've got this, Jason!]

I don't react to the chats but turn to face the final Nephilim, who's sneering at me while slowly turning its head about. I can tell that it's not off guard; it's expecting me to attack at any moment, but it's also doing its level best to see if there's anything in the area that it can exploit.

Unfortunately, there are a *lot* of things in the area that I suspect it'll be able to make use of. I see its eyes settle upon the cans of gasoline, and it suddenly seems to perk up—not by much, but it's there. The Nephilim has a plan, and I imagine that it involves a great deal of explosions.

Thankfully, it doesn't notice that I've noticed (say *that* five times fast) and lowers itself into a stance as if to charge me. I oblige its playacting and jump to the side as if to dodge. Suddenly, sparks fly from its fingertips and it flashes forward.

As I've adequately prepared, though, it doesn't get very far.

My dagger meets its neck, and its body lands with a *thunk* on the metal floor, sliding up just next to the cans. Its head bounces off a crate of ammo, while its sparking hand skitters up to within just a few inches of the gasoline. The sparks start to die down, but not nearly as fast as I'd like, so I run forward and yank the body back. A moment later, the Nephilim is still and cold, and I let out a sigh of relief.

Thud.

The floor shakes *just* a bit, and I glance at the doorway. A shadow falls across the entrance, though it doesn't enter just yet, and I gulp. It's a long and tall sort of shadow, and my mind begins working through the options.

[DarkCynic: I bet that's the elder Nephilim or something similar.]

[ShadowDancer: Yeah! The boss of the Nephilim!]

[FireStorm: But not like a BOSS boss.]

[ChaosRider: Still a bossy boss, I would bet.]

I have to chuckle slightly despite myself. Then, keeping an eye on the doorway, I take a step back next to the cans. Carefully, I bend down and unscrew one of the lids, then lean over and take a sniff. The smell is so strong I almost pass out straightaway. It's like sticking my head into a tank of petroleum. I gasp and lean back, then cautiously glance inside the can.

It's some sort of hydrocarbon, that much is obvious, but it doesn't smell quite like gasoline. It's also quite gelatinous, like . . . Imagine jelly gasoline. I struggle for a moment as I look the stuff over, but some of my chat chimes in to help.

[ShadowDancer: Hey, I think that's napalm!]

[DarkCynic: I totally knew that.]

[ChaosRider: Yeah, that's what it looks like, alright. Be careful, Jason, that stuff is dangerous.]

I slowly bend down and pick up one of the cans, then tip it over. It doesn't exactly come rushing out, but a good bit of it oozes across the floor. "Do you think if it's dangerous to me, it might be dangerous to the Nephilim too?"

The chat explodes with their agreement, and I smile, then look back up at the doorway. The monster standing there still hasn't moved. It's just . . . waiting, and I haven't the slightest idea why. That said, it's giving me time to work, so I don't complain too much. Quickly, I open up several more cans of the napalm and dump them all around the immediate area, splashing the substance across ammo crates and across the floor. With that done, I open up my inventory and pull out my trusty old pistol. It's been ages since I've seen the thing. It was a concealed carry that I brought with me to New York ages ago but got stuck in my inventory when I realized that it was essentially useless against the monsters. Quickly, I slide over to the doorway and point the gun back at the containers on the far side of the room. With that, I risk a quick glance out into the hall.

Another of the Nephilim is standing there, just staring at me intensely. It's a good head taller than any of the others but is still clothed with those same black robes. I pause, locked under its gaze, and it slowly takes a step forward.

"Jason Lee, I believe. It's a pleasure to meet you."

I whip back out of the way and retreat a few steps. It joins me in the room, crossing the threshold calmly. It gives a single glance at the napalm, then at my gun, and then settles its gaze back upon me.

"Do you really think that threatening me will work?"

"No." I shake my head. "I just like having options available to me."

"Indeed." The Nephilim slowly reaches back and draws a sword out from under its robes. It's longer than the others but has functionally the same shape as the curved swords wielded by the other Nephilim. "You are a resourceful man, Jason Lee, and I must congratulate you on that fact."

"Are *you* about to offer me a deal?" I snort. "I already turned down someone else."

"Perhaps you did. I, though, have a somewhat different perspective, I believe." The Nephilim slowly turns the blade over in its hands. "I have very little concern about not trusting someone. I don't trust any of my people. If you were to join me, I would not lose a moment's sleep, even if I knew your conversion, so to speak, to be nothing more than a ruse or a coercion. You cannot make it through this dungeon, not even with all your strength and power. End this little crusade of yours now, while you still can. It will save *everyone* a great deal of trouble."

[IceQueen: Don't listen to him, Jason!!!]

[ChaosRider: I don't know. Might be fun to see Jason suddenly turn dark.]

[ShadowDancer: Are you kidding??? Jason's our only hope against these monsters! If he turns, then we'll be seeing these monsters in real life, not just on a screen!]

[ChaosRider: I mean like as a trick!]

[ShadowDancer: Oh yeah, that could be cool.]

I roll my eyes at the chat, then shrug. "What exactly do you have in mind?"

The Nephilim doesn't answer at first. It certainly doesn't lower its weapon. "What I'm thinking is that you—"

"Skill: Speed."

I activate my skill and throw myself forward. The world slows; though, as the elder Nephilim spins into motion, I know it's not as much as I'd like. It lashes out at me at what seems like an ordinary speed. I strike the blow out of the way, duck past the Nephilim, then step out through the door. The monster spins to follow, and I raise the gun and fire three times.

Bam-bam-bam!

The bullets leave my gun slowly enough that I can actually see them flash across the room and hit the cans of napalm. Fire blossoms outward, and I quickly grab the keycard and yank it back out of the metal. Lights flash red, and the door starts to move downward.

Outside in the hall, guns blaze to life, but with my enhanced speed, I'm able to walk past them pretty easily. I'm about halfway down the hallway when the door slams shut, *just* managing to seal the Nephilim inside. As I reach the end, I feel the ground start to rumble and step around the corner out of range of the turrets. With that, I allow my skill to turn off and cross my arms as the room explodes.

KA-BOOOOOOOOOOOOOOOOOOOOM!

Bam-bam-bam-bam-bam-bam-bam-bam-bam-bam-bam-bam-bam-bam-bam!

Tat-tat-tat-tat-tat-tat-tat-tat-tat-tat-tat-tat-tat-tat-tat-tat-tat-tat-tat-tat-tat-tat-tat-tat-tat-tat-tat-tat-tat-tat-tat-tat-tat-tat-tat-tat-tat-tat-tat-tat-tat-tat-tat-tat-tat-tat-tat-tat!

The impossible heat of the napalm, as I expected, begins to set off loads of other ordinance. The wall right next to my head suddenly bursts open as a tank's shell is fired straight through. I realize that I'm not as safe as I thought, and I turn and run.

Behind me, the explosions grow louder and louder. Fire erupts through the hall after me, crashing around the corners and racing up the corridors like a flood. Ahead of me, I see a group of monsters with a great many tentacles, all of which are armed with spears and axes and other sharp things. They're standing in front of what look to be stairs, or . . . No, the elevators! All of them turn toward me, and I flash them a sloppy sort of salute as I run straight past them and flash into one of the open elevators right as its doors slide shut.

The moment the doors come together, the force of the blast hits from the other side of the steel, and it actually gets dented inward slightly. I hear a monster's sharp scream from the other side, then slowly turn as I hear a gurgle from just behind me.

I accidentally jumped into the elevator *with* one of them! This isn't going to go well . . . Hopefully, though, the monster is the one that will get the worse end of the deal.

CHAPTER ELEVEN

The creature standing just across from me is . . . Well, it's hard to describe. It stands a smidge taller than I do and looks more or less humanoid except for the fact that it seems entirely reptilian. Its face has two enormous compound eyes and a whole slew of tentacles in place of a mouth, which almost makes it look like it's eating a huge mouthful of spaghetti. In any case, it's holding what looks to be a harpoon and doesn't look at all pleased to see me. As it draws back the harpoon to strike, the elevator starts upward with a rumble.

"Are you going up?" I ask, pointing upward.

The monster hesitates, and I fold my hands behind my back. A soft jazzy music starts to play, and I tap my foot against the floor. With a sigh, the monster steps back as well.

[Minor Cthulhu defeated!]

[XP Awarded: 20,000,000]

[. . .]

[Notice: S-Ranked creature defeated!]

[First Kill of a Minor Cthulhu from planet Earth!]
[Extra XP Awarded: 5,000,000]
[. . .]
[You have leveled up!]
[Congratulations! You are now Level 68!]
[. . .]
[Extra reward granted for First Kill of a Minor Cthulhu!]
[Skill Acquired!]
[Cult Hunter (passive)]

This passive skill is much the same as my other passive skills, and I sigh and pretend to be bored as my XP rises and passive abilities grow a bit stronger. I can only assume that the system is crediting me with starting the explosion and thus is granting me XP and credit for each kill that happens because of it. The numbers keep rising, which leads me to suspect that I've just set off *quite* the chain reaction. I don't know what to make of it, but I do hope that I don't accidentally blow myself up in the process.

In any case, the elevator soon grinds to a halt, and the doors pop about halfway open. Two more cthulhu try to step on board, only to freeze as they see me. I give a small wave, then lunge at the monster who rode the elevator with me.

It's a credit to its S-Ranked status as it twirls its harpoon like a baton and whacks me firmly in the chest before I can even come close to it. I'm lifted clean off my feet and slammed into the control panel. Sparks explode from the metal, several lights blink on, and the doors slam back shut. The music comes back on, and the elevator starts to drop. This time, though, the monster doesn't sit back and wait.

It twirls the harpoon again, then lunges, striking at me with an extraordinary force. I only barely manage to evade the blow, and the sharpened hook at the end of the harpoon carves a long gash out of the wall. Through the crack, I see the side of the elevator shaft whirring past. The cthulhu lets out a hiss and attacks again.

I'm forced to do a little bit of dodging as it attacks again and again and again. It's so fast that I can hardly even follow its strikes with the naked eye, and the force with which it hits is enough to tear open metal on all sides of the elevator. It even knocks open a few holes in the floor, allowing the wind to whistle up from below as we continue to drop. What's worse is the fact that it doesn't pause its attack at all to give me a chance to counter. Lower-level monsters will attack once or twice and then give you a smidge of a break, but not this guy.

In any case, it's still pressing me when the elevator rumbles to a stop and the door hisses open. I leap through and spin to the right, then brace myself against the wall and launch myself forward. The cthulhu runs through the gap right as I come crashing into it, and I knock it sideways. I manage to stab it twice, making the monster stagger, before it whacks me upside the head with the harpoon. I miss a step, and it whirls and hits me in the chest. I'm once again lifted clean off my feet and thrown backward into the wall, and it steps back and braces itself, watching me and waiting.

As I peel myself off the wall, another *boom* shakes the room, and I glance around. I'm standing in a massive storage area, something like another hangar bay, which is filled with more tanks and jeeps and other invasion vehicles. Suddenly, though, a warm glow spreads across the ceiling. With a great blast, liquefied stone begins to pour down followed by a great torrent of flame. With a *clunk*, the reactor core falls about halfway through the ceiling, where it sticks as it slowly continues to melt its way through.

Huh. It would seem that blowing up the warehouse is still causing issues.

I grit my teeth, then spin back to the monster as it lunges once more. I narrowly dodge, and it thrusts at me, only to drive its harpoon deep into the stone. That gives me the barest instant to stab it in the shoulder, which makes it roar with anger and pain. I then leap out of the way as it rips the harpoon back out of the rock. A great chunk of the stone remains caught on the harpoon, and I rush forward at it, hoping to take advantage of that very fact. Before I can do anything, though, it spins, twirls its harpoon sharply, and whacks me in the chest. The force of the blow sends me flying up into the air and into the middle of the storage area. I come crashing down on a jeep as the cthulu marches down from the door toward me.

"Oof, I'm going to feel that in the morning," I groan as I sit up and jump down from the jeep. I take a step forward, only for a pulse of metal to come crashing down from the ceiling and utterly incinerate a jeep just in front of me. Great. The heat is tremendously oppressive, and I gasp and take a step back as I glance up at the ceiling. The area directly above me is rapidly turning orange, and I bite my lip.

Master!

Astrid bounds out of my pocket dimension and howls. A

break in the waterfall of molten stone and metal opens up in front of me, and I race forward and leap through to safety. She portals away a moment later, then appears next to me as another great torrent of molten stone comes pouring down from the ceiling. With an unfathomable *boom*, the great orb of the reactor core falls through the ceiling and slams into the floor, melting jeeps and tanks and tires and mechanic carts into slag.

The cthulhu snarls, then charges at me once more. Astrid snarls, and the ground suddenly collapses under its feet. It falls into the depths, and I give a small nod.

"Thanks, Astrid. I owe y—"

Suddenly, the ground cracks open under *my* feet, and with a great blast of sulfur and steam, the monster simply leaps back up as if it has simply bounced off a trampoline or something. It attacks me again with blinding force, and I'm driven backward under the advance. Astrid snarls, but the cthulhu ignores her.

I need to get rid of it, and I need to do it quickly. I try backing up to get it to lunge at me, but it continues advancing at a steady pace. The heat of the flames grows behind me, and I gulp as I realize that I can't go any further backward without stepping into the reactor core and everything else it's melting.

The monster realizes the same thing and launches into an elaborate series of strikes and twirls that will certainly send me into the heart of the reactor if I miss so much as a single step. I throw myself into evasive maneuvers, dodging frantically as it throws a rapid-fire series of attacks my way. Several times the harpoon grazes my skin and armor, but I manage to keep my footing. I watch for an opening, then duck past and thread my way around it to its other side.

Suddenly, our positions are reversed and *I'm* the one with the chance to push my opponent into the reactor core. At least . . . in theory. In order to do it, I'll have to actually land a hit on it, which is proving to be quite a difficult task.

The cthulhu seems to sense this fact as well and suddenly attacks with fury. It's scared, and I can't really blame it. After all, a misstep at this point will result in falling into a ball of fire so intense that we'd be incinerated in mere seconds. I brace myself, then launch myself at it.

As I do so, I hear a growl from the side and recognize it as Balder's snarl. The cthulhu strikes down at me, only for its harpoon to freeze in the air. It's as if the harpoon has hit a force field, and that allows me to lunge inside its range of attack and stab it through the chest. Energy pulses around the blade, and I slam my shoulder into the creature, knocking it backward. The cthulhu flails about as it stumbles, which gives me another opening.

One thing that I've realized in battle is that rarely do both parties whittle each other away slowly and carefully over a long conflict. Most of the time, individual battles are decided when one party makes a mistake and gets their tail handed to them. In this case, that's certainly what happens. My blade flashes back and forth across its gullet, and a great deal of black blood drips down its body as I expose its internal organs to the air. With one final slash, I cut a long gash across its leg, and it falls backward into the reactor core. There's a momentary flash of light, then a shadow of ash left on the surface of the sphere, and then even that fades away.

"And there we have it." I give a nod and turn away from the core, then look up toward the elevator once more. Standing there are half a dozen more of the monsters, and as I watch, the elevator dings and a much larger cthulhu steps through brandishing a club with a great many spikes coming out the end.

"Huh." I let out a long breath. "This is going to be interesting. Who here thinks I can take them all on at once?"

From behind me, there's a sharp rumble as the reactor core falls through the floor, leaving nothing but a pit behind. With an enormous *thud*, it lands on the next floor down, and a wave of heat washes upward. I frown, then risk a single glance over the edge of the pit where I'm now standing.

Below, all I can see is an ocean of fire bubbling upward, churning and boiling as the reactor core sinks into it. There's a flicker as a dragon is sucked into the core and vanishes, and then the core slumps down below the level of the lava. With that, though, the level of the molten stone begins to *rise*, slowly advancing upon my position.

Cthulhu are one thing. Lava flows are something entirely different. If one of them ever starts roaring at me and sporting a health bar, I'll gladly try my hand at fighting it. As it is, I lose no time whatsoever scampering away from the edge of the pit.

The cthulhu all regard me with suspicion and readiness as I race up from the edge of the pit. Suddenly, though, Burnie swoops down over my head and lets out a blinding blast of white-hot fire. The monsters scream and spin out of the way, giving me a path through. I run straight between them all and dodge past the club of the big one as I do. It growls and swings at me, and I feel the air of the club's passing. With that, I leap through the doors into the elevator, spin, and begin pressing as many of the buttons as I can.

The doors groan and start sliding closed. Just before they shut, I'm treated to a view of a dozen cthulhu staring at me, flabbergasted. Behind them, a great fountain of lava bursts upward, twisting and curling about like waves on a stormy ocean. One of them sees it and starts to run toward me, and then the doors close and the elevator rumbles upward. A few moments later, I start getting more notifications about dead cthulhu, and I let out a sigh of relief.

[IceQueen: You're doing great, Jason! Keep it up and you'll have this dungeon taken down in no time!]

[ChaosRider: Yeah! This is totally epic, and we all love you for it!]

[DarkCynic: Yeah, it's pretty entertaining. I wouldn't mind if you raised the stakes, though.]

I snort at the last comment and lean against the wall. Then two things happen.

First, the elevator stops. As it turns out, I pushed one of the lower floors when I *should* have just hit the button for the top floor.

Second, the bottom of the elevator starts to get warm.

Outside the elevator doors, I find myself facing a demon knight chatting with a cthulu. They both snap to attention and take two steps apart from each other as the door opens. It takes them a moment to realize that I'm not one of their coworkers, and I give a small wave before jumping upward. There's a small latch on the ceiling of the elevator, and I make short work of crashing through it. The demon knight and the cthulhu charge into the elevator a second later, and I quickly slash through the cable holding the elevator up. With a whir, the elevator car falls while the cable shoots upward, connected to a distant ballast.

I, of course, catch hold of the cable as it passes by and get launched upward as if I'm being shot from a trebuchet. The car falls straight downward and is swallowed by the rising lava. I'm awarded two more kills—that napalm is apparently the gift that just keeps on giving—and the flight up the shaft suddenly becomes a race: me versus the rising tide of lava.

Thankfully, the lava begins to pour into the floors that I pass. The first floor, where I met the two hapless cross-dungeon friends, isn't quite large enough to swallow the whole tide. The second floor slows it a bit more, and by the third or fourth one, it seems to me to have stopped rising.

I, however, continue to ride the elevator cable all the way to the top. I have a meeting with Krak, and though I don't have an appointment, I have no intentions of missing the rendezvous.

CHAPTER TWELVE

With a mighty crash, I reach the top of the elevator shaft. My intention is to let go ahead of time, and thus sail up through the door at the top with the grace of a dove, ready to take names and knock heads.

Unfortunately, I hang onto the cable just a *smidge* too long and crash into the ceiling. My head rings as I catch hold of a support bar and swing myself out onto the floor, and my chat goes wild.

[ShadowDancer: OUCH! That had to hurt!]

[ViperQueen: Walk it off, Jason, walk it off!]

[DarkCynic: You know, *I* wouldn't have done something like that.]

I shake my head to clear the cobwebs, then get my bearings. The elevator shaft opens into what looks like a command room not unlike many of the others I've seen recently. There are a great many desks and computers and consoles and things, along with a great many different monsters standing around monitoring the situation.

At this moment, I'll admit that I'm a bit impressed with the damage that has been done. There's a large screen on one wall, which displays a status of the dungeon. About half of it is red, and a large red ball marks the reactor core as it slowly sinks through the structure. At present, it seems to be close to the bottom, maybe with one or two more chambers to sink through. In the meantime, the rising lava is wiping out other decks and seems to have entirely cut off several sections of the dungeon.

"This is Command to Tangent Dungeon ChaosRider2," a skeleton says into a microphone. "You are to detach and withdraw to coordinate alpha-niner-eight-seven-five-two-three."

"Roger that," a voice comes back through. A moment later, a large section toward the front of the dungeon blinks and vanishes. Of course, doing *that* causes the lava to flow toward another tangent dungeon—I think—and a minotaur starts yelling instructions into another microphone.

And then, someone notices me.

"Well, well, well."

There's a hiss, and I see another archdemon slowly walk through a door from the side. He's holding a large flaming sword and has a wicked sort of grin on his black face. The other archdemon I fought was almost a joke, but *this* guy looks like he knows his business.

"Pizza's here." I cross my arms. "Sorry, I don't mean to pry, but no one is wanting to pay, and I *do* need either cash or check before I can—"

Fooooooooom!

The archdemon doesn't seem to appreciate my humor, nor does he allow me time to stall. I dive out of the way as he fires a blast of flame from his palm and scorches the stone where I was just standing. As I get back to my feet, the minotaur snarls, snatches a battle axe off his back, and lunges at me.

I snarl back at him, then rise up as he swings down at me. I can tell that this thing's level is a good bit lower than mine and flash up to meet the axe with my dagger. Despite the size difference, I'm able to parry the axe with ease and send it clattering off to the side. The minotaur blinks in surprise, and I slash Beowulf's Dagger across his chest. A great deal of blood comes pouring down, and the top half of the minotaur separates from the bottom half. He collapses in a heap, and the archdemon chuckles.

"I'm afraid most of you will find that the illustrious Jason Lee is a bit more powerful than you could ever hope to be. I suggest that you reconvene at the secondary bridge. Leave him to me."

Another door hisses open, and the assorted monsters charge for freedom and safety. I move to step into the way, but the archdemon raises a hand and makes a wall of fire appear in front of me. I'm fairly certain I could break through it if I wanted to, but . . . most likely, the other monsters are just going to get swallowed up by the lava anyway, so I'd only be wasting my time and putting myself in harm's way. Instead, I stay put, and the archdemon waits until the last of the monsters have run out. The door hisses closed, the wall of fire vanishes, and the creature slowly inclines his head at me.

"You've caused a great deal of chaos. Do you have the faintest idea just how much?"

"Not a bit." I shake my head. "Though I have to imagine that the reactor core isn't doing anything *good* to Krak's plans."

The archdemon snorts, then gestures at the map. "The lower levels of this dungeon, where the reactor core is now located, was an infernal dungeon and the home of myself and the other demons on board. It was filled with lava and magic. My home is being destroyed as we speak."

"I have to say, I'm not really all that choked up," I answer casually.

"Of course not. I wouldn't be either, in your shoes. However, there's something you ought to know." The archdemon raises his hand, and a small bit of flame appears at the very bottom of the map like a pointer. "When the reactor core burns through the edge of this dungeon, it will rupture the boundary between this dungeon and the interdimensional realm we inhabit. When that happens, this dungeon will be inverted."

"What exactly does that mean?" I ask, hardly daring to ask the question.

"That means that everything inside the dungeon will be sucked out into the void," the archdemon answers simply. "Everything will be flung out to drift aimlessly among the universes until the end of time. Or, I suppose, until it hits another dungeon."

"That doesn't sound so bad." I shrug.

"Perhaps not to you." The archdemon slowly starts to walk toward me. "Just consider for a moment, though, that you're in here with us. When that reactor core breaks through, we're all going to be in a world of hurt, and you're going to be coming along for the ride." *That* gives me pause. "Also, I'd like you to consider that the reactor core itself will be flung out into the void. There, it can burn its way into other dungeons . . . or, perhaps, even to Earth."

Now that *really* gives me pause. The archdemon seizes the opportunity and raises a hand, causing a great deal of magic to swirl about it. He lets out a deep and evil sort of laugh, then flings a blast of dark magic at me. I dive out of the way, and a resounding explosion shakes the very foundations of the room. Computers spark and go dead, lights flicker and start to die, and the archdemon snarls and stalks down toward me, slowly and methodically, prepared to put an end to my miserable little existence.

Unfortunately, my reaction to his news made me just a smidge slower than I might have liked, so while I *did* avoid the blast, I'm definitely scorched a bit from it. The monster twirls his sword, then draws it back and strikes with all available force.

Clang!

I parry the weapon—just barely. Infernal sparks explode through the air as his blade slides along my own, and I snarl and break contact, then stab at him with all my might. He narrowly manages to dodge, then performs a spin attack. The blade cleaves wildly through the air, and I drop down into a crouch to avoid it. Of course, that only makes him lash out with his foot, which catches me in the side of the head. I'm sent sprawling, and he laughs. A fiery rope lashes down around my left wrist, and he starts pulling me up.

"You're nothing but a miserable human, and you're going to die like one." The archdemon laughs. "Meet my blade, Jaso—"

I brace myself to pull with all my might and make him stumble forward. At the same time, dagger gripped in my right hand, I stab at him, aiming for his face. A force field appears and intercepts the dagger only a few inches from his black skin, and he laughs. The rope burns my skin, but I ignore the pain and try stabbing him several more times. He dissolves the rope with a laugh, then spins and tries to kick me away.

I react with a flourish as I stagger back to my feet and grip my dagger a bit tighter. An idea springs into the back of my mind, and I open my pocket dimension and call out Gabe. My hound appears next to me, golden fur gleaming, and gives off a blast of light that makes the archdemon flinch. Not by much, but he *does* flinch, and that gives me hope.

"You think that thing will protect you?" The archdemon chuckles.

"I don't think so, no." I shake my head, and my eyes level with his. "I know so."

Gabe howls, and a torrent of light fills the room, which makes the demon stagger backward. At the same time, my pocket dimension opens again and Bjorn comes bounding out, ice clattering in his fur. He tilts his head back in a howl and sends long ice crystals to grow across just about every surface I can see. The archdemon's fiery sword becomes a bit less intense, and he snarls in obvious pain.

"Keep it up!" I call out to my pups as I charge forward. "We've got him now!"

I slightly underestimate the strength of the archdemon. He's hurting from the attacks, but he's far from down. I attack with fury, but he simply lashes out. My blade meets his, and I'm thrown backward with extraordinary force. As I come crashing down on the metal floor, he strides forward and slashes first at Gabe, then Bjorn. Both canines are forced backward, which causes them to let up on their attack.

Which, as it turns out, is just the thing the archdemon needs.

He opens his mouth and lets out his own howl, a horrid, demonic noise that chills me to the bone. The room grows dark, so much so that I can barely see, and is lit only by a few dark red flames that blaze to life all around. A harsh wind begins to whip around the room, forming a great swirl with the demon at the center. I'm stung by a demonic ash that starts to whip up as well, lashing at my cheeks and making me hack and cough as I try to breathe. The monster snarls and advances, swinging his sword back and forth, gesturing for me to come forth.

"You have no power here, Jason Lee, and neither do your pets." He snorts in derision as both Bjorn and Gabe try and fail to use their own effects. "All effects below Rank S are being suppressed and will continue to be until you're defeated. Tell them to go away and we can fight man to man."

"I'd be happy to fight man to man," I answer, "but we both know that you're no man. As long as they're out, you have to use some of your concentration to maintain this, and I'd rather keep it that way."

The archdemon shrugs. "Fair enough."

With that, he charges forward, and I rush up to meet him. Our blades come together again and again, and he slowly forces me backward. His reach with that sword is just too long; I simply can't break in close enough to inflict any real damage. One hit is all I need for my enhanced skills to send him reeling, but I can't even manage that much. I need a break. I need . . .

Wham!

His sword breaks through my block and hits me across the chest before slamming me back into the wall behind me. I groan and sink to my knees, and my chat explodes.

[DarkCynic: GET UP JASON!!! He's about to kill you!!!]

[IceQueen: Yeah! You've got this!!!]

[FireStorm: Please get up! We love you, Jason!!!]

I draw in a deep breath as Ascalon begins to glow warmly on my back and Bearing of a Knight kicks in. The archdemon laughs and shakes his head.

"That isn't going to help you here."

"I suppose we'll just have to find out the hard way."

I run forward and, rather on a whim, reach up and grab hold of Ascalon's hilt. There's a loud *shing* as I pull the sword free with my right hand—I'm still holding Beowulf's Dagger in my left—and a great light shines through the cavern. The archdemon sneers and swings his own sword, and I lash upward to block.

Clang!

As it turns out, duel-wielding a sword and a dagger at the same time isn't a great idea, at least generally speaking. My sword is batted out of the way easily, and I launch into a series of strikes of varying sizes and strengths. The archdemon is able to deflect all of them with relative ease, but he *is* forced onto the defensive, which is the important bit. All his attention is focused on me.

Which means that he doesn't see the two hounds coming up behind him.

With one motion, they leap up and sink their fangs deep into his shoulders and arms, dragging him down. He lets out a howl and flails about. It's not much, but it's enough, and I lunge forward and stab both blades deep into his chest. A demonic, dark squeal emerges from his lips in that moment, followed by a sigh that causes a small burst of ash to float up from his lips. The room goes quiet as the hellstorm dies away.

"I suppose . . . maybe you're not too bad for a human."

I refuse to give the demon any sort of acknowledgement. He slowly relaxes and slumps upon the deck, and I'm awarded a bit more XP. Slowly, I climb back to my feet, then take a look about.

The screen indicating the status of the dungeon shows that the destruction is still continuing at quite an extensive rate, and I whistle. I don't have long before the reactor core hits the bottom of the dungeon and either breaks through into interdimensional space or . . . Well, I don't know what else it might do. Frankly, I don't even know if the archdemon was telling the truth, all I know is that the core *is* about to hit the bottom of the dungeon, and the other dungeon monsters certainly seem to have considered the place a loss. I start looking around for any way out of the control room, any sort of clue that might indicate where Krak is hiding.

And then . . . I hear it.

A low rumble, the sound of stone against stone.

The backside of the command room slowly slides open to reveal a large open cave. A boss chamber, and a big one at that. At the far end of the chamber is a throne, fifty feet high, and upon the throne sits Krak. He stares out at me, amusement and hatred in his eyes.

"Welcome to my throne room, *Master*." He snorts, motioning for me to enter. "It's high time we had a chat."

CHAPTER THIRTEEN

A chat?" I ask as I slowly walk into the room. The door closes behind me as I enter, though that could be as much to keep lava out as to keep me inside. "We need to do more than that. Last time we spoke, you tried to kill me."

"And I intend to do more than just *try* this time." Krak slowly rises from his throne. He's a good fifty feet tall, if not more, and has a massive sword made out of bone. The last time I fought him, I had help. This is going to be tricky, for sure. I'm more powerful, but he's also had a lot of time to prepare, and I imagine he has become a good bit more powerful as well. "You have become quite the pain in my side, Jason Lee, and I do not intend for that to continue."

"I'm hearing a lot of *intends*," I answer him as I take my stance. "I think you'll find that I'm not going to go down easy."

[ShadowDancer: YEAH, JASON!!!!!]

[DarkCynic: I'm not sure he's going to be up for this, but it's going to be cool to see him try.]

[ChaosRider: Have some faith! Jason, you've got this!!!]

Krak and I stare at each other for a long moment. In that gaze, a *lot* passes between us. I have to say that I hate him, and that's not an understatement. I truly despise him. He took advantage of me, he deceived me, he pretended to be my friend, and then he turned his back on me. Sure, he's a dungeon boss and was only doing what he thought was best, following his instincts, but . . . still. On the other hand, I can see that he hates me too. He used me to further his own goals, but instead of launching him into the heavens, I've proved to be more of a stumbling block. It's a unique dynamic, and it's one that I don't foresee being resolved except in the case of one of our deaths.

"Your move, Jason," Krak rumbles after a moment, taking his own stance. "I'll give you that courtesy."

"You're all heart." I run through my assorted attack options. I'm going to need help for this fight, that's for sure. "In that case, I tap two mountains and call in my dogs!"

With a flicker, my pocket dimension opens behind me, and Bjorn, Astrid, Balder, and Gabe all step through. They snarl and walk up next to me, ready for blood. Burnie shoots out over my head and starts to spiral through the sky, and Blub bounces into my hand.

[ShadowDancer: I'm pretty sure that it would take more than two mountains to summon six creatures.]

[ViperQueen: Unless he's already played at least three Mythic Glade cards, which lower summoning cost.]

[LunarEclipse: Guys, this is real life, not Spells: The Get-Together.]

I laugh a bit at the chat, but Krak isn't laughing. Instead, he snarls and begins to march forward swinging his sword. One hit from that thing and I'm dead, I'm sure of it.

That just means that I'll have to be fast.

"Let's go, go, go!" I charge forward. "You all know your business! Make it count!"

Krak snarls and opens up his mouth, and I see fire blossom inside his gullet. That's new. Gabe reacts quickly and fires a brilliant bolt of light that hits Krak in the face. It doesn't do any physical damage, but it does blind him for just a moment. He blinks and covers his eyes with his hand, and Burnie swoops in. A blast of white-hot fire explodes across the monster with extraordinary force, scorching his arms and chest and neck, and Krak howls in pain.

With the distraction, I charge forward, leap up, and slash my dagger across Krak's belly. Beowulf's Dagger triggers its own special effect: higher damage against serpentine creatures. A long gash opens up, far larger than what I actually scored, and Krak growls.

It's not an angry growl. It's a focused, I'm-going-to-kill-you growl.

With that, he spins around and lashes out with his tail. I have only a moment to respond, and I jump up into the air as hard as I can. I'm not quite fast enough, though, and the tail catches my legs and flings me high into the air. I slam into the ceiling, then slowly peel away from the hardened stone and come crashing back down. Before I can land, though, Krak reaches out and snatches me from the air. His jaw opens, and he moves to fling me down into his gullet.

Balder howls loudly and powerfully, and a shock wave hits me like a sledgehammer. I'm pretty sure I feel something break under the impact, and I'm knocked clean out of Krak's hand and to the ground below. I bounce several times upon landing, then come up to my feet, ready for anything.

Bjorn bounds past me as Krak snarls and swings his sword at me. A blast of ice erupts around Krak's hand holding the sword, which makes him mistime his swing. It misses me by a hair, and I give Bjorn a nod. Astrid is next and causes the ground to split open underneath Krak. Blazing-hot fumes erupt upward like a volcano, and he snarls in pain.

The next several moments are ones of absolute chaos. I race about on the ground and slash at Krak with every ounce of energy and speed that I have. Burnie spirals around his head and inflicts immense blasts of heat with every chance he gets. All my hounds do their level best, striking here and there. Krak has an insane amount of health, so I know it's going to be death by a thousand cuts for him. That said, we're sure racking the numbers up; we must have landed at least two or three hundred cuts, which only leaves seven or eight hundred more to go.

[IceQueen: YEAH, Jason! You have no idea how epic this boss battle is turning out to be!]

[RazorEdge: I'm recording it and will be sending it in to ABB. America's Boss Battles, if you haven't heard of it.]

[GoldenShield: Keep up the good work, Jason! Just make sure to watch your left!]

I glance off to my left but find nothing. I frown, only for Krak's tail to flash towards me from that direction. I fall flat on my back this time, and the tail passes just above me. Overhead, Krak rages as he desperately tries to stomp me into goo.

"Give it up, Jason! You're not going to get away with this!"

"You keep saying that, but I'm really not sure I agree." I glance over at Balder. "Can you give me a boost?"

Balder draws in a deep breath, and I run away from him and toward Krak. There's a small outcropping of rock that rises up from the floor, and I run up it and jump into the air. Balder emits a sharp bark a moment later, and a shock wave hits my feet. This time, prepared for it, I ride the shock wave like an elevator and use it to launch myself up at Krak's face.

I slam into his throat with extraordinary force and knock him backward. I'm able to slash across his neck, which makes a *great* deal of black blood trickle down his body. He gasps and stumbles backward, then snarls and raises a fist. Magic swirls around his hand, and I realize that things are about to get very bad.

"Everyone! Back in the portal!"

My creatures obey instantly and zoom back inside the pocket dimension in the blink of an eye. A moment later, the magic detonates, sending a blast of infernal magic swirling throughout the room.

The effect is similar to what the archdemon used, but it's far more powerful. The wind nearly knocks me off my feet, and the fire roaring through the air is so hot that I find myself choking, gasping just to breathe. Krak laughs and slowly walks forward as he forms more fireballs in his hands.

"Do you know, Jason, that when a dungeon boss takes on a lesser dungeon, that boss inherits the skills and abilities that the lesser dungeon boss possessed?" Krak snarls softly as the magic grows ever-more powerful. I actually *am* knocked sideways a bit and stagger as I try to keep my footing. "You believe that you've mortally wounded me, but I say that you've only made me more powerful."

"And I say that you're insane," I snap up at him. "Krak, you saw the bolt of lightning that hit you out on the mesa. Give up this insane quest. Destroy your weapon and just go back to being a normal dungeon boss."

"Destroy my weapon?" Krak laughs. "That's the one piece of immunity that I have. I will not be giving it up, not for you, not for anyone. I will keep it, and I will use it. I will become lord of this world, of all the worlds!"

"Not if you lose to a level-sixty-seven warrior." I shrug. "There's not a chance in the world you'd be able to stand up to a level-one-hundred queen."

That's too much for Krak, and the magic around me grows more and more powerful. I fall to my knees, and Krak stumbles forward. But I can see something that he can't.

The magic, powerful as it is, is eating away at him.

His eyes are sinking into his head, and burns are beginning to show on his hands and around his mouth. He might have access to the skill, but he's not a demon. At least . . . not yet. The thought of a demonic Krak fills my mind, and I push myself back to my feet and charge forward.

"*Ahhhhhhhhhhhhhhhh!*"

I let out the scream mostly to try and scare him, to push

him back, to somehow stem the tide that I face. Krak doesn't flinch, and the two of us come crashing together with extraordinary force.

He swings at me with his immense sword, flames trailing off the blade, and I narrowly duck underneath and lash out at his legs. I land two quick hits, then slip around behind him. He spins to follow, but I spin with him and manage to get around to his tail. There, I sheath Beowulf's Dagger for a brief moment and draw out Ascalon.

The moment the golden sword shines in the air, the firestorm around me seems to dim. Krak looks about, trying to find me, and I slash down at his tail with all my might. My aim is true, and Ascalon is strong. The blade cleaves clean through, and the tail falls to the ground with a resounding *thump*. Krak roars and staggers forward, flailing all about, trying to regain his lost balance. Flames erupt from the wound, and I follow him as fast as I can.

I sheath Ascalon once more, then draw my dagger and strike at his right heel as I try to cut through his tendon. There's a sharp *snap* as I succeed, and he falls flat on his face, howling with pain and fury. I don't give him a moment to recover but leap onto his body and race up him as fast as I can, pounding up toward his head. He snarls and grabs at me, and I cut through one of his wrists, causing even more blood to pour down. A moment later, I'm standing in front of his face, feeling his foul breath blowing against me. He stares at me, fury and resignation filling his eyes.

"You should have known better than to mess with me," I snap at him. "If only you'd played it loyal and stuck by my side, you *could* have toppled the queen. You could have ruled the world, but you would have done it from the *right* side."

"Right side. Wrong side." Krak sighs. "Don't you get it? There *is* no right side and wrong side, just a whole bunch of sides that all want the other ones dead."

"*My* side would never have started killing anyone if you hadn't shown up, guns blazing," I counter, though I know that arguing with a dying dungeon boss likely isn't going to get me anywhere. "In any case, I hope you know that this *is* personal."

"Noted. It would be the same in reverse," Krak hisses. He can't even lift his head, though I'm certain that he's trying to think of a way to escape. He's done it before, more than once.

[FireStorm: Watch out, Jason! He's probably regenerating!]

[IceQueen: Yeah! He's going to explode or spawn a new body or something!]

[DarkCynic: If I were you, I'd call my pets back out right this instant.]

I walk up next to his head, preparing to strike. Krak's eyes start to glaze over, though I don't know if that's from blood loss or from focusing on whatever spell he's about to cast. I draw out Ascalon, ready myself, and—

And a brilliant beam of light shoots down from the ceiling.

It's not a holy light, not the sort that comes from someone who saves you. Actually, it's a rather harsh sort of light, the sort that fills you with pain and misery. Honestly, it's a lot like those daylight bulbs that the government pushes because they're "environmentally friendly" or something. In any case, I flinch back from it, which actually winds up saving my life.

The light floods down across Krak, and his eyes suddenly

come back into focus. Then a monstrous figure comes crashing down and lands on Krak's head with overwhelming force. Bits of bone and blood and scales are blasted across me, and I wince and wipe the gore away from my face. Slowly, I look up . . . and find myself staring at what must be a void behemoth.

CHAPTER FOURTEEN

The creature is colossally large. It has to stoop down to fit inside the cavern, which quite comfortably held the fifty-foot-tall Krak. It's mostly humanoid, I suppose, but has stooped shoulders and a knobby head. Sort of like if you had a first grader mold a human out of clay. The skin is black and knobbly, almost scaly, and it has red eyes that peer down from a misshapen face. The thing snarls softly but doesn't say a word.

[IceQueen: AHHHHHHHHHHHHHHHHHHHHH!!!!!!!!!!!]

[RazorEdge: Jason, I suggest a tactical retreat.]

[ShadowDancer: Yeah, you're going to have to get a *lot* stronger to kill that thing!]

[DarkCynic: Honestly, I don't know if he'll ever be able to do it.]

[FireStorm: Oh, he totally can. Just probably not today.]

"Excuse me." I give a small bow. I know there's no way

I can run from the thing before it squashes me, and I don't have a portal from Mr. Wang to escape through, which doesn't leave me with a whole lot of options. "Forgive me for being so rude, but Krak was *my* kill. I'd rather like the XP that came with his destruction. Ought to raise me to a level seventy at least."

The void behemoth snorts, then slowly raises a hand.

[You have been gifted XP!]

[You have leveled up!]

[Congratulations! You are now Level 70!]

[Please accept from the following rewards:]

[. . .]

I give a nod to the monster. It's the equivalent of a trained ninja tossing a jackknife to a toddler to make him feel better right before he beats him up, and we both know it. The monster snarls once more, and I slowly take a step back.

"Perfect. Now that that's done, why don't you tell me what you're doing here and what I'm to do about it?"

The void behemoth simply straightens up and smashes into the ceiling. A portal opens above it once more, and it's sucked up inside. I watch it go, then whistle and shake my head. It vanishes through the swirling energy, and with a loud *zap*, the portal closes once more.

[DarkCynic: Jason! You should have gone after it!]

[LunarEclipse: Nah. He needs to regroup first. *Then* he'll kill the thing!]

[ChaosRider: Besides, how *could* he have gone after the monster? Jason doesn't exactly have any wings.]

"Very true," I say, then look around the area. The remains

of Krak's body still lie there and are already starting to stink. "Alright, Mr. Wang. I need to get out of here, and probably faster than slower. I don't know if the archdemon was telling the truth about the reactor core, but I'd sure hate to be—"

Boom.

The ground rumbles, and I hear the distant scream of what sounds like a minotaur or a demon. Now, there are very few things that will make monsters scream, which means that either there's another warrior in here with me, or I'm about to be in a world of hurt.

Suddenly, light begins to stream around me, and I get the distinct feeling that the second option is a whole lot more likely.

I look around searching for something to hang onto and find a small outcropping of stone. I run forward and grab hold of it as the world suddenly distorts. I was expecting something like sudden decompression, like you'd see in a space opera movie or something, but the reality is a whole lot different. Instead of just sucking out the air, the hole in the side of the dungeon sucks out *everything*. Matter, energy—it feels like I'm being sucked into a black hole. My whole body stretches outward, I feel myself ripped away from the stone . . . and with that, I'm shot out into the void.

It takes me a few minutes to get my bearings. I'm still alive, which is a positive, but I'm stuck in what really does seem like an infinite void. It's much like I've seen when sucked through Mr. Wang's portals, though the colors are a little different. The brights are brighter and the darks are darker. The floating dungeons also seem more distant, like they're further apart than I realized when I was sucked through the portal tube. It's odd, and I find the whole thing rotating around me as I spin slowly through the space. I can't tell if I'm moving laterally at all or if I'm just spinning.

A few other monsters spiral through the void not all that far from me, waving their arms about or swinging their weapons. The reactor core . . . Honestly, I just don't see it. I also don't see the remains of the dungeon I just came from. I don't see any lava; I don't see a lot of things. It's really quite weird, and that's all there is to it. I should also note that my chat seems to be dead. No one is commenting. It looks like the last message I have is from ChaosRider at the moment the dungeon imploded.

[Video Chat request from Moneybags.]

I blink in surprise, then accept. There's a pause, and Mr. Wang's face appears before mine. He's back in the club, along with Elrith, Paul, Ali, and John.

"He's alive!" Mr. Wang beams. "Jason, can you hear me?"

"Loud and clear." I nod. "How'd you get ahold of me?"

"A bit of interdimensional finagling from our two resident repentant monsters." Mr. Wang smiles. "When the chat went dead, we thought we'd lost you, but Elrith and Paul managed to track you on my sensors. They were then able to route an internet connection through some radar dishes or something. Anyway, it's working, and that's the important part."

"Can you get me out of here?" I ask. "*That's* the important part."

"From where you're at right now, I doubt it." Paul steps

forward into range of the camera. "You're moving too fast for these puny human sensors to lock onto you, at least well enough to generate a wormhole."

"Hey! This is really quite impressive for an underdeveloped race," Elrith says.

"I'm not saying that it's *not* impressive. Just that it's not impressive *enough*," Paul answers him with a small smile. "That said, I think we can give you some nudges. We're going to knock you into a nearby dungeon. Once you're inside, we'll be able to open up a portal and get you back here, no muss, no fuss."

"That sounds good to me," I confirm. "And we're sure that will work?"

"Absolutely." Mr. Wang nods with a smile.

"Probably." Elrith also sounds quite positive.

Paul doesn't say a thing, though his face twists into a rather uncertain sort of grimace. *I'm* certainly not confident, but it's the best option we have.

"Well, do what you have to do, but get me home." I sigh. "I can only assume that the void behemoth is bad news."

"Worse than you know," Paul murmurs. "As soon as he killed Krak, he headed straight for Krak's Astral Dungeon. I honestly don't know if he's heading there to destroy it or if he's taking the dungeon for himself. I could see things going both ways."

"And he's Hella's top general, right?" I just want to confirm.

"One of them, yes," Paul murmurs with a nod. "Some of the actual gods are her top henchmen, but he is probably the highest-rank monster."

"Wonderful." I sigh. "If he really is going there to take over Krak's superweapon, we likely don't have much time."

"The only thing that will buy us a bit more time is the fact that Krak will have troops that the void behemoth will want to kill," Elrith pipes up. "When he invades the Astral Dungeon, he'll almost certainly instigate a battle for control. He'll win, of course, but it'll take him time, which gives *us* time to fight back."

"Good." I nod. "In that case, get a lock on that Astral Dungeon. The moment that I'm back in normal space, I want to be able to invade."

"We'll do everything in our power," Mr. Wang promises. "In the meantime . . . uh . . . don't go anywhere."

"That's sort of hard to do." I scowl. "Trust me, if I had any way of navigating this void, I'd be doing it. About the only *good* thing about this place is that I apparently have plenty of air."

"Actually, you don't," Paul says as he starts to type on a keyboard just out of my sight. "The void preserves everything that enters it. Sort of a magical stasis field, you might say. You don't have plenty of air; you're just not breathing."

I frown, then realize that he's right. I'm not breathing.

"This place just gets better and better." I look around and notice a particularly bright light growing in the distance. It's a blue color, though it's mixed with greens and reds as well. As I watch, it spreads out to form into a long string of lights connected by a silver strand.

"Are you seeing that?" Paul asks softly. "That's the Astral Dungeon. It's moving right now."

"Where to?" I ask. "Also, where exactly am I?"

"You're . . . more or less at the Statue of Liberty, floating back toward land," Elrith answers. "Of course, that's not exact, but it's as close a parallel as I can draw."

"And where's the dungeon heading?"

"At present, we have it on a trajectory off the western side of the city." Paul frowns. "Honestly, I'd say that it's an escape course, a desperate evasion. It might be running from the behemoth, or maybe it's just drifting or something."

"That's good." I nod. "More evidence that we have a bit of time. Aright, are you guys ready to bump me out of here?"

"Almost," Mr. Wang answers. "Hold tight."

"We're actually going to have to sign off," Elrith says as he starts typing on another keyboard. "We only have so much bandwidth, and I'm using quite a few sensors to transmit this call. You'll know it when we bump you. Try to hold still when it happens. If something goes wrong, we'll call you back."

The video vanishes with a flicker, and I sigh and glance around. Most of the monsters in the area have drifted away, leaving me alone in the void. It's kind of lonely, so I amuse myself by watching the flickering lights of the fleeing Astral Dungeon. Suddenly, I see something just behind it and squint my eyes in disbelief.

Flying along behind the dungeon, chasing after the thing, is the void behemoth.

He seems to be coasting magically along, fury upon his face. I instinctively go quiet, hoping that he hasn't noticed me. I haven't the faintest idea how well sound does or doesn't carry in the void, and I have no intention of finding out the hard way. Slowly, the dungeon and the behemoth fade away into the distance, and I sigh and let myself relax a bit.

Suddenly, a thought strikes me. I need to check out the reward I received for getting up to level seventy! Sure, it would be better if my chat could see me, but I have a strange feeling that when I get "bumped" into this new dungeon, I'm going to be fighting for my life from the moment I enter until the moment I leave. Of course, it's possible that they'll bump me into a low-level slime dungeon or something, but I wouldn't bet a whole lot of money on it. Quickly, I open up my interface, scroll down to my rewards notification, and press it with a flourish.

[Please accept from the following rewards:]

[Weapon]

[Monster]

[Skill]

I pause in thought for a moment. It's strange to do so in silence. No one chimes in to tell me what I should do, no one gives me any input on how I should be doing better. I spend a minute glancing it over, then give a nod and select the weapon. I *doubt* that anything's going to be better than Beowulf's Dagger, but it seems like the best option for me. There's a long pause . . .

[Error connecting to system.]

Oh no. A feeling of horror shoots through me. What will I do if I lose the reward? I mean, I'll *survive*, but I already lost out on rewards when I leveled up from Paul's gifted XP. Gabe has been nice, but I could really use another boost as I continue my crusade against the monsters of the rifts.

[Attempting to establish connection.]

[.]

[. .]

[. . .]

[Attempt failed. Will attempt again in 00:00:05.]

[00:00:04]

[00:00:03]

[00:00:02]

[00:00:01]

[Attempt failed.]

By now, I'm really starting to get nervous. This is *really* bad. Like . . . if this glitches out or something, what do I do?

[All further attempts to establish connection have been abandoned.]

[Generating reward locally.]

I blink in surprise. What does *that* mean? It's going to just give me a reward . . . generated locally? Like . . . it's going to give me something new and unique?

[Scanning requisite level . . .]

[. . .]

[Level detected: 70]

[Converting to Rank.]

[. . .]

[Rank determined: S]

[Gathering environmental data.]

[. . .]

[Environment detected: Void]

[Scanning attack types.]

[. . .]

[Favored weapon: Dagger]

[Attack type: Melee]

[Class: Berserker]

"I take offense to that!" I scowl. "I'm more of a rogue than a berserker."

There's no answer. The system runs through a few other classifications and then pauses. Finally, with a flash, a large dagger appears in front of me with a flash.

[Weapon generated: Dagger of the Ancients]

[Rank: S+]

[Details: Always earns a critical hit.]

My jaw drops as I reach out and take hold of the weapon. I can feel the power radiating through it, and I give it a practice swing. It's *strong*. If anything is going to help me defeat a void behemoth, this is it. Critical hits . . . Honestly, I don't know that I've ever seen one before in the dungeons. I suppose maybe you could call severing a tendon a "critical hit," but that was due to my skill and planning, not due to some random factor that allows some hits to become critical. In any case, I slip it into my inventory and sit back—as best I can— to wait as I float through the infinite void.

Thankfully, I don't have to wait much longer.

Another point of light appears in the void and slowly grows brighter and brighter. It looks like a comet, and it's heading straight toward me. I don't know for sure what sort of bump this is going to be, but it certainly doesn't look pleasant in the slightest.

Closer and closer it comes until it's so blinding that I can hardly look at it. I close my eyes and brace for impact, and then . . .

WHAM!

It feels like I've been hit by a freight train. I'm launched through the void, flashing straight past several cthulhu and a handful of small dragons. The thing, whatever it is, presses hot against me as it pushes me onward. A dungeon ahead of me begins to grow larger and larger, and I brace for impact once more. I had thought it to be one of the more distant dungeons, but now, hurtling through space, it actually appears to be one of the closer ones. Fascinating how infinite voids can mess up your perception of things.

Then, all of a sudden, I slam into something solid—the outer sphere of the dungeon. I don't know how fast I'm moving, but it feels like being trapped between a mountain and the business end of the world's largest sledgehammer. Light erupts across me in a waterfall, and with that, I find myself falling . . . down . . . down . . . into nothing but fire.

CHAPTER FIFTEEN

I hit the ground with a resounding *thud* and find my lungs stung by sulfur and smoke. I cough and stagger back to my feet, swaying as fumes and heat flare all around me, and I do my best to get my bearings.

[ChaosRider: Hey! Jason's back! I saw it first!!!!]

[DarkCynic: No, I saw it first! I just have fat fingers!]

[ViperQueen: Who cares who saw him first? He's alive!!!!!!!!!]

I smile and give a thankful nod to the chat, then return to my surroundings. I'm in a place . . . It's actually kind of hard to tell where I am. The floor is made of black obsidian that's covered with small cracks a couple inches wide, through which a great deal of steam is hissing. Dark fires hang from crude chandeliers made out of bone, giving a small amount of light to the area. It's impossibly, oppressively hot. The room I'm in is small, with an arched doorway leading out. I quickly creep over and crouch down next to the doorway, out of the line of sight. Footsteps echo, and I hold my breath.

"Who's there?" I hear a voice call. It's a papery voice, old and decrepit, and I feel a small smidge of relief. If the monsters in here are old, then maybe, just *maybe*, I've lucked out and stumbled upon a low-level dungeon.

I don't answer the call, of course. Equally papery footsteps echo upon the blackened stone, and I draw out both of my daggers and hold them tight. A moment later, a dark figure shuffles into the room, frowning.

The creature wears black robes and has a face hidden by a black hood. It only stands as high as my chest, and for a long moment, it just looks around, staring. Several times the head sweeps past me, but I hold still, and it doesn't react. Finally, it snorts.

"Must have been another fire lizard. I'll have to tell Frank that they keep getting in. Must have burned through the lower vents again."

With that, the creature turns around and shuffles back out. I catch the smallest glance beneath its hood and see scales and a lizard-like snout. I also notice a tail poking out from the backside of its robes, which slides along on the ground, adding to the odd papery sound filling the air. I hold my breath until it's gone, then relax slightly.

[IceQueen: Whoa! Anyone know what that thing is?]

[ShadowDancer: Doesn't look like anything in my reference guides.]

[DarkCynic: It has to be blind, whatever it is.]

[ChaosRider: The question is whether just that one is blind or *all* of them are blind.]

[LunarEclipse: Maybe it's just a lizardman? In a cult?]

[RazorEdge: THAT sounds terrifying!]

I have to agree. Lizardmen can be issues, and that's *with-out* them being involved in some sort of cult. I'm starting to suspect that this dungeon is an infernal type, which opens up a whole lot of doors that I'd rather not deal with. I frown in thought, then open up my chat interface. A keyboard appears in the air in front of me, allowing me to communicate without actually speaking.

[JasonLee: Mr. Wang, have you been able to lock onto my position?]

There's a long pause before anyone answers. I hold my breath even as the chat explodes with speculation.

[DarkCynic: What does he mean? Has he been communicating with Moneybags outside of normal channels?]

[ViperQueen: Jason, you have to tell us what you know!]

[FireStorm: Yeah! Don't leave us in the dark!]

I hold up a hand, trying to calm them down.

[JasonLee: Hang on! I'm hiding in an enemy dungeon. Gimme just a minute, and then I'll fill you in.]

The chat seems to agree with that, at least well enough, and I continue to wait. Finally, an answer comes through.

[Moneybags: Sorry for the delay. We were aiming for a low-level dungeon connected to an ice cream shop over on 83rd Street. If you had landed there, you would have strolled through a candy-cane forest fighting sugar elves and walked back out into the city on your own two feet.]

[JasonLee: Well, that's not where I'm at.]

[Moneybags: Not exactly, no. We sort of missed. But we *did* hit an S-Ranked infernal dungeon! We can't read the stats on anything, but they're high! You'll have plenty of fun clearing it all out.]

[JasonLee: I *want* to be fighting that void behemoth.]

[Moneybags: Yeah, and I'd like to be out earning money, but I'm staying here to help you save the world. We all make sacrifices.]

[JasonLee: Look, can you get me out or not?]

[Moneybags: Ahh . . . Yes! We've been able to target the largest chamber in the dungeon. It's not *too* far from your current position. Sorry, there's enough magical interference coming off the thing that it's making it hard to get a lock. Just make sure you get there before the dungeon moves, or we'll lose the lock.]

I sigh, then give a nod. With that, I close down the keyboard, take out my daggers, and creep forward. My chat continues to ask me questions, but at this point, I just have to ignore them. I reach the edge of the doorway and pause, then slowly glance around the corner and into the hallway.

Standing out there are two more of the creatures, almost identical to the one before. They're striding down the hall in my direction, chatting amongst each other, and I pull back. Thankfully, they don't seem to notice me and slowly walk by, their tails swishing on the ground. I shake my head, then slowly slip out into the hall.

I should note that the hall is so low that my head brushes against the ceiling, and as the whole place has been rather roughly hewn from the rock, I whack my head on small outcroppings here and there as I make my way forward. I move away from the two creatures, not really wanting to engage anyone here in such a tight space. Ahead, I see a few more doorways and creep along a bit faster.

The first doorway leads to what looks like a dining room, with a long table and a great many chairs. The next door leads to a kitchen, where a handful of the monsters chop away at some vegetables and meat. Here, with their sleeves pulled up, I can see their reptilian skin, their claws, as well as deep burn marks. I frown, then keep moving. There's one final door at the end of the hall, and I creep along just a bit faster, then come up to the archway and peer out through the gap.

This next room is nothing like the other parts of the dungeon. The floor is still black, but it doesn't have the cracks that I've seen before. The little lizard-things walk back and forth, but . . . that's not the crazy part.

The crazy part is that they seem to actually be servants for vampires.

That's what they have to be. A particularly tall and powerful-looking vampire wearing a suit and a sweeping black and red cloak sits upon a throne made of black obsidian, carved into the shapes of skulls, people, and flames. Around the rest of the room are a handful of other, smaller thrones upon which a handful of vampires also rest. The lizards are serving them goblets of . . . Well, it *looks* like wine, and I don't really care to find out anything different. I shudder, then size them up.

There are five vampires, one of which is probably an elder vampire. I have no idea if any of my skills will work against them, but I *am* certain that this is going to be quite the battle. However, I am fairly convinced that this isn't the large room that Mr. Wang and his crew are targeting for the portal. I draw in a deep breath, and my chat sends me some encouragement.

[RazorEdge: You've got this, Jason!]

[ShadowDancer: Yeah! Just keep your head level, use your surroundings, all that fun stuff!]

[ChaosRider: Fight well, fight hard, and nothing will be able to touch you!]

I nod, then slowly step out into the open. No one reacts to my presence, so I just stride casually and regally toward the second-highest throne, which is empty. With a flourish, I sit down and lean back, then cross my arms and put one leg over the other.

[GoldenShield: Did he really just do that? Did he REALLY just do that???]

[ChaosRider: Okay, that's going into the book of most epic moves that have yet been performed in the dungeons.]

[ViperQueen: Are you actually making a book? I feel like Jason probably has half the entries at this point!]

The vampires, who all look rather bored, take a moment to notice. The elder vampire is the first to really focus in on me, at which point he laughs.

"It would seem that we have a newcomer, everyone."

The other vampires turn their heads. The two lowest ones leap out of their thrones and draw swords, but the higher two simply chuckle, though nervously. The elder vampire is the only one to seem truly amused, and he waves at the lizard creatures.

"Servants! Bring some food! Something that a human would be able to eat."

"Many thanks." I nod as the servants scamper away. "It's

been ages."

"I can only imagine." The elder vampire takes a sip out of his goblet. "I have to say, I wasn't expecting guests. We weren't planning on linking with Earth until tomorrow, which means that *you* are a creature of interest. If you had come in here swinging, I would have killed you without any real thought or care, but . . . you intrigue me, and I have a feeling that you'd like to talk too."

I flash a smile at him. "I've always heard that vampires are some of the few monsters who can be reasoned with. I'd like to see if that's true or not."

"I think you will find us to be most hospitable, though I, of course, do not guarantee that things will turn out the way you desire."

"Of course not."

There's a pause, and the servants come scampering back up with a platter of apples, oranges, and some bananas. I pick up one of the apples, give it a sniff, then bite into it. It's actually quite good, and I nod in approval.

"I'm glad you approve. We have quite a garden of fruits and vegetables from all over the multiverse." The elder vampire holds up his goblet for a toast. "I myself prefer the leechfruit, which is native to the world of these little cretins." He kicks at one of the servants scurrying by his throne. The motion knocks the hood back, revealing the lizard's face. I give a little start of horror. The monster's eyes have been entirely gouged out, and I do my best to keep my composure as it scurries away. "You seem to disapprove."

"I imagine that we could find many things we disagree

on." I fold my hands. "However, I didn't come here to debate philosophy."

"A pity. The last time I had a good debate from Earth was when we kidnapped . . . What was his name? Aristotle? Something like that. It was really quite entertaining, and I would love something similar once more." The elder vampire sighs. "I shall have to make do with whatever your request may be. Pray tell, what might we be able to do for you?"

"I need passage to the largest chamber of this dungeon," I answer. "My friends will be opening up a portal there, hopefully soon. With that, I can go home and you can be left in peace."

"Indeed?" The elder vampire seems amused. "Humans who know how to open portals. It would seem that this war isn't going as well as the queen might have planned."

He smiles once more, and the other vampires chuckle. Without answering, he takes another long drink from his goblet, then hands the empty vessel to one of the servants. With that, he rises and motions for me to do the same. I decide to oblige him, though I keep my hands near my weapons.

"You wish to pass through our dungeon without resistance. One might wonder why." The elder vampire starts to walk down the length of the room, but I get the feeling that he's not looking for me to follow. I stay put, tensing up. "At least, one *might* wonder, if it wasn't for the saga of Krak the rogue dungeon lord, as well as Harold, the rogue human warrior. There are many strange things among the dungeons these days. I do not like it." He folds his hands under his chin. "If I allow you to pass, then I will be an accomplice to whatever chaos you bring about on the other side of things. I *do* believe that you're attempting to intercept the void behemoth, one of the queen's top generals. To aid you would be tantamount to treason."

"On the other hand, if you face off against me, you risk death," I point out. "I've gone through a lot of dungeons, and I haven't been taken down yet. Sure, you might be the one to do it, but then, you might *not*. Is another thousand years of peaceful rule really worth throwing away for a chance of glory?"

"He has a point." The elder vampire turns to the other nobles. "The queen takes so little notice of us anyway. Why, do you recall when we snapped up all these servants? They were intended as sacrifices to the queen to grant her strength in an upcoming battle against the champion of whatever world we were attacking at that moment. Loki was dismembered and cast into the dungeon for the better part of a century just for stealing one of them, and she outright killed that titan for eating three of them. We managed to get away with almost a hundred, and she never so much as blinked an eye."

I shrug. "Seems like an awfully good reason to help me."

"On the other hand . . ." The elder vampire slowly turns back to me. "There are a lot more eyes upon us right now. Offenses are easy to forgive when you have your hands full with other matters. When things pertain to *the* matter at hand, offenses are nearly impossible to ignore."

"Also true." I take one more bite of the apple, then hand it to one of the servants and fold my hands behind my back. "Then allow me to make my case perfectly clear. If you don't allow me passage, I'll kill each and every one of you. If you *do* allow me passage, I'll head out to stop the detonation of a weapon that has every chance of destroying *you* right along with the Earth."

"Yes, Krak's little project. I would say that I've been watching it with interest, except that superweapons bore me. Someone always puts a stop to things right at the last moment." The elder vampire reaches behind his back, and his cloak falls away. At the same moment, he draws out two daggers, both silver, and a smile spreads across his face, revealing his fangs. "I'm afraid I must turn down your offer, Jason Lee. May the best warrior win."

I draw in a deep breath and settle into my stance. I know it's a cheesy line, but I can't help myself.

"I plan to."

CHAPTER SIXTEEN

The elder vampire snarls and speaks in a black tongue. The two lowest-ranked vampires both leap to their feet, once more draw their swords, and rush at me just as fast as they can go. Their cloaks trail behind them, and they attack in tandem.

Too bad for them, they're low-level as well as low-rank.

I draw out Beowulf's Dagger and lash out at them. One of them I simply dodge, and the second I attack with force, slashing upward as hard as I can. I cut his wrist clean through, leaving a stump in place of a hand. He looks down in horror, and I slash across his neck. He falls to the ground in three pieces, dead, and I spin to the first one.

His eyes are wide, but he pulls himself together quickly. He snarls, showing his fangs, then lunges. His feet clatter across the ground, and he leaps into the air to throw a kick at me. I reach out with my left hand—the dagger is held in my right—and catch his foot.

Wham!

I have to admit, it's sort of fun being the overpowered one. The vampire screams as I slam him to the ground and cut off his leg at the ankle. He slashes out wildly with his sword, desperately trying to hit me, but doesn't come anywhere close. I stomp on his arm and smash it flat against the floor, breaking his wrist, then kick him in the chin as he tries to rise. His head smashes back into the floor, and blood trickles out across the stone. He's dead, and I turn around.

"Who's next?"

The elder vampire gestures at the next two vampires, a man and a woman. They both rise up, looking nervous, but nod and draw out thin rapiers. Instead of attacking together, they come at me staggered, first the man, then the woman.

That's alright by me, I suppose.

I parry the rapier of the man with ease, deflecting him toward the elder vampire's throne, then move onto the woman. She's faster, but I parry her sword as well. She manages to break away and attack again, and I deflect half a dozen attacks in as many seconds. The man behind me recovers himself and lunges forward with anger and rage. I watch them both, then twirl out of the way and bat the man's rapier aside as he rushes past. My aim is perfect, and they slam into each other and stab one another through the guts.

I don't think they really feel pain, but for a moment, they stare at one another, shocked. I finish the deed by slashing across both of their necks in a single blow. Their heads hit the floor with a tandem *thunk*, and I twirl my dagger and turn back to the elder vampire.

"I have little doubt that you're good, but do you really think you have what it takes to defeat me?" I take my stance. "There's still time to take me up on that deal. I'm in a terrible rush, so in this case, I'm willing to forgive that you just ordered my execution."

The elder vampire *does* seem nervous. I'm likely a bit more than he thought he could chew, but that's just life sometimes. The choice is between fighting me, a level-seventy warrior, and Hella, a level-one-hundred queen. The choice is obvious and is the same I would probably make in his shoes. He raises his daggers, and I see his lips move.

With a flash, something seems to hit me in the head, and my vision flickers and goes dark. It's not completely black—I can still see a few shadows—but it's enough to cover his advance. I hear a foot press lightly against the stone, and I spin and lash out. I don't hit him, but I hear him twirl to avoid the attack. A moment later, my vision comes back, and I find the monster almost upon me, twin blades raised like steel fangs.

The elder vampire throws a series of rapid-fire attacks at me. None of them are intended to kill, just to injure, which shows his intelligence. He lands a few strikes against my arms and shoulders, but nothing critical. I grit my teeth against the pain, then launch an offensive of my own. Rolling with the punches, the elder vampire allows me to drive him backward across the floor, though I'm quite certain that it's only for show. He's making a plan, and it only includes me as a corpse.

"You're good. Not many people survive my blinding spell," the vampire comments.

"You're good. Not many people survive . . . me." I grit

my teeth and lunge forward at top speed. The elder vampire dodges and slashes me across the back, then laughs. A sickly feeling spreads over me, and I stagger as a wave of nausea threatens to turn my stomach. I know it's just a trick, but all of a sudden, I want nothing more than to go home and lay down on my couch.

The elder vampire snarls and attacks once more, and *this* time he's hungry for blood. I draw in a deep breath, then throw myself into the attack with all I have in me. Blades crash against blades, and the elder vampire snarls as I successfully weather *another* of his little spells. I have a distinct feeling that a third will be coming, and I'd rather not be around for that.

Moving as fast as I can, I throw myself into a blistering series of attacks. This time *I* manage to land a few hits on him, and bursts of light indicate that Nimrod's Bane works against these fallen creatures. The elder vampire's eyes become a bit more desperate, and I attack once more.

Suddenly, a wave of cold hits me like a wall. My entire body slows, and I glance down to find an ice crystal sticking out of my leg. One of the servants, standing over by the thrones, holds a small slingshot along with a bag of differently colored crystals. I snarl and strike as hard as I can, but I've lost the offensive. The elder vampire easily bats the weapon away, then kicks me in the chest. I'm knocked flat on my back in the middle of the room, and the elder vampire springs upon me with a glorious look of victory in his eyes.

"And now, you die."

I groan, then feign an attack with Beowulf's Dagger. At the

same time, I open up my inventory with my other hand and allow the Dagger of the Ancients to fall into my palm. The vampire doesn't notice and simply blocks Beowulf's Dagger.

"Let me see . . ." The vampire stomps on my wrist, smashing it into the ground, then kicks me in the chin.

[Skill: Bearing of a Knight.]

[Peril Detected.]

"I do believe that was how you treated my dear cousin," the elder vampire snarls down at me. "How does it feel to be in the same shoes?"

"I wish I knew." I slash upward with the Dagger of the Ancients and hit the monster on the leg. A great blast of energy explodes through the room, and the elder vampire falls to the side. I spring back to my feet, and my whole body warms as Ascalon melts away the ice crystal. *That* feels better. "Actually, now that I think about it, I think I'd rather not know."

The elder vampire sneers, then rises back to his feet. A dark look comes over his face, and he begins to change. His skin turns to a gray-green color, and his eyes sink into his head. He grows a good foot or more, and his arms and legs lengthen and grow claws. The transformation destroys his suit.

"The image of an immaculate gentleman, destroyed by the true nature of the heart."

"And I thought you said you *weren't* a philosopher."

I shrug, and a smile spreads across my face. "You pick up a thing or two in the dungeons."

The elder vampire snarls and raises his hands. Blasts of red magic explode from his fingertips, crackling through the air almost like bullets. I dive out of the way and narrowly duck behind one of the thrones. I don't know what that magic involves, but it looks dangerous. This is confirmed a moment later as one of the little bullets of magic hits one of the servants, and the creature is transformed into a desiccated corpse in the blink of an eye.

"Hiding? Not what I expected," the vampire snarls as he approaches.

"No. Just biding my time."

The vampire chuckles. "Same—"

His voice is cut off as I flex my muscles, which have become quite powerful, and rip the throne out of the stone floor. I throw it at him like a bowling ball and smash him against the other wall rather like a comic book character. He groans and peels himself away from the wall as the chair comes tumbling down, and I slowly walk forward toward him.

"Had enough?"

It's a direct taunt, and one that seems to fill him with rage. I can't say that I blame him for that, but he snarls low in his throat, and he slowly brings up both of his daggers again.

"You're going to regret saying that, boy."

He mutters a few more words, and a new effect seems to come over me. This time pure fire seems to explode through my veins, burning me from the inside out. I gasp in pain and fall to my knees, groaning as I try to keep myself from collapsing altogether. My health begins to drop, and the elder vampire slowly advances upon me. He's not taking any chances by rushing me, but he's also not going to sit back and let me heal and come up with a plan.

He's good.

I just have to be better.

As he closes in on me, my health reaches the halfway point. Bearing of a Knight is slowing the degradation, but this fire-blood skill is powerful. I honestly don't know how I'll defeat him, but I grit my teeth and slowly force myself upright. The pain is overwhelming, and I sway a bit, but there I am.

And, suddenly, I see a bag of crystals lying on the ground next to the servant killed by the vampire's blood magic.

I bend down and snatch up an ice crystal. I don't even stab it into my leg or anything, I just wrap my hand around it and squeeze. The crystal cuts through my palm, and the magic is injected straight into my blood. The fire-blood effect wears off, if only enough for me to function again, and the elder vampire snarls and charges at me.

"You fool!"

As my body cools rapidly, I respond by throwing the bloody crystal into his face. It sticks in his cheek, and I follow it with a punch that hits him in the chin. He staggers, and I spin and deliver a roundhouse kick that drives him several feet away. With that, I attack with force, daggers in either hand. The elder vampire faces off against me, daggers against daggers, as we fight for any opening.

As it happens, the vampire finds one first, and he flashes past my defenses to stab me in the right side. The blade sinks into the muscle there, and a great deal of pain floods out through my body. I gasp, and he stabs me in the gut with his second dagger. I choke on blood that burbles up into my mouth, and the elder vampire smiles.

"Well, now. That's how I like it."

I draw in a deep breath, then take a tighter hold on my own daggers and stab him in the back twice, wrapping him in a deadly hug. He's pinned to me all of a sudden and gasps as both daggers emit extra doses of damage from the extra skills attached to them. He groans, and I see his eyes glaze over.

We both break apart, weak, and clatter against the walls. He slumps to the ground, moaning, while I collapse right next to a throne. My daggers are still lodged inside his body, while his daggers are in mine. Vision swimming, I open my inventory and pull out two Pumped! drinks, which I chug as fast as I can. As healing energy begins to pour through me, I pull out the two daggers, and sigh in relief as the wounds heal over.

Suddenly, though, I look up and see the elder vampire doing the same thing. Well, he's guzzling goblets of wine and chomping down fruits as fast as he can, tossing the peels and golden cups across the floor as he finishes them. I grit my teeth angrily, then stand up and throw one of his daggers at him.

It hits him in the wrist as he reaches for another goblet balanced on the arm of a throne just next to him. The force of the blow slams his wrist back into the wall, where it's pinned tightly. He gasps, then reaches around and tries to pull out one of my daggers with his free hand.

"No." I scowl and throw the second dagger. It hits his other hand and pins *it* to the wall. With that, I advance upon him, and he turns even whiter than he already was.

"Please." He looks up at me. "Be reasonable."

"Like you would have done with me had our positions been reversed?" I raise an eyebrow. "I don't think so."

"If our positions were reversed, I would kill you in a

heartbeat." He shrugs. "Just listen to me, though. Spare me and I'll order my soldiers to stand down. You'll have your free walk through my dungeon. Maybe the queen kills me and my people, but . . ." He shrugs. "If you've just taken me down, you'll be able to do that, and siding with you gives me a bit more time."

The offer is an appealing one, but a warning bell rings in the back of my mind. "You should have offered it to me *before* the fight, as a reward for taking you down. As it is, I can't trust someone who's always changing their mind."

"Please, I—"

I kick him in the chest and smash him back against the wall. That drives my daggers into his body up to the hilt, and he groans. Before he can recover, I yank his silver daggers out of the wall and slash across his neck. His head slowly tumbles to the floor with a *thunk*, and I straighten up.

"And that's that," I sigh, then retrieve my daggers. "Another foe down. A whole lot more to go." I look at the exit from the throne room. "Who here thinks that I've really just taken down the most powerful monster in this dungeon?"

My chat immediately responds in the negative, and I have to agree. I don't know exactly why, but that elder vampire was deceptive to the end.

I just have to make sure I can decipher his lie before it kills me.

CHAPTER SEVENTEEN

I take a few moments to heal before I actually leave the chamber behind. The corpse of the elder vampire doesn't move, doesn't twitch, but somehow I feel like I'm being watched. A few of the servants scurry into and out of the room, but none of them bother me.

[RazorEdge: What do you make of those little lizard things? Are they friends or foes?]

[DarkCynic: I say they're foes! Kill them all, Jason!]

[ViperQueen: Oh, come on! They're so pathetic, could you really kill a creature like that? Have some mercy and pity on them!]

I don't say anything out loud. Personally, I pity the little things as well, and I'd happily give them some grace were it not for the fact that one of them shot me with an ice crystal in an obvious attempt to make me lose to the elder vampire. I don't have any problem with the vampire using assistants in his fights—I certainly do the same thing—but . . . there are many questions involved. Was the servant defending a beloved master? Was it trying to hit the vampire and accidentally hit me instead? Was it being forced to do it? Threatened? Did it have any control over its actions at all? I don't have any of the answers, and I don't know that I'm going to get them.

That said, hopefully I don't have to. Slowly, I bend down and pick up the head of the elder vampire, then position Beowulf's Dagger in my right hand and stride out of the room. I don't know what I'll be facing next, but I'd wager that I'm not going to run into anyone particularly hospitable.

"Keep an eye out for any big chambers," I murmur to my chat as I slip down a long hallway. The stone here is more worked, with polished floors and walls and even a few carvings here and there, particularly on doorways. I don't see any other vampires, though servants do scurry here and there doing a wide assortment of things that I would expect from ordinary servants on Earth. "Mr. Wang? If you could give me any assistance, I'd sure appreciate it."

[ShadowDancer: Don't worry, Jason! We'll keep our eyes peeled!]

[FireStorm: Yeah! We'll get you there in one piece!]

[Moneybags: I'm sorry, Jason. We're trying, but we can't get a pinpoint on your location within the dungeon. All I can say is that you'll know it when you see it.]

"I hate it when people say you'll know something when you see it." I scowl. "I almost never do, you know?"

My chat generally agrees with me, and I smile as I stride down the hall a bit faster. I can hear voices ahead of me, and

I grip my dagger a bit tighter. Suddenly, I catch a glimpse of a larger audience hall, and I slip up to the doorway and hide behind a set of curtains that's been strung delicately across about half the entrance.

"We have heard your complaint and will take appropriate actions," a female voice echoes down through the room. "You, however, must accept whatever decision we hand down."

"Of course, your ladyship," a voice answers. "Thank you for listening to me."

Footsteps patter away, and I risk a glimpse out. Sure enough, it's a massive audience hall with a set of thrones at the top of a small flight of stairs, overlooking the area. At the other end, a massive set of doors looks out into what may well just be an open world.

I think I've found my big chamber. I just have to go through an audience hall to get there.

"Next!" the voice calls out.

"I'm sorry, m'lady, there's no one else there," another voice calls out. "That's everyone."

"Another hard day of work for me, another day of lazing around with the servants for my husband." She sighs. "Do we have any idea where he's hiding? Go check the wine cellar, and if he's not there, check the baths. I have some things I need to discuss with him here."

A smile appears on my face, and I press myself up against the wall. A moment later, a guard walks through. He's a vampire and wears leather armor set with an imperial crest in the shape of a skull. He blinks as he sees me, but before he can attack, I slash him across the throat. His body falls to the ground in front of me, but his head bounces back into the throne room. There's a long pause, followed by an annoyed sigh.

"Fredrick, I've *told* you not to kill the servants. It makes them nervous to follow your orders. Now get out here! I need to talk to you, pronto."

I shrug, then pitch the elder vampire's head out onto the floor. It bounces a few times as it rolls across the marble floor, and I take a deep breath and step out. I find a regal queen vampire relaxing upon a throne, gazing down at me with an annoyed look. Flames rise up from fixtures upon the throne, while two large hellhounds sit on either side. The hounds growl and rise up as I enter, but she waves them back down.

"So, you've killed him?" She sighs and straightens up. "Do you expect me to be impressed?"

"I sure hope you'd have at least a bit of respect." I shrug. "Not that I expect you to cede your throne to me, but a little nod might be in order."

A smile breaks across the queen's face as she does just that. "There's your respect. I hope you know that the man you killed was a lazy pig, hardly worthy to be called an elder vampire. He never practiced, never even bothered to spar against the palace guards."

"Yeah, I sort of expected as much." I shrug and scratch the back of my neck. "I've fought goblins that I had more trouble with."

The queen laughs this time. "He'll be rolling in his grave to hear that. Or wherever you left him. Unless it was the dump, it was too good for him." She sighs and raises a hand. "I suppose you're expecting me to come fight you right now?"

"Or you could just let me pass through," I answer. "I'd be totally okay with that. I won't bother you, you won't bother me, and so on."

"I'm sorry, but I'm afraid I have to decline." She sighs again. "I'm afraid that the Watcher wouldn't take too kindly to that, and I'm a *bit* more worried about him than you, if you get my drift."

"How about I kill him for you, and then when he's dead, you give me passage?" I hold up my hands. "Sort of an exchange?"

The queen laughs, and she shakes her head. "That's not how this works, and we both know it. He's watching right now, you know. He sees everything in this dungeon, and"—she shrugs—"he *will* respond accordingly. Fang, Tooth, go get him."

The two hounds bound to their feet and charge down the stairs from the throne. Flames trail from their fur and tails, and sparks fly from their mouths. I brace myself, then attack with due force, my blades carving through the air as I throw myself into battle.

I've only fought hellhounds once before, right before I took down Harold. They weren't easy to defeat then. Thankfully, though, I've since become a bit more powerful. Beowulf's Dagger hits the first hellhound square in the chest, and I lift it clean off the ground with the force of the blow. The queen gives a start and rises up, and I flip the hound over and slam it into the ground.

The second hellhound snarls and latches onto my leg, where it starts to gnaw at me. I glare down at it, then punch it while still holding on to the hilt of Beowulf's Dagger. The hellhound is knocked backward by the force of the blow and looks up at me with something akin to horror.

[GoldenShield: Yeah, Jason! That's the way to do it]

[ShadowDancer: NO WAY!!! It's so cool to see him facing off against these lower-level things, you know. It's sort of exciting.]

[DarkCynic: Yeah, it's cool.]

I advance on the hellhound, and it turns back toward the queen. She glares down at it and points at me, and, reluctantly, it turns back. Flames explode across the whole of its body, and with that, it leaps forward, paws and claws outstretched, ready to tear me limb from limb.

I respond by slashing my dagger across its neck mid-attack. The neck is too thick for me to cut clean through, but the hound comes crashing to the floor, dead, and spills black blood across the obsidian. I let out a long breath, then turn to face the queen.

"Have any more sentries or guards you'd like me to kill? Or are you going to come down so I can just kill you outright? I'm okay either way. I just need to know since I'm sort of on a time crunch."

The queen's face turns red, and she slowly begins to stride down from her throne. "Oh Great One, protect me. Oh Great One, grant me victory."

There's no answer, and I can only assume that she's speaking to the mysterious individual she alluded to right before the hellhounds attacked. I have to admit, it makes me a smidge nervous. Is it a demon that they worship? One of Hella's god-general-things? I don't have the faintest idea, but she's coming down to attack me, which doesn't leave me with a lot of time to think. I'm just going to have to attack her and deal with the consequences later.

[LunarEclipse: You've got this, Jason! It doesn't matter who she's praying to, I'm sure you'll still be able to beat her!]

[RazorEdge: I'm pretty sure you're like a dozen levels higher than she is, so yeah! Just kick her from this side of the universe all the way to the other!]

[ChaosRider: GO GET HER!!!]

I draw in a deep breath as she reaches the bottom of the stairs. Carefully, she reaches up behind her shoulders and draws out an elegant blade. It's pure black, though it has a sheen that reflects the light beautifully. The hilt is set with black diamonds, and the blade has been forged into a rather lovely curve. It's a weapon designed to look good while also being built for combat.

This isn't going to be an easy fight.

I draw out the Dagger of the Ancients and prepare myself with a weapon in either hand. The queen smiles, then slowly marches forward, advancing with a cruel purpose. She begins swinging her sword in a distinctive and intentional attack pattern, carving through the air with a sharp whistle. She knows what she's doing, that much is obvious. I don't move and wait for her to come to me. As she arrives, she lunges, and I block her sword by catching it with my daggers held in an *X* shape.

Her sword rings out against my own steel, and she smiles, then disengages and slashes horizontally across my chest. I block with Beowulf's Dagger and stab at her with the Dagger of the Ancients, but she spins out of the way before I can even get close. Suddenly moving a *great* deal faster, she slashes the sword across my back, and I'm the one who needs to pivot out of the path of destruction. With that, her face hardens, and we launch into battle with one another once more.

She's fast and gets faster by the moment. Strike, spin, strike, spin—she's never in the same spot for more than a few seconds at a time. I'm easily able to block all her attacks, but I can't land a single hit against her. Of course, she's in the same boat, so I'm not all *that* concerned, but I would rather like to be able to knock her down a few pegs. Suddenly, she lets out a snarl and leaps backward as she mutters a few words in her black tongue.

A dark spot forms on the floor under my feet. It's almost impossible to see, given that the floor is already made of polished obsidian, but it's there. I jump nimbly out of the way, and a thunderous *boom* shakes the room as a bolt of lightning shoots down from the ceiling. Well, a bolt of *black* lightning. It leaves a sickly sort of smell in the air, like that of rotting flesh, and I shudder. Slowly, I prepare myself once more, and the queen mutters a few more words.

More bolts of lightning come crashing down, and I'm sent into evasive maneuvers. They're easy enough to dodge, but it's taking time to do it, which is frustrating in the extreme. The queen is watching, and her face is growing darker. A wind begins to blow through the throne room, making her hair blow about her face, and I get nervous. When that happens in the movies, it's usually because things are about to get really bad.

The lightning continues, but suddenly added to the fray are dozens of bats, diving down out of the ceiling. They're big, black, and have glowing red eyes. Likely they're magical constructs of some sort, but whatever the case, they're fast and begin biting at me as they flash down out of nowhere. Several of them bite me on the shoulder and legs, and I wince in pain as I continue to leap about.

"How do you like my little friends?" The queen laughs as she shoots back into the battle. Her sword flashes through the air, and I narrowly block it as several of the bats bite at me. They're not doing much damage at all, and frankly I wouldn't expect them to do much of anything, but they're annoying, and they're all causing bleed damage that's slowly lowering my health. I do my best to ignore them and just focus on fighting the queen, but . . . Have you ever tried to have a conversation while a mosquito is buzzing around your head? It's terribly distracting. As the monsters strike, she manages to land a small nick on one of my arms, and a bolt of lightning strikes a good bit closer than I'd like.

"You're fading, and fading fast." The vampire queen laughs. Suddenly, she throws her sword at me. I bat it out of the way, but she blurs into motion and spins around behind me and grabs my shoulders. I spin too, but her fingers latch down like talons, digging through my armor into my flesh. "Now, it's time for you to learn how a true vampire queen does business."

"I'd rather not." I draw in a deep breath, then intentionally step back into one of the black spots. A lightning bolt hits me an instant later and blasts black electricity over both me and the queen. She shrieks and falls backward to the ground, and in that moment, both the bats and the lightning fade away.

I gasp in pain and turn toward her as she starts to rise. She's far from dead, and her eyes darken. Her lips move, and suddenly, I feel a great sickness spreading through my body.

[Condition: Cursed. You will take . . .]

I ignore the stats as I feel my foot bump up against something. Down on the ground is her old sword, and I kick it as hard as I can. The sword bounces off the ground and hits her in the gut, and she groans. Before she can do anything, I throw myself forward.

My muscles tremble as they start to fail from the curse, but I still have just enough strength to rip the sword out and stab it deep into her chest. With that, darkness swirls around me, and I find myself falling . . . down . . . down to the darkness below.

CHAPTER EIGHTEEN

When I wake up, I find myself sitting at half health and hiding behind one of the full-length tapestries that, apparently, hang around the throne room. I groan and sit up, holding my head, and my chat explodes.

[ShadowDancer: He's back! He's awake again!]

[ChaosRider: Jason! Are you okay?]

[ViperQueen: Give him some space!]

"Yeah. Yeah, I'm okay." I sigh and shake my head, then peer out from behind the tapestry. The throne room is empty save for a few of the lizard servants trying to pull the bodies of the hellhounds out of the room. They're struggling, which is sort of funny to watch, though I feel a bit bad for their pain. "How long was I out?"

[GoldenShield: Five minutes, maybe.]

[IceQueen: I think it was closer to 10, but yeah, not long.]

That makes sense. My health has healed a little bit, but

not much. About what I'd expect from ten minutes of passive healing. A *very* vague memory comes back to me of pulling myself to safety, but I can't be certain if it's real or if I'm just trying to fill in the blanks. I open up a bottle of Pumped! and start trying to sort things out in my mind.

What *was* that curse effect? It was powerful, stronger than any other effect I've ever felt. It knocked me unconscious, sucked the strength from my limbs. I mean . . . it felt like I just about had all the life sucked out of me. I shake my head a few times, then open up my interface. I can't find any record of the effect, which only means that it's worn off.

"Alright, guys. Remind me to get something to negate curses." I sigh and push myself to my feet. "If you know any-one else who's been cursed or have seen any healing items that might be able to defeat curses, I'd sure appreciate a heads-up."

My chat comes back in the affirmative, which I suppose is good enough for me. With that, I draw in a deep breath and walk out from behind the tapestry, stride through the throne room, and come out on the threshold of the vampire castle.

That's what it is, really. Spreading out before the doors of the castle is an infernal wasteland, and I'm reminded of the status of the dungeon. The castle sits upon a small hill over-looking a volcanic plane. The volcano itself rises on the other side of the expanse, spewing black soot into the sky and lava down its slopes. Fiery monsters roam here and there among the rivers of lava, while several small cities seem to be built up on their shores. I whistle slightly, then give a nod to the chat.

"Alright, Mr. Wang. Would this be that really big chamber you're talking about?"

[Moneybags: Yup, this would be the one! We just got the portal open. It's . . . Well, it's somewhere in that mess!]

[IceQueen: Don't worry! We'll look over every frame of video you send us to try and figure out where it's located!]

[DarkCynic: Somehow, I'm not confident he'll find it.]

I sigh and glance around the area. A broad path leads down from the door of the castle, down beside a flow of lava to one of the towns. On either side of the path is a rough land-scape covered in boulders and fissures and little bits of infernal brush. It's a nasty-looking place, for sure. Down below, I can see something moving along the path near the river. It looks like a man on horseback . . . Maybe two men on horseback? I can't tell for sure, but I'm positive that it'll be quite the fight if they catch me.

"Alright, everyone." I draw in a deep breath and take a step out onto the path. "Let's get to this. We've got a lot of ground to cover, and I don't know how much time we have."

Suddenly, from behind me, a bell starts to ring. It's an awful sort of ringing. Think of a church bell but make it darker and more ominous. I spin around and look up at the castle, where I see a brilliant light flashing from one of the towers. I have a bad feeling that it means an alert is being called, and I'm the only person who would merit such an alarm.

"I guess we're going to have company." I smile and start down the path with a bit more purpose. "Let's get this show on th—"

[Condition: Targeted by Chrono Spell. Duration: 01:00:00.]

"A chrono spell?" I freeze. "What does that mean?"

My chat doesn't have any good answers. Suddenly, though,

the ghostly image of a clock appears in the air in front of me. I don't have the faintest idea why that might be. Then it fades away.

And then, just as suddenly, pain shoots through my whole body.

It's the worst pain I've felt since entering the dungeons, and I've been beat up pretty badly. I collapse in a heap—there's no other way of putting it—and then slowly struggle back to my feet.

[Notice: You have been returned to Level 1.]

[All stats have been reset.]

[Duration Remaining: 00:59:48.]

"Wait a minute." I blink a few times. "I've been reset back to level one for the next hour? How . . . What . . ."

Something clatters behind me, and I spin as two low-level vampire guards come running out onto the threshold of the castle. They're armed with simple swords, but I know at a glance that I'll die in seconds against them. I've lost all my speed, all my strength. As I draw out Beowulf's Dagger, it feels heavy and awkward in my hands.

[Notice: You must be at least Level 45 to use S-Ranked items.]

I grit my teeth and shove the weapon back into my inventory. "Alright, then. Bjorn, I need you now."

With a flicker, my pocket dimension opens and Bjorn steps out. He, thankfully, hasn't been affected. As the two guards come running down, he growls, and ice spears explode up from the ground and spear them both through the guts. They groan and slump down, dead, and Bjorn spins to me.

Master, you're . . . little.

"I know." I grab hold of his fur and swing up onto his back. "I know this is a bit unorthodox and is probably insulting for you, but I need you to get me out of here, and I need you to do it now."

Bjorn simply tosses his head. Balder emerges from the pocket dimension as well, and he gives a sharp howl. The doors slam shut, and Bjorn freezes them closed with a blast of ice. With that, my two hounds turn toward the wasteland and bound away as fast as they can go.

Before the apocalypse began, I wasn't the least athletic person in the world. I played basketball and football when I was in high school, and while I didn't get to go to college on a sports scholarship or anything, I certainly collected my fair share of trophies. That said, in the few short days of the apocalypse, I've already forgotten just how much of my strength comes from my levels. Hanging onto Bjorn's fur as he races into the field of boulders and crevices takes every last ounce of effort that I have, and it's nearly not enough. He skids around boulders and the force of the turns nearly rips me from his shoulders. He leaps over crevices and I find myself staring down into depths that I know I won't be able to survive. When he lands, the impact nearly tosses me from his body. It's insane to be so terrified of something that wouldn't have made me blink only a few minutes ago, but that's the situation I find myself in. Suddenly, as Bjorn skids around a corner, I do slip from his back and hit the ground hard.

I roll several times, bounce off an outcropping of stone, and slam into a boulder. My health drops into the red, and I slowly and painfully climb back to my feet.

[DarkCynic: Wait, what's happening? Jason, this is pathetic!]

[ViperQueen: Hey, he's been cursed! He'll still get through this, just watch!]

[ChaosRider: Yeah! You can do it, Jason. Just keep your head level and don't stop fighting until the end!]

I nod to my chat, then open up my inventory and pull out a Pumped! soda. As the liquid runs down into my stomach, my health refills, and I draw myself up with a sigh.

I don't have any weapons that I can actually *use*, since my level is so low. Ascalon is impossibly heavy on my back—it feels like it must weigh a hundred pounds. I grimace, then take it off and stick it in my inventory. Bjorn and Balder, suddenly realizing that I'm not with them, come racing back to stand next to me.

Are you okay, Master? Bjorn asks me as he licks my face. I take a few points of damage from the sandpaper texture of his tongue and scowl at the duration of the curse, which has only dropped by a few minutes.

"I'm alive, but that's a long way from saying that I'm okay." I sigh and scratch him behind his ears. "This dungeon would be able to take down warriors who were level fifty, and I'm back to level one. Honestly, I just don't know what to do."

We'll stand with you. Balder nods firmly. *Don't worry about a thing, Master.*

A loud screech echoes through the air, and two dark creatures flash overhead. They look like small dragons, and they clearly have riders perched upon them as though they were horses. A sharp cry rings out, and the creatures start to descend, slowly spiraling down toward us.

My pups react instantly. Balder lets out a howl, and one of the dragons is struck as if by a mighty hand. Its wings crumple and it comes crashing to the ground not far away. I can't see the point of impact, but a great deal of debris is blasted up into the air. Stones, large and small, are thrown this way and that, and I dive back out of the way as a shotgun blast seems to flash through the area.

"I suddenly have a much greater appreciation for innocent bystanders in a war zone," I mutter as Bjorn lets out a howl as well. Then the second dragon comes shooting down from the sky, thankfully hitting an area a bit further away. Bjorn comes back to stand next to me, and we wait . . . wait . . .

A foot scuffs against a stone, and I spin around as an armored vampire comes charging out from behind the stones. He's wearing a helmet with horns coming out of the forehead and the chin, and I can see his hard eyes through the visor. His sword gleams in the light as he utters a few dark words. The light around me seems to dim . . .

And Balder gives a sharp yip. The guard is lifted off his feet, then slammed back into a boulder just behind him and crushed like a soda can in the hand of a professional wrestler. There's a moment's pause, and a second guard suddenly leaps down from the boulder above me. He kicks me in the head, knocking me backward into the middle of the clearing, and my health falls down into the orange.

The guard laughs. "You're feeling it, aren't you? The bigger they are, the harder they—"

His voice is cut off as a blast of ice erupts from the ground and pins him to the boulder. He groans and slumps slightly, and I rise up, drinking another Pumped! as I do so. He begins to mutter some words as well, casting who-knows-what spell, and I nod to Bjorn. Ice suddenly fills the vampire's mouth, and I walk up to him, reach up, and grab his helmet.

It takes me a few tries to pull off the helmet before I cast it aside. As I do, I find the vampire trembling, though not from fear.

He's trembling from laughter.

"Make one wrong move, and my beasts will kill you," I warn him, then nod to Bjorn. The ice in the vampire's mouth melts, and he lets out a hiss. "I want to know what just happened to me."

"You've been cursed!" The vampire laughs. "It's always horrifying when it first happens, but—"

"Who or *what* is doing it?" I snap. "Answer me."

The man simply shrugs, and his eyes start to glaze over.

"Answer me!" I yell at him. "I need to know!"

The vampire sighs, then shrugs once more. "I suppose . . . I suppose it wouldn't hurt to tell you. It's the lord of this dungeon. He's a . . ." The vampire starts to cough up blood, then leans forward. When he speaks again, his voice is a mere whisper. "Chrono-wraith."

My blood turns to ice at the name, though I admittedly don't really know what it means. With that, the vampire slumps, dead, and I sigh and step back.

"Well, then, that'll just have to do." I shake my head, trying to make sense of it. "Alright, Bjorn, Balder, let's get moving. I don't want to stay in one place, not with me being so weak and the vampires so . . ."

My voice trails off as I turn around. Bjorn and Balder are still there, but . . . well . . .

They've shrunk down to the size of puppies. No, check that. They *are* puppies. Neither of them speaks, and I sigh as a distant screech echoes through the air.

This is *not* going the way I wanted. Not in the slightest.

And I don't have the faintest idea how I'm going to get through it alive.

CHAPTER NINETEEN

I open up my pocket dimension—thankfully, *that* skill
doesn't seem to have a level requirement—and Balder and
Bjorn both jump inside. They don't speak to me, which makes
me suspect that they've reverted to a point in infancy where
they can't form proper words, even through thought-speak.
I cross my arms in thought, then turn away. I need to make
tracks, and fast. They'll be after me, and they're *much* more
adept at navigating the landscape than I am.

"Alright," I murmur as I race off through the boulders.
The ground is uneven and rocky, which forces me to go slow.
I slide down the side of a ravine into the bottom, and, staying
beneath the rocky ledges, I race down my impromptu path.
At this point, I don't care so much about my destination as I
do about staying alive. "I need to know everything that anyone knows about chrono-wraiths. What are they? How do
you kill them?"

[LunarEclipse: I'm looking, Jason, I'm looking!]

[GoldenShield: According to the Monster Battle Logs, no other warrior has yet faced off against one.]

[ChaosRider: Yeah . . . There's a minor entry that someone found in a book titled *Monsters of the Infernal Planes*.]

[DarkCynic: Well?? What does it say???]

[ChaosRider: Only that they're S-Ranked creatures with the ability to manipulate the flow of time. Oh, and that they have low health. A single hit will probably kill him, *if* you can manage to land a blow.]

"Any tricks on how to do that?" I ask. I hear flapping overhead and press myself up against the side of the ravine under a small overhang of stone. I don't see the monster shoot past me, but I doubt that it can see me either. That said, in the distance, I hear a long and low howl.

Hellhounds. Probably to sniff out my trail and track me down.

[ShadowDancer: Maybe you stab him *before* you show up! Or after he's dead or something!]

[DarkCynic: That makes no sense.]

[ChaosRider: I bet it's some sort of timey thing, though.]

I don't disagree with ChaosRider's assessment, but I don't have time to think about it. Abandoning stealth, I race along the floor of the ravine as I desperately fight to get away from the distant hounds. I don't know how far they are behind me, but I suspect that they'll catch up a *lot* faster than I'd like them to.

Suddenly, a chasm looms ahead of me, and I skid to a stop. The ravine ends abruptly where it bisects a massive crack in the ground, ten feet wide, a hundred long, and impossibly deep. The glow of magma flickers from below, and I pull back and stare down in pure and utter horror.

"This isn't good," I mutter. "Not good at all. Uh . . ."

The hounds bray in the distance once more. They're already a *lot* closer. If I was still level seventy, I'd be able to jump across without any real issues. That said, I'm *not* level seventy anymore, and . . . I don't know. Maybe I can make it. Maybe not.

The hounds bray again, even closer, and I know I have to chance it. Quickly, I back up about fifteen feet, then take a running start. I leap into the air with every ounce of effort I have and sail across the distance. A blast of hot air hits me from below, scorching past me with impossible force, and I slam into the crevice's far wall. For a moment, I scramble to find purchase on the stone. My right hand catches on a frail root, and I stop falling.

But I'm still dangling over a ravine, a sitting duck for anyone who finds me.

Knowing that I have only seconds, I look for handholds, anything, and scramble upward as fast as I can go. My chat falls silent as everyone holds their breath. I reach up and grab an outcropping . . . It cracks slightly but doesn't fall. My right foot slips on some gravel, but my left foot stays firm.

After several long moments of fighting, my right hand manages to catch hold of the rim of the crevice. I pull myself upward with all the energy I can muster, throw myself over the edge, and roll behind a boulder sitting there. Not two seconds later, I hear the *very* close braying of the hellhounds, along with the pounding feet of more guards.

"Where is he? The hounds sound like they're upon him!"

"I can see his footprints . . . No. No, they're gone."

"What happened?"

"The dogs are looking into the pit!"

"You think he tried to jump it?"

I do my best to keep my breathing level.

"I reckon he tried. A lot of them do."

"You think he fell?"

"I don't see him up there, do you?" The voice laughs. "Yeah, he fell. Come on, let's go report him."

The footsteps turn away. I hear the sniffing of the hellhounds for a moment longer, but they leave as well. With that, I let out a sigh of relief, then relax and take a look around.

The area is still wild, scattered with boulders and desolation. I rise to my feet, then slowly slip forward. I need a place to hide, that much I'm sure of. Suddenly, off to my right, I catch sight of a small cave underneath an outcropping of stone. It looks like the hole has a good view of the surrounding area and is dark enough that it won't be obvious I'm inside. Off in the distance, I see one of the dragons circling around and quickly run, crouching low, in the direction of the cave.

It takes me only a few seconds to reach it. The thing is small, so even crouching down I can hardly fit inside. That said, I do my level best and quickly slip into the darkened interior. The cave isn't deep, maybe five or six feet, and is around three feet tall. I lie down to stare out across the barren landscape, watching and waiting.

From where I'm at, I can see down across the cracked landscape to one of the towns, which seems alive with activity. A small boat floats across the lava, pushed along by a figure with a pole. It's actually kind of cool to watch. I see more people on horseback darting around and watch them with interest. The dragon riders still swoop here and there looking for me despite the report that I've fallen to my death. As I lie there, I watch the duration of the time curse tick downward.

[00:30:00]

[00:20:00]

[00:10:00]

I still have eight minutes left on the timer when a loud buzzing noise echoes through my ears. It sounds like a mosquito, albeit a *very* large one. I freeze, then slowly back up. With a *thump*, a large bug, two feet long, comes down and lands in front of the hole. It buzzes and fluffs its wings a few times and starts walking toward me.

[FireStorm: Uh-oh! Jason took a demon bug's lair!]

[IceQueen: Hmm. That could be a problem. What level do you think that thing is?]

[DarkCynic: 20, at least.]

I grit my teeth. That's not good. I can only tame animals that are an equal level to me or lower. Quickly, I reach out and grab a large rock, about the size of my fist, and snatch it up. The bug suddenly realizes that I'm there and spreads its wings, buzzing angrily.

I don't give it time to react and throw the rock as hard as I can into its face. The bug crunches under the impact and staggers backward, then rips the stone out of its face with its mandibles and spits it to the side. It snarls and races forward, and I know my only chance is to face it in the open.

I scramble forward and roll out of the hole as fast as I can. I snatch up another stone and punch the bug in the side of the head, knocking it across the ground, then throw the stone at it. My aim is true, but the rock only bounces off the hard shell of the monster and clatters away. With that, the bug rises up in the air, then spreads its mandibles wide.

"That's not good."

A blast of fire erupts from the gullet of the beast, and I dive out of the way. Suddenly, I see several dragons spiral sharply through the air and fly in my direction. I'm making quite the scene, and if I don't get out of sight soon, I'm going to die only minutes from regaining my lost status. I snatch up another rock and throw it again, but by now, the bug is anticipating my moves. It dodges the projectile, then rises up into the air. I brace myself, and with that, it dives back down.

This time it fires a blast of green strafing fire that sticks to the ground wherever it hits. A bit of it splashes on me as I dodge once more and begins to burn through my clothes. I take an extraordinary amount of fire damage from the blast, and though I slap it out quickly enough, I've lost almost half my health. I snarl, then open up my inventory and grab out yet another bottle of Pumped! soda. I'm starting to run low on the stuff—I've had a near-infinite supply ever since I raided that Pumped! warehouse, but I've gone through quite a bit of it— and unfortunately, I don't know when I'll have time to pick up more. That said, I don't have time to worry about rationing, and I chug the bottle as quickly as I can. My health rises once more . . . and an idea springs into my mind.

As the bug comes around for another attack, I take the

empty bottle by the neck. It's not a great weapon, but it'll work well enough. This time the bug swoops down and lets out a great blast of blue fire, and I jump out of the way only to bring the bottle crashing down on its head like a club. Glass shatters under the blow, and the bug buzzes and falls to the ground. I'm left holding a stub of the bottle and almost throw it away . . .

Only to realize that my weapon just got even better, if that's possible.

As the bug struggles up into the air once more, I charge at it and stab at its underbelly with my glass bottle. The sharpened glass cuts deep into the soft stomach, and the bug buzzes and falls to the ground. Quickly, I fall on top of it, wrench its head around to point away from me, and stab it angrily at the back of the head just as hard and fast as I can. It takes several attempts to break through the thin armor there, but I manage it. With a crunch, the glass bottle is driven into the monster's brain matter, and I let out a sigh and climb back to my feet.

"There we go." I kick the thing away from me. "It's dead."

[Demon Dung Beetle defeated!]

[XP Awarded: 70]

[. . .]

[Notice: S-Ranked creature defeated!]

[First Kill of a Demon Dung Beetle from planet Earth!]

[Extra XP Awarded: 35]

[. . .]

[You have leveled up!]

[Congratulations! You are now Level 3!]

[. . .]

[Extra reward granted for First Kill of a Demon Dung Beetle!]

[Skill Acquired!]

[Exterminator (passive)]

I roll my eyes as I groan and push myself back to my feet. Two rewards are presented to me, and I sigh and select "Weapon" for both of them. A Rusted Dagger and a Rusted Sword appear in my hands, and I just have to laugh.

"Ahh, there was a time when I would have loved something like this." I give the weapons a few twirls. "Not that I'm really complaining right now, but—"

Thump.

The ground shakes as two dragons land just in front of me and two guards jump down. They draw their weapons and let out sharp hisses. I shrug, then tuck the sword into my inventory and raise my Rusted Dagger.

"Woe to all who come near me!" I hold up the dagger. "Behold, the dagger that runs red with the blood of my enemies!"

Both guards frown and pause. My only chance is to stall them for . . . it looks like about forty-five seconds.

[LunarEclipse: Is Jason really doing this?]

[IceQueen: I'm telling you, ruling these dungeons isn't as simple as just smashing through everything in your path. Jason's smart.]

[ChaosRider: This is going to be fun to watch!]

"That's a Rusted Dagger," one of the guards says and starts toward me once more. "It can deal five base damage, which won't even break my damage threshold."

"That's what you believe," I counter. Thirty seconds. "What if it's something more powerful, though? I've killed a *lot* of vampires today, you know."

The vampire chuckles, but the second one does hold up a hand.

"Hey, better wait. He's right. That could be an S-Ranked weapon. Weapons don't age, so they're not subject to the same curse."

The first vampire sighs, then turns around. "I know how the curse works, idiot. What *you* don't realize is that S-Ranked items can only be wielded if you're over level forty-five. Then the ranks are fifty-five for S+, sixty-five for SS, seventy-five for SS+, eighty-five for SSS, and so on." He sighs. "Whatever that weapon is, if *he* can hold it, it isn't anything good."

Twenty seconds.

"You're betting a lot of life on that," I point out. "How long will your lifespan be if I don't kill you? A hundred years? Two hundred? A thousand?"

"We are immortal," the first guard snaps.

"Unless I kill you. Which I will." I sigh. "Look, I'm on record throughout this *whole* dungeon: I don't want to fight any of you. I just want to get out of here. If you fight me, I'll kill you, but it'll slow me down, and I'd rather not do that. Just take me to the portal, and I'll leave you alone."

"What portal?" the guard asks. He suddenly seems interested in talking, which *also* makes sure that I stay alive. Ten seconds.

"The one I'm going to use to escape," I answer. "Frankly, I don't exactly know where it is. I just know it's *somewhere* in here."

"I'll put out a report to look for it," the first guard calls out. "That sounds interesting. Let's see if this checks out, and then we'll decide what to do about it."

Five seconds.

"Are you sure?" The guard closest to me frowns. "He can't have much longer on his chrono spell. If we don't get him now, we may lose our chance."

Four seconds.

"Ah, he's got to have at least . . ." The first guard shrugs. "Come on, kid, be honest. How much more time do you have left?"

"Two seconds," I answer honestly.

They both nod, then freeze. The guard closest to me draws his sword and lunges, and I feel power flow through my veins once more.

CHAPTER TWENTY

I punch upward with the dagger, performing a perfect upper-cut into the vampire's chin. The dagger itself explodes into fragments—turns out that it really couldn't break his damage threshold—but my fist does plenty of damage by itself. The vampire is lifted off his feet, and I spin and perform a perfect roundhouse kick. He's slammed into a nearby boulder and is dead before he hits the ground. As the other vampire frantically tries to get his dragon into the air, I snatch up a small rock from the ground and launch it. The stone breaks the sound barrier quite easily as it snaps through the air, and the guard is knocked clean off his beast by the force of the impact. He lands on the ground with a rough *smack* that very clearly indicates he's not getting up again. I give a nod, and my chat explodes with joy.

[DarkCynic: Alright, that was pretty epic.]

[ViperQueen: YEAH! The line, the delivery, it was all so perfect!]

[RazorEdge: Totally amazing!!!]

I smile and give a bow, then slowly start strolling down the wasteland toward town. I don't say anything out loud because I don't want any monsters watching the chat to learn my plans, but my mind whirs frantically as I try to parse through everything.

I've been reverted back to level seventy. Apparently, I don't get to keep the two levels I earned while reverted—lame—but that could get reversed at any moment. I simply don't know the limits of the chrono-wraith. S-Ranked monsters usually have a whole boatload of tricks at their disposal, and in this case, he *sounds* like a creature that doesn't fight using ordinary physical means. He's a trickster, and that means I'm as likely as not to stumble into any sort of trap he leaves for me. I don't know how many times he can activate the chrono spell against me, and I don't know how much more powerful he can make it—can he revert me back to *before* I had any levels? I don't know a whole lot of things. All I do know is that this thing is powerful and isn't something that I want to mess with.

Ahead of me, the town looms larger and larger. I'm not sure why, but I find myself drawn to the location. Sure, it's full of enemies, but that also means more chances to find the portal. I just need *someone* to have seen it, someone to know where it's located, and for that, my best chance is to interact with someone, even if they are people who want me dead.

It takes me about twenty minutes to reach the edge of town. I'm still doing my best to be stealthy, since I don't really want to bring down an entire army upon me. I can fight things off a lot better now, but let's not go looking for trouble, right? In any case, I soon find myself hiding behind a patch of scraggly trees at the edge of the town, watching the residents slowly going about their business.

The people living in the town remind me of the vampire's servants. They're humanoid, but beyond that, I just can't tell much. Their skin is blackened and charred, like they've been burned by the nearby lava flow. Vampires from the castle ride back and forth through the town shouting orders and calling out this thing or that thing, but none of the residents really pay all that much attention. I have a feeling that they do exactly what they're told and not a bit more. I sigh, then slowly rise up and slip into a narrow alley.

[GoldenShield: What's Jason doing?]

[IceQueen: Something epic, I'll bet!]

As I reach the end of the alley, I peer out. It takes me a moment before I really see anything, but I soon catch sight of a man in a long blackened coat walking down the street. He catches sight of me, his eyes pale and yellow, and he freezes. I motion for him to come to me, then slip back into the alley. A moment later, a vampire on a horse flashes past but doesn't say anything. There's a long, *long* pause . . . and the man slowly walks into the alley as well.

"Thanks," I whisper. "Look, I need to get out of here, and I need to do it fast. Have you seen a portal anywhere? Have you heard of a portal suddenly appearing?"

The man doesn't answer. Slowly, he opens up his mouth wide, revealing black and yellow teeth. It takes me a moment before I see what he's showing me.

He has no tongue.

I wince but reach out and pat him on the shoulder. He closes his mouth and nods, then slowly walks back up to the end of the alley and points across the town. I follow him and see that he's not pointing at the town at all, but at the volcano beyond.

"You've seen it?" I feel my hope rising. "You're sure?"

The man pauses, then makes a motion that seems to indicate drinking. He then flashes an elaborate series of sign language symbols with his hands, which I can't even begin to follow. It ends, however, with him pointing up at the volcano.

"So, you were having drinks . . . and you heard someone else talking about it?"

The man nods.

"Perfect." I let out a long sigh. "I guess I've got quite the trip ahead of me, then. Many thanks."

The man slowly bows his head, then motions for me to slip back into the alley. I do so, and with that, he walks out, vanishing down the street. I wait a few moments to ensure that he's away, and then I turn to walk back into the shrubbery around the town.

Only . . . there's an elder vampire standing between me and the cover of the brush.

As a matter of fact, it's the very same elder vampire who I killed back in the little throne room.

"Let me guess." I sigh and draw out my twin daggers. "The chrono-wraith just turned the clock back and brought you back to life?"

"It's not the first time, and it won't be the last." The elder vampire draws his twin daggers as well. "And you, my friend, do not possess his favor, which means that when we strike *you* down, you won't be getting back up."

"You don't exactly possess his favor either." The queen appears out of thin air at the entrance of the alley. She draws out her sword and stares me down in that narrow space. "He only brought you back at my request."

"So you *do* love me," he—the king—sneers.

"No, but I needed someone to keep him contained while I kill him." The queen hisses and bares her fangs. "Now that I've already fought you once, I know your tactics. You won't get away so easily *this* time."

I shrug. "We'll see about that. I'm always up for a bit of a challenge."

"Are you now?" The queen laughs before her face quickly becomes serious again. "Let's test that, shall we?"

She races forward, and her sword flashes through the air. I block it with Beowulf's Dagger, only to dodge backward as the king stabs at me with his daggers. The assortment of blades is quite a lot to deal with in the narrow alley, but . . . Well, as I said to the queen, I *do* like a challenge.

For the next several moments, the three of us fight desperately against each other. I spin back and forth blocking first one weapon and then the next. Neither of them can land a hit on me, and I nod in satisfaction as we break apart for a momentary pause.

"You're not too bad." I gesture to the queen. "You'll make a worthy addition to my wall of defeated monsters."

The queen hisses softly, and the king laughs.

"And you'll be forgotten, as I don't *keep* a wall of defeated warriors," the queen answers softly.

"Each to his own, I suppose." I sigh, then shrug. "Change of topic, but do you like baseball?"

The king blinks in surprise, but the queen's eyes narrow. I see her muttering a few words under her breath, and I open my inventory. Blub drops out into my hand, and I throw him at her with all my might.

KA-BOOM!

The blast shakes the area, shattering stones and making the ground tremble. The queen is knocked flat, and I leap over her body and dash out into the middle of the street, where I'm a bit more open. I don't flee, exactly, but I do need a bit more space if I'm going to make a proper mark.

Hooves clatter down the street, and I look up to see one of the vampire guards racing at me. He raises a lance, and I shrug and throw Beowulf's Dagger into his chest. He groans and falls, and I snatch the dagger back out of him as he tumbles past me. With that, the queen springs out, sword flashing, and the two of us lock together in deadly combat.

Steel rings against steel as the two of us crash together. She begins speaking as we fight, and once more, lightning bolts come flashing down from the sky, blasting chunks of stone out of the cobbles and setting street signs on fire. A few of the slaves run for cover, but most just step back into doorways or watch from windows.

The king suddenly appears from a different alley and charges at me with a grin on his face. He speaks a few dark words and a circle of fire appears on the ground around me.

Suddenly, a curtain of flame rises up, separating me from the other fighters.

"You idiot!" the queen screeches. "Now I can't get to him!"

"You don't need to get to him," the king soothes. "Just wait! This curse is *really* powerful."

The flames swirl faster, and I feel the air getting hotter and hotter. The king may very well be right . . . but if Blub has healed to his full size, I imagine that Bjorn has done the same. I open up my pocket dimension and he steps out. He can barely fit into the ring with me, but fit he does, and he lets out a growl. The air chills to a tolerable amount, and I give him a nod and scratch behind his ears.

"Let's do this fast, alright?" I whisper to him. "When this goes down, hit them hard, and hit them fast."

Bjorn nods. A few moments later, the fire dies away, and Bjorn lets out a powerful howl. The king has only an instant to be surprised before a great blast of ice erupts from the ground and encases him, and I spring upon the queen.

The only thing is . . . she's been using the time to prepare, and I utterly forgot to be ready for her hat trick.

[Condition: Cursed.]

I groan as the world darkens and I feel my strength leave me. I sway with the effort of just standing on my two feet, and the queen charges at me with a shriek. Bjorn staggers toward her, but he falls as well, likely taken down by the same spell.

The queen hits me, hard, as she slashes me across the chest. It's hard to describe what being cut by a sword is like, but trust me, it's tremendously unpleasant. I fall backward across the cobbles, gasping and groaning as she stands above me. I can't move, and my own blood trickles across the cobblestones.

"And here we are, Jason Lee." The queen stares down at me in triumph. "You are nothing, you must realize that. You are nothing but a pathetic human, nothing but a lowly little bug that I will soon crush."

"Yeah . . . ," I whisper. "You're not the first person to tell me that. I don't expect that you'll be the last."

With every remaining ounce of my strength, I roll out of the way as she strikes down at me. Her sword rings out across the cobbles, and she snarls as I come back to my feet. The world is so dark I can barely see, and my body sways, but I'm still a level-seventy warrior. I'm not going to be taken down by some half-baked queen who thinks she's being protected by some chrono-wraith.

She lunges again, and I desperately lift my dagger to bat her sword away. I do the same thing again, and then again. Suddenly, she blurs around behind me, and her claws dig into my shoulder. I feel my legs buckle, and my health begins to drop.

"And so, Jason, you see my true power," she murmurs in my ear. "What will you do now?"

Wait for Bearing of a Knight to kick in.

I think the words, only to gape in horror. I don't have Ascalon on me—I moved it to my inventory because it was too heavy. The queen will kill me in an instant if I try to open up my inventory. I have few options.

And so . . . I drop like a rock.

I simply let myself fold, collapsing as if I were dead. The

queen's talons tear at me, but I fall free nonetheless and strike the ground. A small moan escapes my lips, and I flop over onto my back. The queen stands above me, then snorts and turns away.

So, using the last ounce of my energy I open up my inventory and pull out Ascalon.

The blade gleams in the light as it snaps into my palm, and energy fills me once more as the curse is burned away. The queen spins back, horrified, and I rise up.

"You little—"

I slash the sword across her body before she has a chance to fully process what's happening. The force of the blow splits her from top to bottom, and she slowly collapses, dead long before she hits the ground. The king, still stuck in the block of ice, stares at me as I walk over to his little prison.

I don't say a word but draw back the sword and stab it through the block. It goes in one side and out the other, and the vampire's eyes slowly become lifeless once more. With that, I sigh, draw the sword back out, and turn to Bjorn, who's recovered now that the queen is dead.

"That's one more obstacle down," I mutter to the noble beast, then turn toward the volcano. "Let's get out of here. With luck, we won't see any more of this little chrono-thing."

CHAPTER TWENTY-ONE

I quickly run through the rest of town, keeping an eye out for any more vampires. Only a single grunt challenges me, and I cut through him like he's made of paper. Soon, I come up to the edge of the river of lava where I can look up toward the volcano.

I squint my eyes against the glare from the river of fire, but I don't see anything in particular. If there is a portal up there, it's nothing obvious. Glancing around, though, I see a small boat, one of the same ones I saw earlier. That's my best chance, I know, and I quickly climb into the thing. There's a long pole lying in the bottom, which I pick up and dip down into the lava. With that, I shove off and start pushing steadily up toward the distant volcano.

As soon as I set out on the river, I start to regret the decision, but there's nothing I can *really* do about it. The heat rising up from the lava is fantastically hot, and cinders sting at my skin. Here and there, bubbles form and pop, which spray both the boat and me with bits of molten stone. It feels like I'm paddling straight into the bowels of hell, and I'm still a *long* way from the really hot stuff at the mouth of the eruption.

That said, I also do think that the boat is my best option for travel. Glancing at the wilderness, there's only one road that goes along the river, and it passes through a handful of small towns, all of which look to be crawling with vampires. Out here there are a few fire monsters wandering back and forth among the lava fields, but they're keeping to themselves, and I don't give them any reason to attack.

My chat falls mostly silent as I push on slowly and steadily. It's a lot more boring than most of my adventures, and it doesn't get more interesting very quickly. I pass by first one town and then the next. Minutes turn into hours, and I lose all track of time. All I know is the flow of the river, the thumping of the pole, the burbling of the lava. All I want to do is reach the portal so I can get home.

As I pass by the final town, my arms really start to burn, and I push the boat over toward a small island in the middle of the river. The bottom of the boat rumbles against the gravel on the riverbed, and I happily climb out onto solid land once more. There, I sit down on the narrow stretch of land and look out across the area.

[Condition: Dehydrated.]

I scowl at the notification but open up my inventory and pull out another Pumped! bottle. It hisses as I crack it open and tastes simply *wonderful* as I tilt my head back and guzzle it all up. With that, I sigh and shake my head.

"How long has it been since I boarded that boat?"

[DarkCynic: About five hours.]

[ViperQueen: Yeah, it's like eleven o'clock at night.]

[ChaosRider: Do you think you'll sign off for the night soon? My mom is yelling at me to get to bed.]

I have to laugh at that last one. "I don't have a clue when I'll be signing off, honestly. I can't really fall asleep right here in the middle of a lava flow, but I have to admit that I'm plumb exhausted." I yawn, then shake my head. "I could sure use a few z's, but—"

Something cracks, and the ground shakes slightly. I rise back to my feet, and the stone in front of me cracks once more. That's a slight problem, no matter which way you look at it. A sharp blast of steam comes shooting up, and my chat begins quite eagerly telling me that I ought to be getting out of there. I have to agree with them, and I race into the boat and push off as fast as possible. Though it hurts me to do so, I let myself float back down the river slightly. I'm not going to be able to pole myself upstream fast enough to avoid whatever that is, and I'd rather not die in a minor volcanic eruption.

Crack!

HISSSSSSS!

KA-BOOOOOOOOOM!

Steam explodes up into the air from the strip of land— steam that turns to black smoke after only a few moments. Suddenly, the simple eruption of steam and smoke turns into a proper explosion, and fire and lava shoot high into the sky.

And then, emerging from the chaos is a dark form.

It shoots out of the ground, rising up on the plume of black smoke like an arrow. As it reaches the pinnacle of the cloud, it spreads two leathery wings and spirals outward, becoming a very distinctive form that I know quite well by this point.

It's a dragon.

Not a big one, mind you, but a dragon is a dragon. I frown, then put my pole in the lava and start to steer over to the shore. Before I can, though, the dragon shoots down from the sky and slams into the boat with impossible force. I'm launched high into the air, then, fortunately, I come down hard on the ground among the boulders. I groan, but my health doesn't fall all that far, which is good. Slowly, I pick myself up and turn to face the thing.

The dragon is just emerging from the river of lava. It's about five feet long and is cloaked in flame. It has black scales, yellow eyes, and just looks . . . evil. I mean, I have yet to meet a truly *good* dragon, but this one takes the cake. It just looks like something that would love nothing more than to drag you to hell and leave you burning in the deepest pit that it can find. I watch it closely, and it shakes itself to rid its body of the last bit of lava.

"Alright." I draw out two of my daggers and prepare myself for a fight. "Are you really ready to take me on?"

The dragon hisses, then spreads its wings wide. Suddenly, I see the ghostly image of a clock appear before it, and I frown. I don't know what *that* means, but I get my answer after a moment. It starts growing . . . and growing . . . and growing.

The beast expands from a simple five-foot baby dragon to a *much* larger two-hundred-foot beast in the span of about ten seconds. Its tail uncoils with a flourish across the shoreline, knocking boulders into the lava with immense power. Its wings generate a hurricane of wind as it simply settles itself, and its growl makes my chest ache.

"I am the bringer of death," the dragon growls down at me, "a demonic dragon, the highest classification, aged to my prime. What are you? A little level-seventy human? Pathetic."

"I personally find that monsters who deal in insults are rarely the ones I have to worry about," I answer as I prepare myself for battle. "Why don't you just—"

WHOOOOOOOSH!

The dragon flaps its wings, and a powerful blast of wind hits me with unfathomable force. I'm lifted off my feet and sent flashing backward to bounce across the wasteland like a toy. The dragon takes to the skies only to unleash a great blast of flame that burns across the ground as it swoops toward me. As I come to a stop, I catch sight of another of the demon bug holes. I quickly dive inside, squishing half a dozen of them as I do so, and the dragon roars overhead with a torrent of fire. The heat lowers my health by a hundred or so points, and I roll back out as the dragon swoops past and rises up into the sky, then circles back to check on its work.

"Alright, Balder!" I cry out, charging across the ground. "I need you!"

Balder leaps out of the pocket dimension. I jump up onto a boulder and leap into the air, and he gives a sharp bark that flings me high into the sky. The dragon doesn't see me coming . . . at least, not until it's too late.

I shoot right past its head and flash it a sloppy salute, then land on its back and catch hold of a spine there. Fire erupts from the point of impact—it *is* a demonic creature, after all—but I ignore the pain, draw my Dagger of the Ancients, and stab it between two scales. A great explosion of light erupts off the blade as I stab it down into the monster, and the dragon howls in pain.

With that, the dragon dives, spiraling sharply, and I hang on for dear life. It pulls up as it nears the ground, then slams into the rock, digging in with its claws. I'm flung from my perch and come crashing down in front of it, only to catch myself and run right back at the thing. It stares down at me, then opens its mouth and lets out a piercing blast of flame.

I respond by ducking behind a large boulder. Flames roar past on both sides, and the rock slowly begins to melt under the force of the blast. I stay put as it dies away, and with a rumble, the dragon steps forward to look around the boulder to see if I've perished or survived.

With this monster, I know I can't make a single misstep, so I throw myself into motion the instant that I can. While it looks around the right side of my rock, I dart around the left and break for its body as fast as I can go.

"Skill: Speed."

The world slows, albeit not by much, and I run forward at the beast. As I come up to it, I jump into the air and slash both my daggers across the monster's right paw. Both weapons are powerful, and with the passive skills I've been building against both demonic and serpentine creatures, I'm able to cut through the tendon with ease. The dragon howls and stumbles, putting me within striking distance of its belly. Before I can get to it, though, it flaps its wings and shoots up into the air once more, rising up into the sky.

"Alright, everyone!" I call out. "I need it downed, and I need at least . . . thirty seconds, I'd say."

I can do it, Master!

Gabe bounds out to stand next to me. I give him a nod, then stare up at the circling monster. "Do it and I'll make sure you have luxury kibble for the rest of your life."

Gabe closes his eyes and draws in a long deep breath. Finally, he opens his eyes again right as the dragon swoops down and begins another strafing run. Fire hits the ground about two hundred feet away, rapidly burning toward us.

Ooooooooooooooooooooooooooooooooooowwwwwwwww!

The howl is long and piercing, and the sun suddenly grows a hundred times brighter. The dragon screams and falls to the ground under the assault, flinging boulders and stones up into the air as if they're nothing but rubble. Gabe jumps back into the pocket dimension while I charge forward at the beast.

An avalanche precedes the dragon, with boulders bouncing about like marbles. I duck through it with as much speed and skill as I can manage and jump up onto the wing of the creature as it rumbles to a halt. Slowly, it starts to pull itself up, shaking the boulders off. I don't think it even notices me, what with all the other bits and pieces of stone spread across its body. Which is all for the better. I reach its back and race up between its two wings, up to the base of its spine. Quickly, I cross my two daggers, take a deep breath, and lash out with every ounce of strength I have.

Thankfully, that's quite a lot of strength at this point.

Two pure-white blades cross right at the link between two of the dragon's vertebrae, and twin blasts of light tear through its neck. The blow doesn't sever the dragon's neck entirely, but it does drop the dragon to the ground, where it groans and falls limp. I race up toward its head, preparing a final, fatal blow to the back of its skull. As I reach the head, though, I see the faint image of a clock and sigh in annoyance.

Flash!

The dragon vanishes in a blast of energy. Or rather, it shrinks back down to a five-foot hatchling, located where the dragon's chest just was. It looks about, then flaps its wings as it rises up into the air.

Gabe walks out of my pocket dimension again to stand next to me.

Well, that's a good thing, Master!

"You think you can get it again?" I ask.

Gabe responds by drawing in a deep breath. While he's preparing himself, I snatch up a stone, draw back my arm . . . aim . . . and let fly.

The stone once more breaks the sound barrier as it races toward the dragon. My aim isn't quite perfect; I was aiming for its head but hit its body instead. In any case, the blast knocks the dragon from the air, and it tumbles, head over wing, back down toward the ground. At that same moment, Gabe howls, and a torrent of light hits the thing with incredible force.

It's hard to describe quite what happens in that moment. Under the immense blast of light and energy, the little hatchling simply evaporates, turning to nothing but ash and dust. A little bit of it dribbles down to the ground, but not more than a pile, and even that much is quickly blown away by the wind. I'm informed that I'm the first human to have killed a demonic dragon and receive a great many rewards.

[You have leveled up!]

[Congratulations! You are now Level 73!]

Three levels from the demonic dragon? It's the first time I've leveled up in the infernal dungeon, and I nod in approval. With that, I clap my hands and slowly turn to look back up at the volcano.

[ChaosRider: NOW are you going to sign off, Jason?]

[ViperQueen: How is he even still awake? I feel like I'm about to drop, and I'm not fighting monsters.]

[FireStorm: In fairness, you might feel differently if you were out there in the trenches.]

I laugh, then draw in a deep breath. "Oh, trust me. I'm signing off the *moment* that I get a chance." Slowly, I start off through the field of destruction, a smile growing on my face. "I think I see the portal. I'm almost home, and I'm not planning on stopping until I get there."

CHAPTER TWENTY-TWO

It's a true enough statement. High up on the volcanic slopes, I can see a small flicker of dark energy that looks just like a portal. Even better, it's on my side of the river of lava, which means I don't have to deal with crossing a whole river of liquid flame. I quickly walk away from the desolate battlefield left by my fight with the dragon and begin winding my way through the boulders as I head up toward the portal. As I do, I call out Burnie, who flaps down to land on my shoulder.

"I want you to fly up into the sky and keep an eye out for anything odd," I order him. "If you see any more dragons, or if those vampire lords get resurrected or anything, I want to know about it."

You've got it, Master.

Burnie shoots up into the sky, where he begins to spiral about, swooping first this way and then that. I take off at a trot, forcing my weary limbs to move faster across the landscape. Wiry and scorched plants catch at my arms and legs, and the fumes from the area burn my lungs. I realize that I really don't know at this point how long I've been inside this dungeon. How much damage have I done to my body simply from exposing myself to all of this? I don't have the faintest idea. In any case, I can see my destination, and I'm not going to stop until I get to safety.

Master?

Burnie's voice echoes in my head, and I frown and glance up at him. "What is it?" I don't know if he can hear my voice or not, but I certainly hope so.

There's something coming. I think it's the chrono-wraith.

I don't know how Burnie would know a thing like that, but I'm not going to take any chances. I put on a burst of speed, activating my speed skill to do it, and race across the wasteland and up the mountain as fast as I can.

As I reach the slope of the volcano and start upward, I risk a glance backward. I don't scare easily, but in that moment, I rather wish I hadn't done that. A mist is following me, covering a more or less circular space on the ground about twenty feet across, drifting around the boulders and over the crevices after me. It doesn't look like it's moving all that fast, but as I watch it a bit more closely, I realize that it's probably doing double my own speed.

[LunarEclipse: Yeah, that's for sure the chrono-wraith.]

[ViperQueen: RUN, Jason, RUN!!!]

[ChaosRider: On the bright side, you ought to get loads of XP and cool stuff for beating this thing!]

I don't disagree with that, but I also know that the wraiths are supposed to be particularly difficult to kill. A good warrior takes fights as they come, but he doesn't seek them out, and I have a feeling that seeking out this fight will likely cause me to blunder into something I'm not prepared for.

With that in mind, I turn my focus upward and run just as hard and fast as I possibly can. My breath comes in ragged gasps, and my legs burn, but there I go. Behind me, I start to hear the steady ticking of a clock growing steadily louder as the wraith gets closer and closer. Ahead, the portal grows larger and larger, and I close my eyes as I push on desperately.

I'm two hundred feet away.

One hundred feet from my goal.

Fifty.

Twenty.

Ten!

The portal is within my grasp when the wraith reaches me. Mist swirls around me, and with my hand only inches from the dark energy of the portal, my body freezes. The ticking noise becomes oppressive and cacophonous, and I scream in frustration.

At least, I try to. Truth be told, my body won't move. I've been paralyzed before, and this isn't the same feeling. I'm just . . . motionless. My body won't budge one way or another. I can't blink, I can't speak, I can't do anything except think.

It's like I've been paused, just like a movie or something.

"Here you are, Jason Lee," the voice of the chrono-wraith echoes in my head. "Helpless, like a little baby. You've done a number on my people, I'll grant you that. Few could claim a record as good as yours, and I have to admit, I'm impressed. But in the end, here you are."

[DarkCynic: If only you hadn't stopped to look back! You might have made it!]

[RazorEdge: Yeah, bummer! Oh well. He thinks he has you trapped. Now's your time to really show him what you're made of!]

[ViperQueen: Kill the chrono!!!]

My jaw unseals, though the rest of me is still frozen. I work it back and forth a few times, then sigh. "So, what happens now? I just remain stuck here until the end of time?"

"Hardly!" The wraith laughs. "You will die, and you will do it in exactly the way that I intend. Is that clear?"

"Clear as mud." I snort. "How are you going to kill me, then?"

"There are lots of ways I could do it," the chrono-wraith muses. "I could starve you. I could age you. I could turn you back into an infant and leave you to die, but . . . none of that sounds interesting enough to me."

"Do tell," I snarl softly.

"Oh, I will. Actually . . ."

There's a flash and the mountainside suddenly fades away. The mist remains, though, as a hazy sort of background. I find myself standing on a metal floor, almost like I'm in an arena. A figure emerges from the mist across from me.

It's . . . It's me.

Not-Jason draws out Beowulf's Dagger, then the Dagger of the Ancients. He settles into his stance, then nods at me. With a crackle, my body reanimates, and I slowly take my own stance.

"You're going to kill me yourself?" I raise an eyebrow. "The way I understand it, if I land so much as a single hit on you, you're dead."

"You'll just have to find out for yourself," Not-Jason answers.

I growl. "No one takes my body and gets away with it."

Not-Jason flashes a smile at me, then charges. His stance is all wrong, his body entirely off-balance. I don't move a muscle but wait for him to reach me. As he reaches me and swings, I duck easily underneath his blows and stab him in the gut. The force of the attack lifts him off his feet and flings him backward across the arena, and he groans. I rush forward to follow up the attack, and—

Flash!

The arena resets. Not-Jason has healed, and I'm put back in my original position. Not-Jason frowns, then adjusts his stance slightly.

"Like this? Yeah, that's right."

My eyes open slightly. He can just heal himself? And then learn from his mistakes? I realize that I need to end this, and I need to do it immediately.

[DarkCynic: Alright, Jason, this is going to be a tough one, but I think you can do it if you really pull yourself together.]

[LunarEclipse: You've got this! Just keep yourself focused!]

[IceQueen: This is going to be so cool!]

I charge at my doppelgänger, ready to cut his head clean from his body. Not-Jason sees me coming and takes a defensive stance. As I attack, he spins out of the way and lands a few quick blows against me before retreating. Following him,

I continue slashing and attacking with every ounce of strength I have. He mostly just ducks and dodges, and I press harder.

Flash!

I didn't even land a blow against him, but the arena resets anyway. This time I only have a moment's preparation before the chrono-wraith comes at me swinging just as hard and fast as I was doing a moment before. This time I'm forced to defend myself, striking and parrying as quickly as I can. He forces me backward across the arena, using the exact same tactics that I used only a few moments earlier.

"This isn't fair," I grunt as he slams a knee into my gut and knocks me back into the swirling mist that marks the edge of the arena. I slam into something solid, though it's hard to tell exactly what.

"Life isn't fair," Not-Jason mocks me. "If I kill you, it will be because these blades have cut you open, making it impossible for your body to sustain itself. That's about as fair as it gets."

I let out an enraged yell and launch myself forward, activating Speed as I do so. I flash across the arena and hit him in the gut, and he's slammed back into the misty wall. Something cracks in Not-Jason's body, and the arena resets again with a flash.

We regard each other with a bit more suspicion before we attack once more. Once again he uses my own tactics against me. I'm training this guy how to kill me, but I don't have a clue how not to. He suddenly activates Speed and charges me, and I react instinctively by spinning out of the way and slashing him across the neck. He just manages to deflect the blow away from his neck, but I still land a long slash across his face. With another flash, the arena resets again, and he eyes me warily.

I soon start to lose track of how many times the arena has reset. He attacks, usually using some tactic that I taught him in the previous clash, and I defend against him. It happens over and over, again and again, until finally, breathing heavily, I manage to stab him twice in the back. He groans and falls to his knees, then vanishes in a burst of light right before I can behead him. My dagger carves through the air where his body just was, and I snarl and stomp around the arena.

"Get back here! If you're going to challenge me, at least acknowledge when you've—"

FLASH!

"—lost," I murmur, finishing up the sentence. The little arena has faded away, and I find myself standing on top of a skyscraper, looking out over the ruins of a once-great massive city. As far as I can see, the buildings have been bombed-out or are simply run down, with broken windows, rusted frames, and a great deal of blackened fire damage. I grit my teeth and walk up to the edge of the skyscraper, where I look down to find desolate streets far below strewn with broken cars and white bones.

"I know when I've lost." Not-Jason appears behind me, daggers in his hands. "This is the moment when we lost, when my world fell to the dungeons. This is the last image that I have of my world, the last moment in time when I looked out over my city, knowing that after everything, after every last drop of blood that we had spent trying to keep the tide of destruction at bay, we had lost. I know when I've lost. The question is, do you?"

I slowly wrap my fingers a bit tighter around the handles of my daggers. "So what, you lost your world to the dungeons and decided to just go join them? Become of some sort of magical time wizard?"

"You didn't live my life."

"No, but I've lived mine!" I snap as I spin around to face Not-Jason. "And I know this: if the Earth fell, I wouldn't stop fighting until I had ensured that no other world faced what I did. If you give in, then you're not better than the monsters you hate so much."

"Let me tell you something, Jason," Not-Jason sneers. "In the multiverse, everyone who doesn't come from your world is your enemy. You walked into my world, the dungeon I carved out for myself, and immediately began killing everything."

"Only because they fought me," I point out. "Why did you bring me here?"

"So you could share in my pain," Not-Jason snarls. "So you, too, could see what I have to live with every day!"

With a flash, the scene around me changes. Instead of an alien city, I find myself standing on a skyscraper in New York. I see the Statue of Liberty. I see the Empire State Building.

And I see it all in ruins. Smoke, fire. Just like the old world. I snarl softly, then turn toward Not-Jason with fury.

"You kill me here and you'll be complicit in this reality."

"It can't be stopped," the wraith sneers. "I see all of time before me."

"Do you see your own death?" I counter. "Because I reckon that it's coming up a lot faster than you're expecting."

With that, I charge forward at Not-Jason. My feet fly over

the rooftop, and I throw my daggers at the monster as hard as I can. It's a tactic I haven't yet used, and it's effective. They hit Not-Jason in the chest and stomach, and he staggers backward. Before he can move, I slam into him, keep running, and throw both of us off the side of the building.

Down we go, down . . . down . . . down. The wraith screams, and I pull out both of my daggers and kick him as hard as I can, pushing him downward just a bit faster. He flashes down toward the sidewalk and hits a bare instant before I do.

Flash!

I don't feel the impact and instead find myself back on the rocky mountainside, staring at the portal once more.

[Chrono-Wraith defeated!]

[XP Awarded: 50,000,000]

[. . .]

[Notice: S-Ranked creature defeated!]

[First Kill of a Chrono-Wraith from planet Earth!]

[Extra XP Awarded: 10,000,000]

[. . .]

[You have leveled up!]

[Congratulations! You are now Level 75!]

[. . .]

[Extra reward granted for First Kill of a Chrono-Wraith!]

[Item: Pocket Watch]

With a flash, a small pocket watch appears in my hand. I've seen them before—my grandfather had one when I was growing up. It has a shiny brass cover and a little dial you can twist to wind it up. A smile spreads across my face, and I flip it open. On the inside cover are a handful of letters, and I squint down at them.

[Uses: Three]

[Effect: Turn back time. Duration: 00:05:00.]

I gape in shock. Now that's a powerful item if it really works that way. I quickly stick the item in my inventory, amid a great deal of speculation in my chat, and step toward the portal.

And then I hear ticking once more.

With a flicker, a shape takes form just next to me, shadowy and dark, which looks rather like a dark lord. It sneers from beneath a misty hood, and I get a bad feeling about things.

"If you're seeing this, it means that you've just killed me and have survived the process," the chrono-wraith snarls softly. "I don't take such things lightly. Accept this reward for your . . . success."

[Skill Acquired!]

[Hardcore (passive): Gain no XP from kills. Gain no rewards from leveling.]

"Well . . ." I stroke my chin. "That's certainly not good."

My chat explodes with indignation, but I suppose there's nothing to do about it for the moment. I'm exhausted, and I need to get some sleep. I'll see if Mr. Wang and his crew can do anything about it. Until then . . . well . . . I'm not going to worry too much about it.

CHAPTER TWENTY-THREE

When I emerge from the portal, I find the club is a hive of activity. Through the enormous windows the sky is dark. Inside, though, there are dozens of warriors, all standing in ranks and watching the portal with interest.

I stagger through, weary and exhausted, and Mr. Wang calls out loudly, "He's through! Shut it down!"

The portal dies with a sharp clatter, and several attendants rush over to me. Mr. Wang saunters up, a smile on his face, as the warriors all begin to disperse.

"Sorry for the to-do. We've had that portal open for almost five hours. If something ventured through from the other side, we'd need to be able to kill it before it killed us."

"You'd have had quite a time doing it," I murmur. "What's the status of . . . everything?"

"There's a lot to discuss, but before we can go over any of it, *you* need to get some sleep." Mr. Wang points upward to the bedrooms that have been set aside for warriors to get some sleep between their dungeons. "Go rest, and we'll talk about it when you wake up in the morning. There's nothing so imminent that it can't wait, and even if there were, you're in no shape to do anything right now."

"Fine, fine." I yawn, then nod and stagger toward the bedrooms. "But I'll see you . . . soon . . ."

My vision swims before me, and I find that I'm being led by an attendant toward the room, having apparently fallen asleep standing up. I don't resist, and a moment later I'm falling into bed. I have *got* to get better rest, that's for sure. The bed is soft, and there are no monsters, and within seconds, I'm out like a light.

My sleep is rough and uneven, filled with nightmares of a burning New York. Now, I'm not a native of New York, so that part *specifically* doesn't bother me as much, but I know that New York is representative in this case of the entire world. From New York to Los Angeles, from Moscow to Beijing, the monsters in the dungeons want to raze the Earth to the ground. I'd like to prevent it, but . . . what am I up against, especially now that I can't level up?

I don't wake up until late in the day. Sunlight streams through the windows, and I stagger to my feet and make my way to the door. There, I sweep out into the hall and down into the main room, where I find Mr. Wang, Ali, John, Elrith, Paul, and a great many others sitting around in what looks like some sort of meeting. Ali looks up and waves, and Mr. Wang turns around and smiles.

"Jason! Good to see you up and about! Have you had a shower or breakfast or anything?"

"No, to any of it." I shake my head. "I'll take some food while we talk, but a shower can wait. I'll just run into the dungeons and get covered with sweat and monster blood all over again."

"Suit yourself." Mr. Wang shrugs and points to an empty chair. "We've got a lot to go over."

I nod and drop into the chair, where I lean back and sigh. My body *aches*, though I don't dare show too much weakness. An attendant rushes over with a plate full of sausage and eggs, and I feel a smile grow on my face. I take the whole thing and tuck in while the conference begins.

"Alright . . . Let's see." Mr. Wang stands up. "We were just getting together, Jason, so your timing is perfect. Our first order of business is Krak's Astral Dungeon. Elrith and Paul were able to extend our sensor net, allowing us to peer into the multiverse across a tri-state area, and thus, we were able to locate the dungeon and the weapon near Lake Erie. The void behemoth appears to have caught up with it there and has since been engaged in taking it over."

"Has he succeeded?" John asks.

"Impossible to know for sure, but the dungeon *is* heading back this way," Mr. Wang says. "I estimate that it'll be in the metropolitan area within two hours. It seems to be on a direct course for this very tower, and while there *are* other points of interest along the way, I think it's safe to assume that we're the target, or at the very least that we're intended to *think* that we're the target."

"That's not good," I murmur, thinking about the burning image of New York that the wraith showed to me. "Do we have any way of getting someone inside?"

"Yes-ish." Paul stands up. "We can anticipate its motion and shoot someone on a collision course. It'll be . . . Well . . ."

"If we launch me into the void and the dungeon changes direction, we'll be in trouble," I mutter.

"Yes. However, our technology should be able to pull you back out before you just go zooming off for infinity!" Paul sounds pleased.

"There are a lot of variables in that." I sigh, but shrug. "Not that I think we really have any other option. Trust me, I'd mention one if I could come up with it, but I do think that's the best choice."

"Good." Mr. Wang sighs and crosses his arms. "I wish I could say that I knew what the plans of the dungeon are, but we simply don't know. We know that Krak built a weapon in it. Maybe the void behemoth disabled the weapon and is now coming to connect the dungeon to New York, just like any ordinary Astral Dungeon."

"I don't think any of us really believe that." I shake my head.

"No," Ali murmurs. "Will Jason be the only one going?"

"At present, yes," Mr. Wang confirms. "Jason is level seventy-five and will be facing monsters upward of level ninety. The next-highest warrior in the entire *world* is level fifty-two, and he lives in China. I've put in a request to have him sent here, but the authorities there are resisting. After that, there are a handful of people in the forties—John here is among them—but that's less than *half* where the void behemoth is sitting. It would be suicide for anyone except Jason to enter."

"And it's still possibly suicide for me," I groan, "but *someone's* got to do it."

"Exactly. I truly wish it could be someone else, but that's the way it goes." Mr. Wang nods. "All other warriors under my command will be deployed through the city to respond to dungeon breaks once it arrives."

"Fair enough." John nods. He stands up and walks over to me, then claps me on the shoulder. "Do me a favor and don't let anything through that's over level sixty, alright?"

I laugh and nod. "I'll do what I can."

The room begins to break up as everyone stands up and starts to walk away. Mr. Wang walks over and sits next to me, and I focus more of my efforts on finishing up the lovely breakfast provided for me. His face becomes serious, and I disconnect my chat. When that's done, he begins to speak, his voice low.

"I don't think I need to tell you how serious this is, Jason." Mr. Wang glances at the computer array over by the portal generator. "Paul told us a bit more about the weapon that Krak built. You remember the reactor core that you knocked down in Krak's first dungeon?"

"Hard not to." I flash a small smile. "What about it?"

"He built another one. All reports indicate that the second one is about ten times the size."

That makes me choke on my breakfast. "Ten times?"

"It runs on some magical gemstones in the core or something." Mr. Wang grimaces. "As near as we can tell, it can generate about as much energy as a small star. Nothing impressive compared to our sun, but the sun is also a good eight light-minutes away from us. If this reactor comes into contact with the Earth, it'll be able to burn everything on the face of the planet to the ground within a matter of minutes. Bright side: most people won't even feel a thing. Less bright side: we're talking somewhere in the ballpark of"—Mr. Wang shrugs and waves his hands around through the air—"zero survivors."

"Zero survivors." I whistle softly. "That's insane. Are we certain?"

Mr. Wang nods slightly. "Paul managed to get in touch with some of his old contacts, people who didn't necessarily mind his transition from dragon to human and who would probably follow in his footsteps if they could. It sounds like it's quite the tool."

"I knew it was powerful, but that's incredible." I shake my head. "I thought Paul said initially that it could destroy dungeons too."

"You saw the way the reactor core burned through the dungeon wall and inverted the whole thing." Mr. Wang shrugs. "If you focused the blast, this new weapon could fairly easily do the same thing, at least according to the simulations that we're running."

"Great." I hand my plate to a nearby servant. "In that case, what's the MO of the void behemoth? I know we sort of touched on that just a few minutes ago, but do we think he's coming here to burn the world down?"

"That's our best guess." Mr. Wang nods. "He needs to

attach to New York due to the whole leveled-warrior thing. Astral Dungeons can only be attached to the planet if you get a warrior over level sixty-five, but as a *further* protection, it can only attach to the warrior's specific area. That way you don't have a warrior break the barrier here, then have an Astral Dungeon open up in China or Korea or Canada or something."

"No, it makes sense." I grimace. "In that case, why don't we just have me move away?"

"He'd only follow you. Besides, there's a theory among the dungeon bosses that it doesn't have to do with a warrior's exact location, but instead with where he's from." Mr. Wang holds up his hands. "You're from here, so that's where it's allowed. If you left, the zone would remain."

"Wonderful." I sit there for a moment longer, then slap my thigh and climb to my feet. "Well, there's nothing to be done about it, I suppose. I'll just have to get shot into the dungeon and take it on from there. Just make sure you don't miss, because if I go shooting off into the void, our goose is cooked."

"We'll do our best." Mr. Wang smiles. "To help facilitate things, we'll actually be firing a handful of dummies out into the void along with you. Chances are good that the behemoth already knows our plan, but if he sees multiple launches, he'll have to decide which one he wants to deal with."

"And what if he chooses correctly?"

There's no good answer for that one. "At least you'll have a better chance than otherwise." Mr. Wang sighs and stands up as well. "I'm terribly sorry, Jason, but I'm afraid that the future of our world really is in your hands and will likely remain that way until Hella is defeated. If you fail, billions may die."

"And if I win, what will the death toll come to?" I groan.

"You'll do as well as you possibly can." Mr. Wang smiles. "Now, is there anything else we can cover before you disembark?"

I almost turn my chat back on but pause. "Yes, one quick thing. Apparently, I can't level up, gain XP, anything. That's going to be a problem."

"Yes, indeed." Mr. Wang sighs. "I was afraid you were going to ask about that. The short answer is that we don't know what to do about it. It's a passive skill, right?"

"One that I can't turn off," I confirm.

"We've had our experts working on it around the clock," Mr. Wang answers. "There are some theories, but it's nothing that appears in any of the guidebooks or reference material that we can locate. Our best bet is that you'll have to find another skill that lets you control passive skills."

"And where do I find *that?*" I ask.

"Ah . . ." Mr. Wang turns slightly red. "There's a five per-cent chance of getting it when you choose a skill for a level-up reward, once at level eighty and above."

I stare at Mr. Wang, wondering if he's gone bonkers.

"Also, all skills *can* be earned through physical means. It's certainly possible that you'll encounter the skill as a drop." Mr. Wang shrugs.

"Yeah, I think I'll take my chances with magically level-ing up and then scoring a random drop." I sigh and shake my head. "You said that was your best bet. What's your worst bet?"

"Well . . . I don't know about *worst*, but . . . do you remember the stardust?"

I snort with laughter and annoyance. "I try not to. Why?"

"Because you're about to enter an Astral Dungeon, which is the one place in the universe where stardust can be created."

Gears start to turn in my head. "How exactly do I get my hands on some?"

"Stardust is a product created by refining fallen stars," Mr. Wang answers. "They're *extremely* powerful entities that sometimes appear in Astral Dungeons."

"How often is 'sometimes?'" I demand.

"Ordinarily, about point-zero-one percent of the time," Mr. Wang answers frankly. "Given that Krak built this dungeon from scratch, I'd say the odds are a lot higher. If he knew where one was, he almost certainly brought it along for the ride. *If* you can find a fallen star and *if* you can defeat it, then you might be able to get some stardust, which *may* have a slight chance of healing you."

"There are a lot of possibilities in that statement," I mutter.

"You *did* ask what our worst idea was." He holds up his hands. "I wish I could give you something better. Do keep in mind, Jason, that you're level seventy-five. That's nothing to sniff at."

"Yeah, but I've got a level-one-hundred goddess who's coming here to raze the planet." I start walking toward the portal generator. "Nothing less than that is going to be enough."

Mr. Wang doesn't answer, but soon, the portal generator flickers to life. A portal forms, full of crackling, black energy, and Paul steps up next to the computer and gives me a nod.

"Ready in three . . ."

I turn my chat back on and fall into my stance.

". . . two . . ."

My chat explodes with questions about what's happening and when I'm going to be getting back into the fight.

". . . one . . ."

I draw in a deep breath. This is going to be the fight of my life, no matter which way I look at it.

". . . GO!"

CHAPTER TWENTY-FOUR

When I leap into the portal, it truly feels like I've been fired from a gun. I'm launched out into interdimensional space like a bullet, flashing through the void past smaller dungeons, out through the great inky darkness that surrounds the small points of light. In that instant, the dungeons almost seem to me like leeches swimming through the ocean of the void only to attach themselves to universes they intend to suck dry.

Ahead of me, I see the Astral Dungeon. It's brilliant and bright, though quite distant. I fly past hundreds of smaller dungeons, and that's not an exaggeration in any sense of the word. As I pass beyond the boundary of New York City, I find countless dungeons waiting in the wings, biding their time as they await their own turn to rain death and destruction upon the humans. I also pass by a number of dungeons that have attached themselves out in the country. I have no idea how much chaos must be taking place out that way, but I'm sure it's a lot. In any case, on I go, on toward the great Astral Dungeon.

The closer I get, the larger the thing becomes, and I suddenly realize just what I've gotten myself into. It is incredibly enormous. I mean, it must be larger than all of New York City put together, if I'm not mistaken. It sure looks like I'm heading right for the center of it, but it's hard to know for sure. A sudden thought strikes me, and I glance over my shoulder.

It takes me a moment to make out the other objects that have been launched alongside me, but I soon locate the streaks against the darkness. There are a dozen of them, launched out like a spray of pellets from a shotgun. I smile a bit, then turn my attention back to the dungeon ahead. I find myself approaching it rapidly, and the brilliance grows to impossible proportions.

Jason Lee.

The voice echoes in my head long before I've actually struck the dungeon.

I know you are coming. We could have killed you. We have chosen to let you enter.

"I'll bet," I mutter. "And why exactly are you granting me such a privilege?"

There's no direct answer, but the voice says, *We know you are level seventy-five, without any hope of leveling up. I would like to test you myself. The queen likes to take recruits from the heroes of the worlds she slays. Usually, at least a few of them come over to her side once their worlds are reduced to rubble. Come to me, and if you make it in one piece, we'll have a little interview. If you pass, I'll let you watch while I burn Earth to a cinder.*

The voice goes away, and I snort and shake my head.

"I don't care. I'm always going to—"

WHAM!

I slam into the edge of the dungeon and get punched straight through the outer barrier, just like the last time. Once again, I'm thrown out of a portal and slam into the floor, and I let out a groan.

"Alright, guys. I know this is *your* favorite new way to travel, but I have to say, it's not my . . . favorite . . ."

My voice trails off as I climb back to my feet and look around. So *this* is an Astral Dungeon. I'm not going to lie, I've been burning with curiosity ever since I first heard the term, and this . . . this is everything I thought it would be.

The floor, the walls, the ceiling, they're all a swirl of energy that seems to move, to grow, to shrink, to fold upon itself, to flow and ebb like something living. I'm standing on solid ground, but that solid ground is alive, a membrane of energy. Honestly, it's hard to describe.

In any case, the room I'm in is mostly a mixture of different shades of red and is about thirty or forty feet across. There are no entrances or exits, which I find to be somewhat concerning. Slowly, I start walking forward, angling toward one of the walls. Behind me, the portal flickers and vanishes. I'm alone in here now. Whatever happens, there's no way back.

"Jason Lee."

The voice is deep and authoritative. It comes from behind me, and I spin around. The wall ripples, then fades away to reveal an arched doorway. There are stairs inside the doorway leading upward. Of course, there's also a figure on the stairs, who slowly steps down into the room.

"A mind flayer," I mutter. "I'd recognize your kind anywhere."

The mind flayer simply inclines his head. He's more or less humanoid but has four tentacles dropping down from his face where his mouth ought to be. His arms and legs are long and covered in octopus-like flesh. He wears purple robes that look like they belong to a magician, and he has large eyes that could belong to an insect. He slowly raises his hands and bolts of purple lightning flash back and forth between his fingertips.

"I had hoped that I would be the one to welcome you here." The mind flayer sounds pleasant, though I know that's one of his tricks. "Would you like to attack first, or should I? I'll give you that courtesy."

"I have to say that you have me at a disadvantage." I draw my daggers and prepare myself. "How about you take me to your leader and no one has to get hurt?"

"Defeat me, and I'll give you what you want."

"Fair enough." I shrug and charge at the mind flayer. I know that attacking first is often a recipe for disaster, but I also know that if I stand around, the monster is only going to come up with some sort of an illusion to trick me. You defeat these sorts of things by staying fast and ignoring distractions, and that's just what I have to do.

The mind flayer laughs, then points one of his hands at me. A blast of purple lightning erupts outward and forms a net of crackling energy in front of me. I ignore it and charge right on through. The net wraps around my body as I run at the monster, and, suddenly, a blast of energy crackles across me.

[DarkCynic: Jason! Why'd you do that?]

[ChaosRider: You could *see* it!!!]

[ViperQueen: Come on, Jason. I don't want to find another favorite, but I will if I have to.]

The purple lightning hurts, but I ignore the pain and slash at the mind flayer. He vanishes along with the lightning, and I glance at my health. It's fallen a smidge, but not much. As I suspected, the lightning was more of an illusion than anything else. I glance around the area and finally locate him back on the other side. He raises his hands and forms a spectral sword. He twirls it a few times, then points it at me and lets go.

That one I avoid by dodging to the side as it shoots through the air and slashes at me. It chases me for a moment, hacking and slashing, and I allow it to direct me around the side of the room, back toward the mind flayer. I block a few strikes that get too close, but mostly, I just watch. Then, with all my effort, I spring backward and slash my daggers through the mind flayer.

Once more, he vanishes with a small flicker of energy, and I let out a grunt of frustration.

"Don't be too hard on yourself, Jason," the mind flayer calls out. "Most people don't kill a mind flayer on the first attempt. Of course, they don't usually get a second one, but—"

I grunt and slash at the air where the noise is coming from. There's a laugh, and the mind flayer sighs, "This is too easy, you know that?"

He appears again on the far side of the room, where he

raises a hand. Purple energy forms in his palm, and he casually flings a ball of destruction at me. I dodge it and rush at him, straight down the middle of the room. The energy spins around and follows me, crackling and roaring, and the mind flayer forms a second one.

This time, as he throws the ball, I jump to the side and slash at an empty corner of the room. There's a sharp yelp, and the Dagger of the Ancients comes away red. The mind flayer appears as the illusion, along with the two balls, vanishes, and he howls.

"Impudent little creature!"

A blast of pure-white lightning crackles between his hands, and he thrusts his palms at me. I'm lifted off the ground and slammed back against the wall by the force of the blast. Trust me, *that* hurts. I groan and slump to the ground, twitching, as he advances.

"I suppose you *are* better than some. In that case, I'll do you a favor and kill you faster."

He snarls and thrusts a hand at me again, and a painful ringing noise breaks out in my head. It's like having my head inside a tornado klaxon, and I instinctively clap my hands over my ears—dropping my daggers in the process. I realize my mistake an instant after I make it, and the mind flayer rushes forward.

He makes a sharp gesture with his right arm and a spectral blade forms, then slashes downward across my chest, knocking me to the floor. With that, he springs upon me and smashes a foot into my chest. Another sphere of energy forms in his hands, and he lifts it with both arms high above my head. It's a kill shot, whatever it is, and I groan and punch upward at him with every ounce of strength I have left.

I hit him in the leg, which makes him stagger *just* a bit, and snatch up my daggers as I jump to my feet. An instant later, he hits me with the ball of red energy, which pulses across my whole body . . . and then fades away without doing a lick of damage.

"I . . ." The world starts to sway. My sense of balance is off. I can't really tell which way is up or down or sideways. "Wow."

"Wow, indeed." The mind flayer takes a few steps backward. "You've been a worthy—"

Ooooooooooooooooooooooooooooooooowwwwwwwww!

Balder's sharp howl cuts through the air, and the mind flayer is lifted off the floor and slammed into the wall. I regain my sense of balance almost immediately and draw in a deep breath. "I know I've been a worthy opponent. So have you."

The mind flayer looks terrified as I charge at him. He lifts a single finger and gives it a flick, but nothing happens. I smile and jump at him—

Ooooooooooooooooooooooooooooooooowwwwwwwww!

A shock wave hits me an instant before I strike the mind flayer, and I'm slammed into the wall just next to him. Balder jumps on me a moment later, snarling and growling and biting. He bites down on my left arm, hard, and draws blood. His eyes have become black, and I grit my teeth.

"Sorry, Balder. Hope you'll forgive me."

I punch him in the nose as hard as I can, which makes him loosen his grip. The moment I'm free, I spin and kick him across the room, trying to get him away from the action. He slams into the far wall and slumps to the ground, and I spin toward the flayer.

By that time, the monster has already climbed back to his feet, cackling, and is retreating to a safe distance. I also can't be certain if it's the real one or not, or if the monster has just cast another illusion. I grit my teeth and try to think through my options, but I don't see many of them. Balder is picking himself up off the ground and growling, and I charge at the mind flayer once more.

Balder springs into action and bounds across the floor at me. I watch him come, then dodge right as he leaps at me. As he passes me by, I grab his tail, then sling him around me in a wide arc. With a huge burst of my remaining strength, I throw him toward the other side of the room, where a corner stands mysteriously empty.

When I say, "mysteriously empty," I mean that my mind *knows* it's empty, so much so that when I look in that direction, my brain screams at me that I should look away because there's nothing there. And *that* tells me that something's up. As it turns out, I'm right, as Balder slams into the mind flayer. The illusion vanishes, and the mind flayer scrambles back to his feet.

Seemingly snapped out of his stupor by the blow, Balder growls, shaking the room, and snaps at the flayer. The monster screams and tries to run, but Balder chomps down on his leg, drawing a great deal of blood. Quickly, the mind flayer lifts a finger and points it at the pup . . . but by then, I've already reached him.

My daggers flash through the air, and I cut off the monster's head in the blink of an eye. It falls to the ground with a thump, and the whole thing dissolves into energy. I sigh and stand back up, then slowly look around. Balder nuzzles my hand, and I scratch him behind the ears.

Nicely done, the voice of the mind flayer whispers in my mind. *You've passed the first test.*

"Do you grade on a curve?" I snort as I start walking toward the hall.

As promised, I will give you what you desire. A map. An image appears in my mind, crystal-clear, as if I'm seeing it in front of my face. *Use the knowledge here wisely.*

With that, the voice of the mind flayer fades away, and I nod and start up the stairs. According to the map, I need . . . well, I need to go quite a distance.

Which just means that I need to get started as quickly as I can.

CHAPTER TWENTY-FIVE

I head up the stairs, keeping an eye on the map as best I can. The map . . . It's hard to explain, exactly. Since it's mental and not physical, I can zoom in on things, on anything I want. If I have a question, the answers—within reason—appear before me. At the same time, though, there are some details that are very clearly wanting. There are corridors that just seem to end without any explanation. There are rooms without doors, and some of the labels seem to be moving. Maybe that's just the nature of an Astral Dungeon; I honestly don't know.

In any case, the stairs take me up to a blank wall made of the same energy as before. A door forms for me, and I slip through into a broad hallway. Pillars of light and energy rise up on both sides, flanking the path just like in an old audience hall. It's really quite impressive, and I slowly start through the area. The map seems to indicate that I need to go down the length of it and through a few more rooms before I make it to the reactor, the weapon, or the behemoth.

To my confusion (and delight), nothing attacks me as I slip through the hallway. At the end, two doors open up into a dining room, complete with chairs and tables and everything else you might expect in a castle. It's all made of living energy, of course, and here the colors are blues and greens instead of reds. Nothing attacks me, even though things are getting a bit . . . stranger.

Here, there are bodies.

Great alien ant-like things lay scattered all about. Some of them have energy weapons that look almost like plasma guns, others have plasma staves, and a few of them have energy swords. They've all been cut down, and I'm reminded of the behemoth chasing after the dungeon. Were these soldiers loyal to Krak? Soldiers who defied their new overlord? I don't have the faintest idea. As I slip through the room, I keep a close eye on everyone, but they all appear dead.

My only question is what killed them . . . and am I going to be next?

At the end of that room, I find another, much smaller doorway. This time, as I step through, I come up short, and for a moment, I just stare out at something truly incredible.

[ShadowDancer: WHOA.]

[IceQueen: What exactly am I looking at?]

[ChaosRider: This . . . this is beautiful. Deadly, but beautiful.]

The door opens onto a small floating platform of greenish light. Below the platform is a wide starfield, twinkling and sparkling with a brilliant radiance. More platforms float here and there as they drift back and forth across the void. Little boats seem to race across the starfield between platforms, ferrying monsters back and forth.

And, at this moment, there are quite a few of them in use.

Pew-pew-pew-pew-pew-pew-pew-pew-pew-pew-pew-pew!
Zat-zat! Zat-zat! Zat-zat! Zat-zat!

Energy weapons flash and discharge this way and that as alien-looking monsters battle among themselves. A huge armored dragon swoops down over several platforms defended by some of the ants and opens its mouth. A piercing laser blast shoots down and incinerates dozens of them, and heavily armored soldiers, whose race I can't identify, disembark from several small boats. The few remaining aliens return fire and manage to shoot down one of the boats, but the rest approach quite quickly.

"This is incredible," I whisper, looking around. There's a boat up against my platform, and I close my eyes. "Alright. I need to get over to . . . that platform right there." I quickly step into the boat. "Let's get this d—" Responding to my mental command, it goes shooting across the stars.

A low rumble fills the air, and I glance over my shoulder. Two more of the boats shoot along after me filled with the armored guards I saw earlier. Up close, they look more like robots than people, albeit robots stuffed into old medieval armor, and they raise their guns.

Pew-pew-pew-pew-pew!

Blasts of energy streak past my boat. I duck down, wishing I had some way to return fire. The platform looms ahead, almost in reach, but a blast hits my boat. It starts to sink down, and I know I'm out of time. Quickly, I race forward and jump up into the air, sailing across the last of the distance. My hand catches on the edge of the platform, and I grit my teeth and swing up and onto the safety of solid land—well, solid energy, but you know how it goes.

"Halt!" The robots reach me and leap onto the platform, pointing their guns directly at my head. "Don't move!"

I scowl, then quickly spin and sweep the legs of the one on my left. He falls, while the second fires his weapon into the ground. I quickly stand up and grab hold of the stock of his gun and stop it solidly as he tries to twist it around to point at me.

Pew-pew-pew!

Several blasts of plasma shoot off into the void, and I grit my teeth and rip the gun out of his hands. Before he can move, I flip it around and shoot him through the chest. Smoke rises up from the small hole, along with a few sparks. I scowl, then add a few more holes for good measure. Slowly, he falls backward and tumbles off into the void.

The second robot starts to rise, so I bend down, grab him by the chest, and lift him up into the air.

"Forgive me for saying so, but you guys seem a bit low level for a dungeon like this."

"We do as we are told," the robot answers. "There is victory in numbers."

"I'll bet," I snort. "Do you work for Krak or for the behemoth?"

"Those loyal to Krak must die!"

"I don't disagree, but I'm afraid that puts me at odds with your boss." I sigh and toss the robot off the edge of the platform. "Catch you later, metal—"

Clunk.

I scowl as the loud sound echoes up from below. As I glance over the edge of the platform, something rises up from beneath. The armored dragon. The robot is on its head, grinning from ear to metal ear.

"*Now* you look properly leveled for this dungeon." I raise the gun and shoot the robot through the gut. He stays standing for a moment, then slowly falls to the side and tumbles down into the depths. With that, I spin toward the doorway and run toward it.

Voooooooooooooom!

A green light blazes around me and I find myself lifted into the air. I sigh and glance back at the dragon, which now has a tractor beam shooting out of its chest.

"Wonderful. Everything's high tech these days." I brace myself as I'm drawn up closer and closer to the monster. "Burnie! You're up!"

With a flash, Burnie shoots out of my pocket dimension and spirals sharply around me. The dragon lets out a roar, but Burnie curls around its head and flashes up into the air. There's a pause, and then a brilliant light cuts through the void.

Burnie's flames hit the dragon in the back of the head, and the armor there turns orange under the blast. The dragon roars and spins upward, and the tractor beam dies. I fall downward, and I momentarily rejoice.

Except . . . there's nothing below me but an empty starfield.

I stretch outward as I fall and just manage to catch hold of one of the little boats. It sags to the side but stays aloft, and I quickly haul myself back upright. Overhead, Burnie and the dragon spiral through the sky. Suddenly, Burnie shoots downward, flashing between several of the platforms. The dragon follows—and smashes the platforms of light into nothing but sparks. A few warriors, robots and insects alike, are tossed asunder by the blows. I brace myself as I watch the trajectory of the two. Suddenly, Burnie curls back around, flies underneath the platforms, and shoots back upward right next to the platform where I'm standing. The dragon follows a second later. Except this time I'm ready.

I rush forward, leap out into space, and catch hold of the dragon's back. The beast roars, and several blinking lights on its armor turn from green to red. Small hatches pop open to reveal turrets, which in turn spin toward me and open fire.

I yelp and let myself drop slightly, then slide backward along the dragon's back. Bullets spark off the metal around me, and one or two of them hit home. They don't break skin, but they hurt, and my health drops a lot more than I'd like. I catch sight of one of the small hatches and swing myself over to it. I quickly pop it open and crawl inside, landing with a clunk on a metal walkway.

I find myself surrounded by spinning gears, whirring cogs, and flickering machinery. My heart begins to pound, and I rush forward, ignoring the temptation to just start smashing everything. Soon, I reach the front of the dragon, where a single hatch guards the way to the neck. Another of the low-level robot guards stands in front of it, at attention.

I shoot him through the head before his sensors even register my presence.

The robot freezes, then tumbles forward and lands on the metal walkway with a clatter. I run up and throw the hatch open, then start down the long twisting hallway up to the head. Two robots sitting in the pilots' seats glance back at me, and one of them draws a plasma gun and starts shooting.

Pew-pew-pew!

One of the blasts of energy hits me in the arm, and a bit of smoke drifts upward. I snarl and return fire and hit him three times across the torso. As he slumps in his seat, the second robot is forced to reach over and push buttons on that side of the cockpit. Clearly, the dragon isn't meant to be flown by a single person.

I rush forward, pounding down the hall, and reach the cockpit a moment later. The surviving robot draws a pistol, but I grab his head with my left hand before he can manage to get off a shot. I squeeze, hard, and crush it like a soda can, and a great deal of smoke drifts upward. With that, the dragon starts to tilt, and I look out through the front windows.

It actually sort of hurts my head to do so, since the glass bubbles are warped to form the eyes of the beast, but I can clearly see Burnie flashing around, harassing the dragon where he can. Now, though, the scene begins to point sharply downward as the dragon falls from the sky, and I grit my teeth.

"This is going to hurt," I mutter. Quickly, I throw myself against the glass bubbles and smash one out, then pull myself through. Broken glass cuts at my skin, but I ignore it as I climb out onto the head of the mechanical beast. Far below,

I see the platforms moving about, and I jump away from the monster, timing it as best I can.

Wham!

I land a few seconds later, shaking the platform with the force of my impact. The dragon flashes down into the abyss below, and I groan and climb back to my feet. It explodes an instant later, and I give a nod as Burnie comes down and lands on my shoulder.

"And there we go," I mutter. "Good as gone. Come on, we need to keep moving."

Burnie's voice drifts through my head as I walk up to the doorway and pull it open.

You know, Master, you could have just ducked through the doorway while I drew the dragon off. You didn't have to kill it.

"True enough . . ." I pause as I look out into a hallway of lights and colors. ". . . I guess. Hmm." Burnie laughs, as does my chat. I force a grin as well, then step through the door.

Maybe that's true, and if it is, well . . . I killed it, in any case, so no harm done. But, that said, I *do* have to stay focused. The minions are nothing in this dungeon. All that matters is the boss . . . and making sure that the weapon is destroyed before it gets to Earth.

CHAPTER TWENTY-SIX

The hallway I find myself in is a long one, and I honestly don't know where exactly on the map I am, but I press on, nonetheless. I can't go back to the cosmic room, that's for sure. There are too many destroyed platforms and too high a chance of falling to my death. I need to stay focused. I need to press on toward my goal.

Ahead, I catch sight of another blank wall and slow down. Checking the map, I do my best to see if I can figure out where I'm at, but I just can't tell for sure. With a sigh, I slip up closer to the wall, and a flickering door appears a moment later.

"Alright, guys." I take hold of the doorknob. "Any idea what we'll be walking into?"

[DarkCynic: I bet it's another cosmic chamber!]

[LunarEclipse: Nah, I'm betting it's a boss chamber!]

[ViperQueen: Mini-boss, maybe? Hard to tell for sure.]

There are a lot of other theories, and I smile as I push the door aside. With that, I step inside . . . and I have to admit, I'm impressed.

The room is simply colossal and is made of metal mixed with the cosmic-energy stuff. At the middle of the room is the reactor core, and it's so huge that I find it hard to look at. I mean . . . this thing is hundreds of feet across and suspended on a dozen or more beams that are as thick as I am. There are, of course, countless computer stations set up around those beams. The doorway opens onto a little platform situated about twenty feet above the floor, with a staircase running down to the ground level. That, though, isn't the most impressive part.

Coming out of the bottom of the reactor core is a *massive* cable, probably thirty or forty feet thick, that runs out the back of the room, straight through a wall. There's a coupling around the cable where it meets the wall, sealing things up nicely, but I have to imagine that the weapon is in that direction. I check the map once more and give a nod of satisfaction.

"Alright, I know well enough where we're at now," I murmur and start walking along. "Let's get this party started."

As I reach the floor, which, again, is hundreds of feet wide and long, I start to notice the bodies. They're translucent, almost like they're made of glass, and lay scattered left and right across the area. They all hold swords made of the same material—well, swords and daggers and bows—and seem to have fallen in defense of the hidden weapon. Suddenly, I pause and really blink in surprise.

Draped across the cable, just next to the core itself, is

a dragon. No . . . Two dragons. Three? I can't tell for sure. They're so clear that they're hard to pin down for certain, but there they are, huge and dead, and I don't have a clue what might have cut them down. I whistle softly, then slowly start forward, picking my way through the desolation.

"Anyone have any idea what these things are?" I ask. "I'd sure like to know their stats so I know what I'm up against."

[IceQueen: Uh . . . I think they're called glasslings.]

[FireStorm: I think you just made that up!]

[ChaosRider: No, that's a thing, I saw it somewhere myself. They're pretty high-level. I think a step stronger than infernal creatures.]

"A step above demons, and I don't see a single body," I mutter. "There's something odd about that. Keep an eye out for—"

Whoosh.

Something moves through the air, and I freeze. I look up slowly and see something crackle around the sphere of energy. Great. Just what I need. I draw out my daggers, and with a blast of energy, a creature shoots down and lands right in front of me.

It's humanoid, but taller and thinner, and wears thick armor marked with deadly-looking spikes. It also seems to be made out of pure light and is wielding a long spear that I *just* bet shoots energy.

"Halt." The creature slams the butt of its—his?—spear against the metal, sending out a shock wave that rattles my boots. "Halt, in the name of Her Majesty."

"You mean Hella?" I ask.

"Do not dare to say her name!" the creature howls. "It is too perfect a name for such a creature as you!"

"You know, her name in my tongue actually derives from a place." I cross my arms. "Do you know what it is?"

The creature seems to freeze, as if he had been expecting defiance. "What?"

"Hell. Hella, hell, the underworld. A place of unending torment, fire, general unpleasantness." I shrug. "I have to imagine that there's a social media platform that only shares embarrassing pictures of you."

The creature trembles with rage. "How dare you associate our glorious queen with such a horrid reality?"

"Well"—I shrug—"if the boot fits . . ."

That's too much, and the warrior attacks. His spear flashes through the air as he twirls it sharply, and I dodge out of the way. At least, I try to. He's tremendously fast and whacks me on the left side just as hard as he can. I'm lifted off my feet and tossed about twenty feet to the side, where I land with a loud *whack*.

"You should not even be here." The warrior stalks toward me. His spear begins to glow, and he points it right at my chest. "Leave now!"

A piercing blast of light shoots out and hits me squarely. I'm thrown backward quite a bit further and come down hard. Smoke rises up from my shirt, and I sigh as I climb back to my feet.

"How about you tell me just exactly who you are?"

"My name is of no consequence. I relinquished my individuality when I entered into service of the queen!" the warrior snaps. "I am a celestial warrior. Second in rank to the Valkyries themselves! I will not be taken down by you, a mere mortal!"

"Others have said the same thing." I size the guy up. My health has dropped by a good bit more than I'd like, but I'm noticing some weaknesses. At least I *hope* they're weaknesses. "You mind telling me what the plan for this dungeon is?"

The warrior seems to smile. "You'd like to know, wouldn't you?"

He flashes forward and attacks with force. His spear twirls sharply through the air and strikes at my head, my torso, my legs, my arms. I block about half of them, but the other half land. One in particular hits me on the temple, and I sway as I try to keep from falling to my knees.

"I rarely ask questions that I don't want the answers to," I snort as I recover myself. "It'll let me know whether I need to worry about killing you immediately, or if I can take my time and enjoy things."

The warrior laughs. "If you wish to save your precious Earth, I wouldn't waste much time if I were you. Krak intended to rebel against us, but in doing so, he gave us a weapon that our grand queen has long sought."

"Really?" I have to laugh at that. "Hella *wants* to burn down worlds?"

The warrior attacks with extraordinary force, and I'm reminded of the fact that he doesn't like me saying the name of his queen. I block a few more strikes this time as I start to learn his attack pattern. High-low-high-high-low-low-high-low-high. I still miss a few, though, and he sweeps my legs. I only narrowly roll out of the way as he stabs down at me, and

I come back to my feet just in time to be hit in the chest by a piercing blast of energy.

It *hurts*, and I'm flung across the room to land underneath the great sphere of swirling energy. As I come back to my feet, the celestial warrior slowly stalks forward, twirling his spear. I still have yet to land a single strike against him, which is a problem. Quickly, I open up my inventory and chug a bottle of Pumped! to heal, then take a deep breath and charge forward at him.

He smiles and attacks with fury, and the two of us come crashing together. This time I take the offensive, slashing and hacking, but he blocks each and every hit. I really can't emphasize just how fast this guy is. I'd bring out my pets, but I have a feeling that he'd only cut them down faster than I could blink, and I'd rather not deal with watching my beloved animals get killed. Plus, I'd rather save them for the final fight. I slash harder and faster and manage to catch his spear between my two blades. For a moment we lock together, and he answers my previous question.

"Does our grand queen want to burn down worlds? Yes, she does, particularly yours. Yours has been a thorn in her side for thousands of years now."

"Ah yes, the old Norse folk." I snort. "I'm trying to imagine a Viking entering the dungeons, taking names and kicking butt. It's a fun picture. Personally, though, I don't get it. Why *destroy* worlds when you could just rule them?"

"It is not my place to expose all our grand plans to you, *mortal*," the celestial warrior snaps. "And now, you die!"

The warrior and I lock together, only for him to twist

sharply. Once more, he's on the offensive and is driving me steadily backward across the battlefield.

[DarkCynic: Hey, you're going to have to do better than this if you're going to clear this dungeon!]

[ChaosRider: Come on, stay focused! That guy's open on the right, I think!]

[ViperQueen: Yeah, I see it too!]

I grit my teeth and mostly ignore the advice. It's true, the warrior *is* consistently leaving his right side open, but to me, it looks like he's trying to bait me in, not that he's actually weak on that side. This guy is good, and there's simply no other way to look at it. An idea pops into my head, and I start backing up a bit faster than he's ready for. He follows along well, but it does throw him slightly off his pace.

Suddenly, I launch myself forward and strike with fury and force. To my delight, I manage to land a strike on him, slashing down one arm, and he howls with pain. Apparently, he's not used to being injured. Before I can react, he spins sharply and whacks me across the chest with the butt end of his spear. I'm knocked flat on my back, but I do manage to get back to my feet before he can stab me.

"Going for tricks, then?" He laughs. "Two can play that game!"

Light flares around him, almost like he's charging up, and he points his spear at me. I get a flash of intuition and jump back out of the way as he rockets forward like he's been shot from a cannon. He streaks past me in a blur of light, comes to a stop, turns, and shoots back at me.

I'm thrown into a game of dodge as he flashes back and

forth across the battlefield in a deadly dance. I'm soon out of breath, and he's not showing any sign of stopping. Growing frustrated, I grip down tightly on my dagger and prepare myself.

"This is going to hurt," I mutter to the chat. "Get ready to send me some healing items."

There are a few confused messages, but most people respond positively. The celestial warrior skids to a stop, turns, and launches himself back at me . . . and this time I jump forward to meet him.

I manage to miss the spearhead, which was my primary goal, and hit him dead-on. Beowulf's Dagger slams into his chest, and our two bodies crash together.

It's really, *really* hard to explain just how much it hurts.

Something (maybe several things) cracks inside my body, and I come to a sharp halt. That said, he's brought to a stop too, and the spear falls down from his hands. Apparently, he wasn't expecting something like that. With all the effort I can muster, I lunge forward, pushing him backward, and shove him to the ground. He slams to the floor an instant later, blood trickling out from his glittery armor, and I flip the weapon around.

It would be the perfect time for a quip, but I know that if I give this guy any quarter, he'll get up, so I keep silent and stab down at him as hard as I can. There's an odd whine as I stab him a second time, and light suddenly flares across me.

ZZZZZZZZZZ—BOOM!

With a resounding blast, I'm launched from his body and go rolling across the floor toward the banks of computers set up underneath the reactor core. My body gets cut several times on the weapons and bodies scattered about, and I slowly rise to my feet at the same time as the celestial warrior. He raises his hand and the spear *thunks* back into his palm. Slowly, he squares his shoulders, lifts his spear, and plants the butt end on the ground. Light starts to gather around the spearhead, and I turn and run as fast as I can.

Peeeeeeeeeeeeeeeeeeeeeeew!

A scorching ray of light erupts from the spearhead and burns across the room, melting the floor and burning through fallen bodies. I manage to leap mostly out of the way, though my left legs gets a bit scorched. The celestial warrior laughs and thunks the ground with his spear as I reach the banks of computers.

"You think you'll win this? You're a fool!"

"I beg to differ," I snarl, then leap over the row of computers to look at their screens. A great deal of data is displayed there, giving a wide array of information that I don't really understand. At that moment, though, a thought strikes my mind.

If I can set off the weapon while we're still in interdimensional space, then maybe, just maybe, Earth can be spared.

There are a *great* many issues with this plan, notably the question of how I'd ever get out of the dungeon, but I decide to worry about that later. Quickly, I start looking around for any sort of a trigger, a key, a button, a—

Peeeeeeeeeeeeeeeeeeeeeeew!

Another blast of light burns through the computers and leaves nothing but a heap of slag. I frown, then look up as the warrior advances.

"I sure hope you weren't needing that."

"If we do, we will rebuild it later."

The celestial warrior laughs and begins charging up his weapon once more. "Unfortunately for you, you won't be around to see it."

I ball my hands into fists and run through my options in my head.

[GoldenShield: Kill him now, Jason, while he's charging up!]

[ViperQueen: YEAH! That's your best hope!]

[ChaosRider: Quick quick quick!]

I nod, then charge forward. As I do, though, I send out a mental command. Behind the warrior, a portal to my pocket dimension opens, and Bjorn steps out. He draws in a deep breath and howls, and a cap of ice forms around the spearhead. The celestial warrior looks up at it, distracted, and I put in every last ounce of speed that I have.

Peee-eew-eew-eew-eew-eew-eew-eew-eew-eew!

Split by the ice like light through a prism, beams of the deadly energy erupt across the whole room, burning long crevices through the walls and floors. The celestial warrior balks and spins toward Bjorn, only to be hit by a blast of freezing air that coats him in ice. He smashes through after a couple moments, but by then I've reached him.

I come up hard and fast and stab him in the back just as hard as I can. Beowulf's Dagger flashes in my hand, and I inflict half a dozen wounds in the span of a split second. The warrior snarls and spins as he lashes out at me with his spear, but I've seen his attacks too many times by now. I duck the blow and stab him in the chest twice, then once in the neck. His body goes rigid, then slowly relaxes.

"You're . . . you're good, kid."

With that, the warrior topples over backward and slams into the ground with enough force to shake the floor. I let out a sigh, then slowly sheath my weapons and nod to Bjorn, who slips back into the pocket dimension.

[Celestial Warrior defeated!]

[XP Awarded: N/A]

[. . .]

[Notice: S-Ranked creature defeated!]

[First Kill of a Celestial Warrior from planet Earth!]

[Extra XP Awarded: N/A]

[. . .]

[Extra reward granted for First Kill of a Celestial Warrior!]

[Weapon Acquired: Celestial Dagger]

I frown as, with a flash, the dagger appears in my hands. Slowly, I lift up the item, letting it gleam in the light. My chat goes wild, and I feel my heart beat a bit faster as I look the weapon over.

[Rank: SS]

[Details: Delivers extraordinary damage.]

Okay, so it's a pretty boring description, but the weapon itself does the talking. It's made of pure light, is a bit longer than Beowulf's Dagger, and is light as a feather. I give it a few practice swings, then nod and slide it into my inventory.

"That works for me." I cross my arms. "It's not a new level, but it'll keep me satisfied until then." I slowly look about and my eyes harden. "Now, let's get this place cleared."

CHAPTER TWENTY-SEVEN

After I spend a few moments admiring the Celestial Dagger, I turn and look about the room, then consult my map. The control room is located along the path of the cable. From what I can tell, the cable carries the energy along the length of the dungeon, past the control room, and into the blast chamber, which doubles as the dungeon's entrance. That settled, I start looking for a door and soon find one just next to the enormous coupling that the cable runs through. I start in that direction, only to pause as something flickers across my chat.

[LunarEclipse: Hey, what's that off to your left?]

[ChaosRider: That door right there? Yeah, that's really odd!]

[RazorEdge: Jason, you should go check it out!]

I pause, then actually turn and look in that direction. It takes me a few moments before I'm able to figure out what they're looking at. Sure enough, there's a small doorway there made out of metal and ringed with a number of warning signs. A handful of cables snake out from couplings in the door itself and run across the floor to the computers that control the reactor core. I frown, then slowly start in that direction.

"Now, why would Krak need to set up something like that?" I wonder out loud. "Do the computers at the reactor control whatever's in this room? Or vice versa?"

There are a handful of speculations in my chat, but I ignore them all as I approach the strange opening. Several new warning signs appear the closer I get and red flashing lights illuminate some of the others.

It may as well have a great big neon Please Explore Me! sign.

I reach for the doorknob and open it up, where I find a small hallway made of purple light. The cables are strung up on the wall, and I frown and walk inside. The hallway curves, which prevents me from immediately seeing where it leads. Soon, though, I come to a metal blast door that has at least three separate locks, a tiny window, and half a dozen *more* warning signs. Carefully, I peer through the window, wondering what Krak could *possibly* have inside.

And my heart almost stops.

There's a small platform surrounded by a great many cables. Sitting on the platform are three radar dishes, all pointed at the same point in space. And, of course, there's a giant red button labeled *Spawn*.

"So, this is a spawn point for something," I muse as I look at the cables. "And it takes an enormous amount of energy to do it, which is what the reactor core is used for."

No one answers me, though I know it's true. Carefully, I

reach out and undo the locks on the door, then step inside. I have an odd feeling that I know what the spawn point is used to generate, though it might simply be wishful thinking. As I walk into the room, I close the door behind me, then realize that it can't be bolted or latched from the inside. Curious. Slowly, I look around, getting a feel for the place. It's about thirty feet across with a domed ceiling.

"Alright. Who wants to see me push this button?" I ask, pointing at the red spawn button.

[ShadowDancer: Do it!!!! Do it!!!!!!!!]

[DarkCynic: I don't mean to be a wet blanket, but are you *sure* that's the best idea?]

[RazorEdge: Sure it is! He can defeat whatever comes out, I'm sure of it!]

The chat continues for some time with people debating the pros and cons of it. In the end, I simply reach out and push the button—which everyone knew I was going to do in the first place. Something begins to charge up, and lighting crackles across the coils of cables. Suddenly, beams of light lance upward from the radar dishes and meet about five feet off the ground, where they pulse together and begin to form a crackling, writhing ball of energy. I draw out the Celestial Dagger and Beowulf's Dagger, then take a step back.

"Alright, everyone. Start up a poll to see what we've got," I murmur. "I can only assume that Krak was using this to generate warriors for his dungeon, but . . . I don't know. Whoever's the closest, I'll give you a shoutout."

The chat goes *wild* with speculation, but I don't really get to see any of it as a blast of light erupts outward.

[Spawn successful!]

The light clears away, and I look up, only to gasp.

Floating there is a fallen star.

That's what it has to be. Well, what *she* has to be. A woman floats in the air dressed in long flowing robes that sort of look elvish. Her skin looks like it was once fair but has since become a burnt, almost fiery color, while her hair blazes with white flame. Her eyes are sunken in her head, and her face is angular and sharp. Picture a wicked stepmother out of just about any movie, and that's who you're looking at.

"Why have you summoned me?" the fallen star asks. Flames crackle down from her hands, and she sneers at me.

"Honestly, there was a button and I pushed it." I shrug. "That said, if you'll give me a bit of stardust, I'll let you go free. Krak was the one who set this whole thing up, and I see no reason to unjustly imprison you or anything."

[FireStorm: Careful, Jason! Fallen stars are listed in the guidebooks as being fallen creatures.]

[ShadowDancer: Duh.]

[ViperQueen: What FireStorm means is that they're cousins to the Nephilim! They're evil through and through!]

"Stardust is the essence of who I am," the fallen star snaps.

"Who you are or who you *were?*" I counter. "Sounds like the sort of thing that you lose access to when you fall away."

The fallen star's face becomes cloudy, and she lets out a sharp hiss. As she lifts her hands, I start to question the wisdom of insulting a monster who wants to kill me. Light explodes from her palms and hits me like a torrent of arrows.

Needless to say, I'm slammed back into the wall behind

me. My health drops to about half, and I blink in surprise. I remember hearing that fallen stars were dangerous, but *wow*, they can pack a punch! I push myself away from the wall and dive out of the way as she unleashes another blast of light, one that almost certainly would have killed me.

"Stop running," she orders. Fire explodes across the wall in front of me, and I pull up short. "You are an embarrassment of a warrior."

"Then try this out for size."

I spin and throw Beowulf's Dagger into her chest. She's knocked backward by the blow and grabs at the hilt as she drifts into the far wall. I charge forward, jumping up into the air as I do so, and stab her with the Celestial Dagger. She lets out a scream and drops to the ground, and with that, I rip out Beowulf's Dagger and attack with force.

Shing!

A shield of light appears around her, and both of my daggers come up a few inches short of her body. She flashes a small smile, then raises her hand. The shield inverts and blasts me across the room again, and she strides forward. Fire flows down from both of her hands now, and she turns both of her palms toward me to blast streams of deadly fire in my direction.

I dive forward, ducking under the flames, and come up close. Before she can react, I leap upward and slash both of my daggers across her torso. She screams and staggers, only to spin and thrust out her right hand. A concussive blast erupts through the air, but I'm just fast enough to spin out of the way and dodge it entirely. With every last ounce of my strength, I slash upward and cut clean through her wrist.

The fallen star lets out a shriek. Her hand drops to the ground, turning to stone as it does so. She snarls, then launches herself into the air, spinning rapidly. Streams of spiraling fire erupt off her body and explode in torrents across the room. The walls shake, the ground rumbles, and I find myself surrounded by flame. My health *plummets,* and I drop to my knees to avoid as much of it as I can.

[Skill: Bearing of a Knight.]

[Peril Detected.]

A soft glow forms around me, warding off some of the flame as her attack subsides. I grit my teeth and rise up, ready to attack once more. Strength flows through my veins, and my health begins to regenerate.

"Die, beast!" She spins around, flies up into the air, and opens her mouth. A beam of pure destruction shoots out, only for a spectral shield to form in the air just in front of me. The energy meets the shield with a resounding *boom* and sends out a shock wave that blasts the door off its hinges.

Anticipating her move, I leap into the doorway just as she dives for freedom. She hits me with extraordinary force and drives me backward along the hall even as I fight for traction. Unfortunately, there's not a lot of traction to be found in a hallway made of light. I'm pushed steadily back toward the reactor, and it suddenly comes into my mind that she likely intends to toss me into the reactor core. At the least, she'll probably think it up once she sees the reactor. I slam both of my daggers into the wall—where, fortunately, they stick—and our progress becomes much slower. Finally, she disengages and draws back, hissing and spitting, and I charge her, giving no quarter.

Wham!

I lash out with a kick to her chest, then follow the attack with a rapid series of strikes and spins and as many other attacks as I can mete out. She returns fire just as fast as she can, sending out concussive blasts that shake the room, bolts of lightning, and streaks of fire. We're at an even standstill, and I draw in a deep breath.

"I'm not going down to you!"

The words don't mean much, practically, but they allow me a moment to collect myself. The fallen star falls back slightly, then flashes forward. I come charging forward to meet her, daggers flashing, and we crash together. I swing as hard as I can, she launches bolts of energy and fire . . . and, suddenly, the hallway falls quiet.

It takes me a moment to realize that she's dead. Slowly, I look down at a stone body that's broken into pieces, like a statue that's held vigil in some ancient ruin for the better part of a millennium or two.

"And there you have it." I nod. "Now . . . all we have to do is figure out how to process the star."

That's the other part of the issue involving the stardust. The stuff isn't a simple drop from fallen stars; you actually have to process it. Thankfully, my chat comes to my assistance.

[DarkCynic: Just head back into the spawn room! I think it's all right there!]

[ViperQueen: There's a panel just by the entrance!]

[LunarEclipse: Hopefully it still works.]

I frown, then slowly walk back into the spawn room. It takes me a moment to locate the panel, but . . . sure enough, it's right there, and I stifle a laugh. There are a few other switches there too, one labeled *Kill*, the other labeled *Process*.

"Are you telling me"—I can hardly keep a straight face—"that all I had to do was flip these switches? I could have spawned one in, then killed it and processed it, all without lifting a finger?"

[ShadowDancer: Well . . . technically you would have had to lift a few fingers, but only to push the right buttons.]

[RazorEdge: Yup, that's about how it looks. But on the bright side, you got to have an epic fight instead!]

[IceQueen: Yeah! That would have been boring for us to watch!]

I don't disagree with the boring aspect, but I also would have much rather avoided all the mortal peril. In any case, the spawn button was smashed into bits by our fight, which rules out any further cheesing of the system. Quickly, I pick up the pieces of the body and haul them back to the platform, where I set them all in a large pile. That done, I walk over to the small platform and flick the process switch, though I prepare to step back out of the way if necessary. I don't know how much other damage was done, and I don't really want to survive a fallen star attack only to get blown up by a faulty connection point or something.

Light begins to pulse out of the radar dishes, and to my surprise, they start panning around as if they're looking for something. Suddenly, they all rotate downward and lock onto the stone body parts. The light turns red, as does the light that makes up the room itself, and I cross my arms.

This ought to be interesting.

There's a loud cracking sound and steam starts to hiss up from the body. Light flashes as well, and I see bits and pieces of powdery dust drift down from the chunks of rock, even as the stone itself seems to simply evaporate into thin air. I hold my breath, not wanting to scatter the precious grains, and watch closely. Down trickles more dust . . . and then more . . . and then, with a pop, the last of the rock itself is burned away leaving only a small pile of sparkly dust on the ground.

"Wonderful," I whisper as I step up to the platform. Carefully, I reach down and look it over. There's *maybe* half an ounce of the dust, and it's scattered. I'd sure like every grain I can get, so I take out a small glass vial from my inventory—don't ask me where I got it; it must have come from some random monster drop *somewhere* along the line—and I gather up as much as I can. Soon, I've gathered up every speck that I can retrieve, and I stand back up.

[ChaosRider: That's so epic, Jason! You're going to rock this dungeon now!]

[IceQueen: Yeah! This is going to be amazing! Get rid of that passive skill and get back to leveling up! How many levels do you think a void behemoth will give you?]

[ShadowDancer: Squeeeeeeeeeee! I can't wait!]

"I can't wait either." A smile spreads across my face, and I slowly lift the vial to my mouth. I've used the stardust before but only once on myself. Every other time has been on others, so . . . I don't know. I just really hope it works.

"Bottoms up!"

CHAPTER TWENTY-EIGHT

With a flourish, I tilt back my head and dump the contents of the vial into my mouth. It tastes terrible, but I swallow it down just as quickly as I can. A great many things start to happen, and I gasp in . . . astonishment? It's not pain exactly, but it's also not pleasant in the slightest.

[GoldenShield: Are you okay, Jason?]

[ViperQueen: Let us know! Can you hear me?]

[ChaosRider: JASON!!! Speak up!]

"I . . . I feel stronger." I slowly hold up my hands, then clench my fists. From what I remember, every grain of stardust enhances every single stat by 0.5 percent. I don't know how many grains are in half an ounce, but I imagine that I must have swallowed at least a thousand or two.

In any case, my stats jump up a *lot*. There are a handful of added effects as well, but they scroll past fast enough that I can't read them. They're mostly things like added damage resistance. Anyway, I have a single thing that I need to focus on. The stat increases are nice, but they're temporary at best.

"Remove skill: Hardcore."

There's a long pause, and a bit of code flashes across my vision.

[Confirm remove skill: Hardcore?]

"Yes."

[Stardust Healing Effect: Removing skill.]

[. . .]

[Skill Removed!]

I smile as I race down the hall and across the floor of the reactor room. Above me the huge core crackles and rages, but I ignore it. Instead, I rush up to the door leading into the next room and punch it as hard as I can.

BAM—ping!

The door flies off its hinges and clatters inward, and I rush inside. There, I find a long room and the cable running across the floor. A hundred feet or more overhead, I see a floating platform beneath a field of stars—*now* the stars are above me—on which stands a singularly enormous creature. Stairs made out of a rainbow of light lead in a spiral up to the platform, and I charge at the stairs with every ounce of strength that I have.

Jason Lee. I have to admit, I'm impressed. The voice of the void behemoth rings in my head, and I grit my teeth. *But you will fall, and you will do so at my pleasure.*

"Don't count on it."

"Behold!" the behemoth cries out. "My legions!"

With a flicker, bursts of light appear across the floor as

they form small portals. Lights flash up from each and every one of them and I suddenly find myself facing what must be a hundred celestial warriors, along with a few fallen stars as well.

"If that's your choice, I suppose I don't mind if you lose a few of your troops." I smile and don't change my trajectory at all. "Bring it on."

The warriors snarl and all begin to charge at me. Some of them raise spears, some of them draw swords, some have daggers. Others have still more weapons. Flails, maces, clubs, just about every single thing you could imagine. Meanwhile, the fallen stars all rise up into the air and take positions around the stairs.

This is going to be interesting. And . . . if I'm not mistaken . . . even a little bit fun.

The first warrior meets me wielding a large sword. He swings at me, and I simply raise my hand and catch the blade in my palm. He emits a startled yelp, and I smash my fist into his chest, flinging him backward across the floor. The next warrior is equipped with a mace and brings it smashing down on my head, where it shatters. Bits and pieces of the spiked mace head bounce around the room, and I slash my Celestial Dagger clean through his neck, removing his head. Body, head, and weapon clatter to the floor, and I charge onward.

The crowd of warriors snarls and forms up in front of me, desperate to keep me from their master, but at this point I might as well be cutting through an army of slimes. I put a dagger in either hand, then spin as I lunge forward and slash through half a dozen of the warriors in a single attack.

[LunarEclipse: Now this is the Jason we love to see!]

[ChaosRider: I . . . I'm speechless.]

[DarkCynic: That stardust stuff really needs to get nerfed. It's kinda OP.]

[IceQueen: Are we really going to complain about that??? It's helping Jason, let's just let it be!]

I smile as I continue to charge forward, hacking and chopping and slashing my way through the minions. As I reach the stairs, one of the warriors lunges forward and grabs me by the shoulders. I snarl and elbow him in the face, crushing his helmet inward. He falls backward, dead before he hits the ground, and I sigh.

I'm going to miss this strength when it runs out.

With that, I start up the stairs, only for the fallen stars to begin their attack. Staying well out of range of my daggers, they begin to swoop back and forth as they fire bolts of light and energy at me. None of it really does that much damage, and what damage *is* dealt out quickly heals, but it's annoying.

[GoldenShield: Come on, Jason! We know you can find a way to take them down!]

[ViperQueen: And if you don't, they'll just come back to bite you as soon as the stardust wears off.]

[ChaosRider: Mmm, true enough.]

I draw a deep breath, then sheath both of my weapons. If only I had a boomerang or something. Unfortunately, we're not living in Australia, so I scroll through my inventory for a moment until I find a bit of rubble that I've picked up. With a flash, I pull it out: a handful of small stones. The fallen stars snarl and move in closer, and I thumb one of the stones into my right hand and fling it with all my might.

Pop!

The fallen star turns to stone as the pebble is blasted straight through her head. She falls from the sky, crushing one of the celestial warriors below, and I grin. With that, I charge upward even faster while flinging rubble at everything that gets close. The fallen stars drop all around me, and my grin widens. I throw a few bits of rubble down at the warriors below until there are none left, all killed in a heartbeat.

And with that, I race up the last of the stairs.

As I mount the final stair and step onto the platform, the air around me seems to ripple. Suddenly, the platform becomes much larger—like . . . *much* larger. Maybe two hundred feet across, maybe three. I don't know for sure. Standing in the middle of it is a figure that I instantly recognize and who stares down at me with fury and hatred abounding.

"So, here you are," the void behemoth rumbles. "Here you finally are. I've waited a long time for this, and now it's here."

"You could have just teleported me straight from my entry point up to you." I shrug. "Not really my fault if it's taken me a while to get through your little dungeon."

The void behemoth chuckles, then slowly raises a hand.

[Stardust has expired.]

[You have leveled up!]

[Congratulations! You are now Level 75!]

"Only seventy-five?" I grumble. "That many kills would have netted me like four levels at any other time."

"Stardust reduces the amount of XP gained as an offset to the extraordinary power it offers," the void behemoth rumbles. He slowly looks up at the starfield and points. "What do you see?"

"Someone in need of some serious beatdown," I mutter and start forward. The behemoth snorts and a force field appears around me. I'm pretty sure I can smash through it, but if he's wanting to play games, I'll let him play for a moment.

"Forgive me." The behemoth turns back to me, and a smile splits his claylike face. "I would like to have a word. You were persistent in your demands through the infernal dungeon. I would have you listen to me."

"Fair enough." I sigh and hold up my hands. "What can I do for you?"

"Right there"—the void behemoth points up at the sky again—"that little green dot. That's your world. Earth."

"The planet that you're about to destroy," I snap. "How long until you fire this old weapon?"

"That depends on you." The void behemoth turns back to me, and fire blazes in his eyes. "I would love to destroy it, but . . . there are other things I would like more. This weapon, this dungeon, it gives a person a sense of power."

"You want to go after the queen together," I surmise aloud.

"You're resourceful. Join me and I'll spare Earth. If we kill the queen together, I'll announce the retreat. The dungeons will leave, and we'll go terrorize other worlds, never to return again."

"You know what my answer has to be," I snap. "There's a hidden part of this deal. You'll go back on your word, or there will be a hidden clause, or . . . something. I'm not going to help you, and I don't think you'll help me. You don't know me except as a warrior tearing through your dungeons, and I don't know you except as a general for the person trying their hardest to lay waste to my world."

"Ahh . . . So naive," the void behemoth sighs. "You see . . . you're wrong on a few points there. We actually know each other quite well."

"Is that so?" I smirk. "Explain *that* one."

"Actually, I'd like *you* to," the void behemoth answers, and a smile cracks across his face. "*Master.*"

Horror spikes through my gut even as all the pieces fall into place. My chat goes crazy, and a single word escapes my lips.

"*Krak?*"

CHAPTER TWENTY-NINE

K rak?" I ask once more. "It's really you? I sort of figured you'd find a way to stay alive, but . . . this?"

"In fairness, I was intending on transferring my consciousness into *your* body, not this thing," Krak rumbles. "Then *he* killed me instead of you, so . . . I decided to take the win and go with it. I have to say, I'm impressed with the capabilities. A massive improvement over my old body."

"Then I suppose I'll just have to kill you a second time." I sigh, ball my hands into fists, and punch the force field. It shatters and I step out.

"You kill me?" Krak laughs. "I'm twice the size as before, have ten times the health, and a hundred times the ways of killing *you*. Even with you all the way up to level seventy-five, you're still no match for me."

"Maybe not," I say through gritted teeth, "but I have to protect my world. If that means that I have to kill you a hundred times over, I'll do it. You're nothing to me, Krak, not anymore. Once, we were friends, but you've lost that over and over again."

[ShadowDancer: WAIT!!!!!]

[ChaosRider: I have so many questions!]

[DarkCynic: Yeah! If that really *is* Krak, why did he attack his own dungeon?]

"I can see your messages, you know." Krak chuckles. "One of the advantages of this new body. In any case, the answer is a simple one. No one knew that it was me. If I had showed up and tried to tell the truth, all my minions would have attacked anyway. Thus, I gathered together some of Hella's minions so that no one on *that* side of the universe would realize what was happening until it was too late. Now it is." Krak turns to face the stars once more. "Hella's dungeon is invisible, connected to the Earth, and it's not one that she can move very easily. I imagine that she's scrambling to detach it as we speak, but there are limits even to what the goddess of death can manage. I'll attach this weapon to her dungeon and detonate the chamber. It will kill her and most of her generals and will probably desolate a good portion of the Earth along with it. I'll hit level one hundred from the carnage and settle into my new reign as king."

"Until someone else stabs *you* in the back," I snap up at Krak. "Give this up. It can't end well and you know it."

"All I know is that you're a problem, and unless you stand by my side, I intend to stomp you like a bug," Krak growls.

"I have no intention of standing by you," I retort.

"A pity. I would have enjoyed fighting alongside you once more."

Krak rumbles, and he lifts a massive foot to stomp on me. I race out of the way, and the foot comes crashing down, shaking the whole platform, and he laughs. With that, he rather joyfully begins walking around, slowly following me, just stomping left and right.

"One single blow from these feet killed an S-Ranked lizardman boss!" He laughs. "What will it do to you, I wonder?"

"I haven't a clue," I answer. "And I have no plans to let you find out!"

As he stomps down as hard as he can, I race straight at his foot and leap up and over the shock wave as it erupts outward. When I land, I'm only a few feet away from his leg, and I lash out with all my might.

My Celestial Dagger blazes in one hand, Beowulf's Dagger in the other. Both bite deep into his flesh, and I start to hack and stab just as quickly as I can. His skin is thick, almost six inches, and it falls to the ground with sickening *thumps* as I desperately try to inflict damage. Krak howls and moves away, but he's slow, and I follow as fast as I can while continuing to attack with pure and utter fury.

Well . . . I suppose that *fury* isn't the right word. The last time I faced Krak, I found myself truly despising him, hating everything that he stood for, and only wanting him dead. This time I actually find that I don't hate him.

I can't.

I have a planet to protect and a superweapon that's about to burn it to a crisp. There are no hard feelings. There's no anger. All that exists is a simple desire to kill and avoid being killed.

I flash about his feet, moving faster than ever, and land long slices up and down the length of them. I know I'm not landing any kill shots, but until I figure out what his new attack patterns are, I'm going to have to content myself with smaller victories. I know he can use magic; the question is exactly what he'll pull out, and when.

I've just moved to attacking his other foot when he lets out a powerful and angry roar.

"Enough of this!"

Something whistles through the air, and I step back just in time to see something streaking down from the sky. It's fiery red and has a long trail of flame behind it.

A meteor.

Boom!

Flame explodes outward from the point of impact as it hits only a few feet away. The ground heals as soon as the meteor itself fades away—after all, it's made of living light—but that doesn't give me any consolation. More meteors begin to shoot down from above, and Krak laughs and begins to jump up and down, sending out shock waves that ripple across the whole area. I'm forced to dodge both the shock waves *and* the meteors, which is *far* from the easiest task.

Wham!

One of the meteors shoots out of the blue from behind me and hits me on the shoulder, spinning me around and slamming me to the floor. An instant later, one of the shock waves hits me and sends me rolling toward the edge of the platform. I groan and catch myself just a few feet from the edge and look up to see Krak laughing at me.

"And how do you like that, I wonder? Let's see how you can handle some of my other skills, eh?"

With a laugh, he claps his hands, and dark magic swirls about his head. Lightning bolts shoot down at me, and I'm forced to dodge. I pull up short as a lightning bolt suddenly hits in front of me.

They're anticipating my movements!

I let out a cry of shock, spin out of the way, and throw myself into what is, hopefully, a random defensive pattern. Lightning falls all around me until, finally, it fades away. High above, Krak laughs, and I grit my teeth.

"Balder, I need to get up there, now!"

With a flash, Balder appears next to me. I run forward, then jump up into the air. It's a move we've started to perfect, and the shock wave from his howl launches me high into the sky. Of course, I still only hit Krak on his belly, but that's enough for me. I dig my daggers into his thick flesh and slide to a stop, and Krak growls.

"None of that, eh?"

Below me, Balder barks again, and I scramble upward. Krak thumps his chest, but by then, I'm on my way upward once more. I flash up past his chest and manage to catch hold just next to his shoulder. He snarls and raises a hand to squash me, and I quickly scramble up on top of his shoulder and duck up close to his neck.

Wham!

The hand hits his rocky flesh with extraordinary force, and I grit my teeth as I'm forced to simply brave the shock wave. It *hurts* and drops my health to a mere fraction of what it used to be. I quickly pull out a Pumped! drink even as Bearing of a Knight kicks in, though I'm honestly not sure if the skill will be of any use. Thinking as fast as I can, and knowing that I have mere seconds until he swats at me again, I jump up and grab hold of his ear, then swing up on top of his head. For a moment, the monster rocks back and forth, turning about as he tries to find me. Below, Balder seems to have scampered back into the pocket dimension, which is fortunate.

What to do, what to do? I don't know how much health Krak has left, but I'm woefully underprepared for this battle. To take on a monster of this size, I need to be able to deliver crushing blows of a million or more damage points. I need to be able to use epic skills myself. I need to be able to do a *whole* lot more than what I'm doing now. Sure, I can sit down on top of his head and stab him until he dies, but . . .

"I need John and Ali," I mutter. "I need help. My pets are good, but this is beyond even them. Of course, it would be beyond John and Ali too, but . . ." I groan as I run through the possibilities in my head. Anyone else, even the second-most-powerful warrior in the world, is too low to be able to help me. I need another *me*. I need . . .

A thought springs through my head, and a smile grows on my face.

"That's it."

[DarkCynic: What's it?]

[ViperQueen: You have a plan?]

[FireStorm: Whatever it is, it'll be great!]

"It will be." I take a deep breath. "Get ready, everyone, for your minds to be blown!" I open up my inventory and scroll for a moment until I come to the pocket watch I received for defeating the chrono-wraith. "Now, let's just hope that this works the way I want it to!"

Flash!

With a pop, I appear on the top of the stairs and watch myself as I stare (or stared) up at Krak. I smile and ready my daggers. The battle begins, and Past-Jason charges at the feet of the void behemoth. I watch him for a moment, then run up onto the platform and charge at Krak as well.

I attack the foot that Past-Jason isn't attacking and throw myself into the hacking and slashing just as quickly as I can. Past-Jason looks up at me in surprise, and I give him a nod.

"Do I die?" he calls out loudly.

"No, but I thought I could use some help." I shrug. "And since everyone else is—I'm not going to say *weak*, but . . ."

"Got it!"

Past-Jason and I throw ourselves into a blistering attack against Krak's feet. The monstrous giant roars in surprise, and I feel a grin spreading across my face.

"Ready to really scare him?" I wink at Past-Jason, and we both call out at the same time, "Balder!"

With a flash, two Balders come racing out. They look at each other in surprise but sit back and prepare to do just what they know we need. The two of us Jasons are launched upward, and then upward again, where we quickly attack Krak's head and neck with as much force as we can manage. Krak howls and waves his arms about, and I puff out my cheeks.

"It's working!" Past-Jason calls out.

"Not by enough." I scowl, then glance down at the watch. "Ready to give this another try?"

Past-Jason pulls out his own watch and gives a nod. "Let's do it."

Flash!

I appear at the top of the stairs right next to Past-Jason, now Jason Number Two. Number Two nods at me, then gestures over at Jason Number One.

"Ready to scare the pants off him?"

"Given that they're *our* pants too, I'd rather not." I frown in thought. "Also, given that I'm the most knowledgeable person here at this point, would you mind terribly if I give some input?"

"Not at all." Number Two shakes his head.

"Call out our pets." I think for a moment longer. "Let's start with Burnie, see what he can cook up."

"Right you are."

When Number One charges the feet of the behemoth, Number Two and I run forward to meet him. He attacks one of the feet with vigor, and, instead of going to the other one, both of us join him. He jumps slightly in surprise as the two of us strike with fury and force, hacking and slashing just as hard and fast as we can.

[IceQueen: Okay, guys, I know this is insane, but like . . . there are THREE of them now!]

[DarkCynic: I have to admit, even I wasn't expecting this. I wonder what three of *me* would do?]

[ChaosRider: Who cares? Just sit back and watch the show!]

The three of us, with our six combined blades, tear into Krak's foot with extraordinary vigor. Flesh falls to the ground like rain, and blood pours out across the floor, making it slick.

[Notice: You have disabled the right foot of the Void Behemoth.]

Krak howls in pain and frustration, and he steps back to glare down at us. At that moment, all three Burnies flash up, fire blazing from their wings, and his eyes open wide.

FOOOOOOOOOOOOOOOOOOM!

Three piercing blasts of fire hit him in the face and wrap around his head, burning his neck, his shoulders, his face, and more.

[Notice: You have disabled the eyes of the Void Behemoth.]
[Notice: You have disabled the ears of the Void Behemoth.]
[Notice: You have disabled the nose of the Void Behemoth.]

Krak raises his hands and meteors start to fall down from the sky above. Burnie, all three of him, throws himself into evasive maneuvers, forcing him to let up on the concentrated blasts. All three Jasons do the same, and while it's a great deal easier than before since Krak isn't hopping around like a toddler playing hopscotch, we all suffer a few scrapes. As the blasts die down, I let out a long sigh, then glance at the other two.

"I've got one more use." I pull out the pocket watch. "You know what they say about the third time."

"I don't believe in luck," Number One replies.

"Nor do I." I shrug, and a smile crosses my face. "But I do believe that four of us, all working together, will likely make a pretty good team."

FLASH!

I appear once more at the top of the steps with Numbers Two and Three. Both look to me with questioning eyes, and I draw in a deep breath.

"Even with all of us, this is going to be hard. Get out your pets, all of them. His body can be disabled, so that's what we have to do. Knock out his feet, knock out his hands. Once that's done"—I shrug—"I honestly don't know. We still have to find some way to reduce his health."

"One thing at a time," Number Two answers. "Let's go!"

This time we charge before Number One does anything. Krak gives a start as all four of us come charging forward.

"Illusions will not help you, trickster!" he growls.

"Oh, I'm no trickster," I answer back. "Just a desperate warrior willing to do *anything* to protect planet Earth."

Four Burnies swoop over my head and flash up through the sky toward Krak's head. They spread out, and he lifts his hands. It's truly difficult to express the magnitude of the blast as all four of them fire blistering white beams of energy at him, but . . . it's impressive. Almost instantly, everything on Krak's head is disabled, but the Burnies don't let up for an instant.

Down on the ground, we don't either. All four of us hit the right foot and disable it within seconds. Krak falls to his knee, and we race over to his left foot and disable *that* one within a few more seconds. He falls to his other knee, and, as he looks for all the world like he's pleading for his life, I call in the hounds.

OOOOOOOOOOOOOOOOOOOOOOOOOOOOWWW!

Four Bjorns cause enormous spikes of ice to erupt from the ground, which stab into his belly and legs. Four Astrids cause rivers of fire to erupt under his skin—in different places than the ice, of course—blackening his body and causing immense (I hope) internal fire damage. Four Balders cause shock waves that twist his arms around and around until the right one is pulled out of its socket and the left one breaks. Four Gabes cause a spear of light to fall from the sky and spear him through the chest, pinning him to the astral floor. Four Blubs . . . Well, they don't actually do all that much against a creature so large, but it's entertaining to watch them exploding and bouncing around.

The chaos continues for the full five minutes we're allotted. Then, as time runs out, each of the other three Jasons pulls out his pocket watch to teleport back in time.

"You've got him!" Jason One says before he waves and vanishes.

"Yeah! Tell me all about it!" Jason Two says before he salutes and teleports away.

"Dude . . . *please* try not to die," Jason Three adds.

With that, I'm left alone on the platform once more. My pups gather around me, Burnie circles slowly through the air around Krak's head, and I stand there to wait.

I know it sounds silly, just standing there, but there's not a lot else I can do. Maybe the internal bleed and burn damage is finishing up the job, and I just have to wait. Maybe Krak has hardly been hurt at all. I honestly, truly don't know.

Most likely, if I'm being honest, he's trying to work on a way to get out of the situation.

"Jason," he finally says, his voice low and rumbling. "You . . . I underestimated you."

"Why, thank you," I say while giving a small bow, even knowing that he likely can't hear or see me.

"I didn't think you would beat me back when I was just Krak. I *certainly* didn't think you would beat me now that I'm a void behemoth." Krak sighs. "You . . . You're something else. I truly wish I could have had you at my side. We might have actually succeeded in topping the queen. Pfft, I'd have happily been your top general if *you* wanted to be king. Everyone knows you deserve it."

I'm not exactly sure where this statement is going, but . . . suddenly, I'm starting to get nervous.

"Mr. Wang, if you have a way to pull me out of here, I need you to do it now," I murmur softly.

[Moneybags: We're working on it, Jason! Just give us a few minutes. Is there any way you could bring the dungeon to a stop? You're still on a collision course with New York.]

"I don't think I can do a thing with the trajectory of the dungeon, nor do we have a few minutes." I bounce on the balls of my feet as Krak tries to pull himself upright, wincing in pain.

"Anyway," Krak sighs. "What I'm trying to say is that . . . Jason, you're going to go far. If I let you live, that is. Even when I wanted to take over everything, I was still loyal to my side. To this side of the universe, to the dungeons. If I die right now, you'll have access to this weapon. Mr. Wang and his little team will turn this thing into the best weapon, the greatest ship that humanity has ever seen. I can't allow that to happen. Goodbye, Jason. I hope you know that I hold you in the highest regard, and I'm so sorry that you have to die this way."

With that, Krak lifts his hands—or, at least, the stumps that used to be his hands—and mutters a few dark words.

[Notice: Detonation in progress.]

[All exits have been sealed.]

[No target has been specified.]

[Catastrophic destruction will take place in 00:00:30.]

I blink in horror at those words. I have thirty seconds to live.

I suppose it means I'd better make them count.

CHAPTER THIRTY

A timer appears in my vision, ticking steadily downward as I race from the platform. I take a few steps down the stairs, then glance at my health: 75 percent. It's going to hurt, but I'll survive. Quickly, I leap from the stairs and fall the rest of the distance. When I land, something pops in my knees, but I rise up and charge onward, now with my health at 25 percent instead. My chat goes wild, but I don't have time to explain.

Lightning begins to pulse up and down the length of the massive cable as it prepares the weapon for detonation.

[00:00:20]

I burst through the door into the reactor room, where I find the core crackling with energy. Great blasts of it arc through the room and hit the walls, as the cable simply isn't large enough to contain it all.

"Everyone, back into the portal! Burnie, I need you!"

[00:00:15]

As the rest of my creatures return to the pocket dimension, Burnie flies down and lands on my shoulder, and I nod. "I need you to cut through those supports."

Burnie nods back to me, then spreads his wings and shoots up into the air. I watch him loop around the sphere once, and then he lets his attack loose.

FOOOOOOOOOOM!

I've never seen him send out such a sharp and focused blast of fire. It cuts clean through the first support, then the second, then the third. The reactor core tilts, then groans and comes crashing to the ground. Almost instantly, sparks explode upward from the point of impact. It starts to sink through the floor, dragging the cable along with it, and I turn and run in the opposite direction.

[00:00:05]

Burnie flashes back into the pocket dimension, and I put on a burst of speed. The massive coupling on the wall suddenly explodes into bits as the cable is sucked across the floor, winding toward the hole that the reactor core is cutting through the Astral Dungeon.

[00:00:03]

"Alright, fans!" I call out. "Even if this *does* work, I don't know what's going to happen, so—"

FLASH!

Light flares up and down the walls, and I suddenly freeze. It's just like the last time I inverted a dungeon, and I feel myself lifted off my feet. Light and color and sound and energy swirl around me, and with that, I'm shot out into the void.

Boom.

The blast is, in reality, much louder and more forceful, but I can't really put it into mere words. I'm given a brief glimpse of the core inverting and blasting just about every ounce of its energy down the length of the cable. At the end of the cable is a large focusing device, which, as it waves about wildly, is blasting energy out into the void as the entire dungeon is sucked out into the inky blackness.

[XP Awarded: 10,000,000]

[XP Awarded: 50,000,000]

[XP Awarded: 100,000,000]

I begin to rack up the kills as the weapon sprays its deadly energy all throughout the cosmos. Nearby dungeons collapse in on themselves as the weapon cuts through their borders. Monsters floating through the void, just happy to be alive, are vaporized under the torrent. Most notably—well, perhaps I'd better just show you as best I can.

As I float through the void, watching it all happen, a dark blob catches my eye. It's several hundred feet distant and looks broken and defeated, but it is instantly recognizable. Krak. The void behemoth stretches, and for a moment, he seems to heal. I'm reminded that he can survive in the void quite well as he turns his head back and forth. Suddenly, his eyes lock onto mine and a smile cracks his face.

"Well done, Jason. Well done."

An instant later, a beam of deadly energy cuts him in half, and I'm awarded a staggering one billion XP.

[You have leveled up!]

[Congratulations! You are now Level 76!]

[You have leveled up!]

[Congratulations! You are now Level 77!]

[You have leveled up!]

[Congratulations! You are now Level 78!]

When the blast finally dies down, I'm left floating alone in the void, and I sigh deeply.

"Alright, Mr. Wang, if you can hear me, I'd sure appreciate it if you could just zap me back to the headquarters instead of knocking me into a dungeon." There's no answer. My chat isn't working, and I don't get a video feed. "Alright, then. I'll just wait."

I sit back and do my best to get comfortable in the void. It's surprisingly hard, but I manage after a few tries. Just as I finally succeed, I see a light growing in the distance, the same one I saw the last time I was stuck out here into the void.

"Oh, great. They're going to—"

Wham!

Thankfully, I've healed up in the time I was waiting. A few moments later, I'm blasted through the wall of yet another dungeon. I fall to the floor, landing with a *splat* in a pile of goop, then slowly rise to my feet to find myself standing in a fairly normal-looking cave, albeit a cave that a giant seems to have sneezed over. I frown, then take a step forward. My foot squishes against something on the floor, and notifications appear.

[Mega Slime defeated!]

[XP Awarded: 1]

[. . .]

[Notice: S-Ranked creature defeated!]

[First Kill of a Mega Slime from planet Earth!]

[Extra XP Awarded: 0.5]

I have to laugh as I slowly start through the dungeon. It's easily the easiest dungeon I've ever taken on, and, working as quickly as I can, I slide my way through the long corridors and goop-filled passages until I arrive at the flickering portal. There, I happily kill the S-Ranked master slime by *sneezing* on it, then make my way through the portal and back into New York City.

The next few hours aren't really anything of note. A jeticopter sent by Mr. Wang takes me back to the tower, where I take a *long* shower—turns out that slime goop isn't water-soluble, which makes getting it out of your hair a real issue—eat a bit of food, and then, finally, sit down with Mr. Wang, Ali, John, Elrith, and Paul. It's truly a great joy to fall onto the couch cushions, and Mr. Wang smiles and nods at me.

"Well, how does it feel to be a hero yet again?"

I shrug. "I don't know. I wasn't the one who disabled the weapon. Truth be told, I didn't really have any clue how to do it. If Krak hadn't blown it up for us . . ."

"Well, the fact of the matter is that Krak *did* blow it up," Elrith says. "Not only that, the blast actually took out over a hundred smaller dungeons. In that blast, I'd say that half of New York was cleared up."

Horror shoots through me. "Were any warriors killed?"

"No, no!" John shakes his head. "Mr. Wang had us all lined up in battalions to face whatever might come through the portal if Krak indeed landed any forces. There wasn't a warrior in the dungeons in all of New York, which, for once, actually worked in our favor."

"That's good." I let out a sigh of relief. "And any new dungeons? Have they started coming?"

"Actually, more good news on that front," Paul says. "It would seem that the blast spread some sort of radiation through the area. New dungeons can't even join the same plane of existence as us, let alone attach themselves."

With that, a ray of hope starts to shine over me. "How . . . how long would you say that the radiation field will hold out?"

"Potentially forever." Paul shrugs. "I've only seen this happen once before. It was on a world we were invading two or three thousand years ago. Almost the same thing went down. Someone built a reactor core from dragon crystals, and it exploded, and that was really the end of it. New dungeons couldn't link up, and since the residents were being so problematic, Hella ordered everyone to leave. All the dungeons that were already attached were allowed to fight it out. Some of them successfully repelled the warriors that entered, which allowed the dungeon bosses to gain power and prestige. Others were cleared out. Either way, we left the world behind."

"What are the odds that something similar happens here?" I ask, feeling that ray of hope grow.

Paul and Elrith share a look and a smile, and Mr. Wang leans forward. "The order has already been sent out. Here, take a look at it."

He passes a note to me, and I look it over. My eyes grow wide, and I slowly lean back into my seat.

"'Attention all dungeon bosses, rift leaders, and monsters

loyal to the cause.'" I speak slowly as I start to read through it; I assume everyone else in the room has seen it, but I still find myself reading it out loud. "'Earth is being moved from Green status to Yellow. No new points of contact. Repeat: no new points of contact. Breaches of this protocol will be considered acts of treason and will be dealt with accordingly. Beginning Ragnarok Protocol.'

"What is 'Ragnarok Protocol'?" I ask, even though the mere mention of it fills me with dread. I know a smidge about Norse mythology, and it doesn't sound pleasant.

"It's never been enacted before in the dungeons, though we were all taught what to do in the event that it was." Paul shrugs. He glances over at Elrith, who gives a nod. With that, he continues. "In short, Hella's dungeon, along with the dungeons of her top generals, the gods themselves, have likely already attached to Earth. They're essentially impossible to detect, no matter what technology you use. It's standard protocol for them to attach at the beginning of an invasion. That way they can't be located when the target world becomes better at fighting back as time goes on."

I nod slowly. "That makes sense, I suppose. So . . . what? They come out, hammers swinging?"

"More or less." Paul nods. "It essentially tells everyone else to stay back, stay in your dungeons, only engage the enemy if they come to you. Meanwhile, her real champions will come thundering forth to—pardon the pun in your language—rain hell down upon the world."

"Great." I cross my arms. "If that's right, then we're about to face a full-scale invasion force?"

"Something like that," Elrith confirms. "Now, the single bright side is that you still have to hit level ninety-five before Hella herself can enter. There are a few rules that they still have to follow, which is the only thing that's going to save us."

"I need a list of them, and I need to know where to strike first." I slowly stand up and cross my arms. "I need a list of all her generals. Are we looking at the full Norse pantheon or only one or two? Is there any chance that they'll fight each other, or are they all loyal to Hella? Are there any other entities out there? Zeus, Poseidon, and so on? Can you get ahold of Beowulf again? I have a feeling we could use his help." I sigh and put my head in my hands. "And *why*, if Earth is just being attacked right now, do we know the identities of these people?"

"I can answer the last one!" Elrith stands up with a smile. "The short answer is that they attempted an invasion a couple thousand years ago. Your people didn't take kindly to it. Vikings, Mayans, Persians . . . You know, the Roman Empire actually took over a few dungeons and was planning to use them to invade North America, I think."

I snort and shake my head. "That sounds about right. Get me those lists and get them to me yesterday." I slowly walk up to the glass windows looking out across New York. It isn't burning yet, and I don't intend to let it start. "We're going to get this."

I stand there for a long time, soaking in the view. For whatever reason, it feels like everyone is waiting, just looking at each other. For so long now, it's been a jump from one dungeon to the next dungeon to the next dungeon, with hardly enough room in between to breathe. Now, we're just watching . . . waiting for the other person to blink. The world has come to a standstill, and I don't really know what to think of it.

"Hey." John walks up next to me, a smile on his face. "You've got this."

I smile and turn to him, only to notice that he's in his full gear. "You heading out?"

"Yeah. Mr. Wang is assigning a whole bunch of us to go start clearing out all the dungeons attached to the city right now." John holds up his wrist, which has an odd device attached to it. It looks something like a watch but has a whole lot of little wires and things coming out of it.

"What's that?" I frown in confusion.

"Mr. Wang cooked it up. Well, he had the idea, and then Elrith and Paul managed to get it working." John chuckles. "I can't even begin to understand how it works, but it amplifies the amount of XP that you get from each kill. The goal is to level us up faster so that we can serve as more of an official fighting force alongside you when Hella does come through."

"Can I have one too?" My eyes sparkle.

John only laughs. "Not a chance! If you get one of these, she'll be able to come through the portal in the next fifteen minutes. Give us a chance to get to the point where we can hold our own. You'll still be more powerful than the rest of us put together." I laugh a bit, and he continues. "Plus, it can only handle a certain amount of XP anyway. If it gets too high, it'll just short out, and I'm *certain* you're over that range."

"Probably so." I shake my head. "Well, best of luck."

"Luck has nothing to do with it." John flashes a salute and walks away. "Catch you around!"

I watch him go and notice Ali going with him. With that, I turn back to the city, looking for any sign of trouble. Mr. Wang walks toward me, a smile on his face, and opens his mouth to speak.

And then I hear something.

Laughter.

It starts out quietly, then begins to grow louder and louder and louder. The floor trembles, and everyone freezes. I draw my daggers and look about, watching for anything at all, but nothing presents itself.

Louder and louder and louder it becomes.

Crash!

The windows all break at the same moment, and the jeti-copter out on the landing pad falls on its side and bursts into flame. I turn to look at it in horror, then spin back to Mr. Wang.

Except . . . he's not there anymore.

No one else is there anymore.

The club has emptied, leaving only me and the strange laughter. I grit my teeth and brace for whatever's coming next.

"Whoever you are, I *will* kill you!"

One last mocking laugh is all I hear, and a bolt of lightning flashes down from the ceiling and hits me in the chest. Portal energy swirls around me, and I'm taken away.

Where to? I haven't the faintest idea . . .

But when I find out, I'm going to kill whoever brought me there.

ABOUT THE AUTHOR

Kaz Hunter is the author of the Apocalypse Reincarnation, System Bound, and Rise of the Strongest Sovereign series. A graduate of Texas A&M University (go, Aggies!), he started writing on Wuxiaworld and Webnovel. He has since moved on.

Podium

DISCOVER MORE

STORIES UNBOUND

PodiumEntertainment.com

* 9 7 8 1 0 3 9 4 5 4 6 3 7 *